People of the Bear

Lindy watched in terror as the bear dropped its head to stare into her eyes again. She knew it wanted to kill her, could almost see the deadly determination in its eyes. It huffed in her face, deep panted exhalations from the adrenaline coursing through its body, and stood immobile for a long time, just watching her, daring her to move.

The ebony fur of its chest began to move closer to her face, making her recoil deeper into the litter of the forest floor when suddenly the bear backed up and arched away from her. In one fluid movement, its thick forelimbs lifted off the ground, slimming and lengthening to become muscular human arms. The furred hind legs stretched into smooth, powerful human legs. The long, tooth-filled muzzle shortened into a human face that looked down at her.

What had been dark fur was now smooth olive skin. With his legs straddling her, the man towered above her and glared down with hate on his face.

For my brother
Dave
who helped make this dream reality

A note of thanks:
To my family for your love and support
To the Mundania Press team for your excellence
To those who give of themselves to care for wild creatures
And to God, from whom all blessings flow

Books by Lori Johnson

The Bearwalker Series
People of the Bear
Heart of the Bear
Legacy of the Bear

People of the Bear

Book 1 in the Bearwalker Series

Lori Johnson

Mundania Press

A Mundania Press Production
Mundania Press LLC
6470A Glenway Avenue, #109
Cincinnati, Ohio 45211-5222

To order additional copies of this book, contact:
books@mundania.com
www.mundania.com

Cover Art © 2008 by Trace Edward Zaber
Cover Details by SkyeWolf Images (http://www.skyewolfimages.com)
Book Design, Production, and Layout by Daniel J. Reitz, Sr.
Marketing and Promotion by Bob Sanders
Edited by Michele Dowdey
Copyedited by Kent R. Miller

Trade Paperback ISBN: 978-1-59426-466-5
eBook ISBN: 978-1-59426-465-8

First Edition • March 2008

Production by Mundania Press LLC
Printed in the United States of America
10 9 8 7 6 5 4 3 2 1

Chapter One

Lindy Anderson slammed the phone down, cursing her ex-husband for causing this miserable divorce. Why did she even pick up the phone and listen to his ridiculous excuses again? It had been nine months since the split and he still called incessantly, begging her to forget what he'd done and come back. "*I'll never go back to that jerk. Hell, I'll never look at another man again—ever,*" she swore under her breath.

She sank back against the wall and gazed to her left through the kitchen window where the dark forest stretched out beyond sight. Thank God for the seclusion of this Minnesota cabin, where the nearest man lived six miles away. That suited her just fine. Her gaze fell from the frost-dusted pines to a fresh muddy trail leading through the yard to her back porch. Her eyes followed the trail up the porch steps and widened in shock at the sight of a naked man sprawled shivering on the porch steps.

She threw the door open and stepped out into the cold evening air, wondering if she was seeing things. But the man moaned softly and opened his eyes to look at her as she knelt by his side. She was definitely not hallucinating.

"Are you all right?" she asked, instantly regretting the question. One quick look at him told her that he wasn't all right at all. Fresh blood seeped from a vicious wound in his right shoulder and ran down his chest in congealing reddish-brown streaks. His teeth chattered violently inside his trembling blue lips. A quick glance over her shoulder at the thermometer nailed to the porch railing showed the air temperature hovering at 30 degrees and she knew he had to be freezing. The man opened his mouth to speak but his words wouldn't come. He panted heavily between shivers, his breaths puffing out in thick white vapor that crystallized in the cold air, and looked up at her with frightened brown eyes the color of thick, rich honey. They clearly spoke the plea for help he couldn't voice. He struggled to wrap his uninjured arm across his chest, as if that would shield him from the cold, but it couldn't.

"What on earth…" Lindy said. She slipped her arms beneath his back to raise him up off the icy concrete steps. "You need to get into the house," she said, hoping that he would have enough strength to help her get him inside. He nodded that he understood and leaned forward to let her help him up. Though he was weak and unsteady on his feet, he was alert enough to stand up beside her. She thanked her lucky stars for that.

She tightened her grip around him and helped him through the door. He wobbled precariously, and she saw for the first time that his back was caked with frozen blood the color of mud. *What the hell happened to you?* she wanted to ask. But she didn't, knowing that the questions would have to come later. Her first priority was to get him warmed up and keep him alive.

She led him into the kitchen, through the small dining room and rounded the corner into the family room. They headed toward the opposite wall where a fire burned warmly inside the brick fireplace. Her steps were slow and tiny to match his own, and twice she felt him falter and almost fall, but she held on tight. He wasn't a big man, but he was almost dead weight and it was a struggle maneuvering him across the room. Even through her knit sweater, the cold from his flesh seeped into the warmth of her arm and made her shudder. *How long has he been out there in the cold?* she wondered. She hadn't even heard him come up on the porch, but then she knew she wouldn't have heard him during the shouting match with her ex.

The man leaned heavily against her, allowing himself to be led without question, though he watched her from beneath half-closed eyelids. Then his eyes closed again as though it took too much strength to keep them open.

She swept her gaze over him as they made their way toward the fireplace. At a little over her 5'7" height, he was short for a man. His build was slight and lean with the musculature of a runner. Under a crop of shaggy cinnamon colored hair, his boyish face was smooth and hairless except for the russet hued brows and eyelashes above his honey-colored eyes. He appeared to be in his mid-twenties, about five years younger than herself.

Her gaze dropped lower, over his smooth stomach and narrow hips, and came to rest on the mound of reddish hair between his thighs. He wasn't large, but was nicely proportioned. Her gaze lingered there for a moment. Why on earth was he completely naked out here in the middle of nowhere on a cold spring night? Lindy shook her head and forced her gaze away. *Good God, what am I doing?* she scolded herself, feeling a warm surge of shame brighten her cheeks. The poor man was probably embarrassed enough without her gawking at him.

They stumbled together onto the large braided rug in front of the fireplace and the man sank down on it in a heap. He leaned closer to the fire until its heat spilled over him and the flames' light played off his body, casting him in a molten gold glow. Despite the blood on him, he was nice looking. She couldn't imagine how he'd gotten into such a sorry condition.

Lindy ran to the bedroom for the wool blanket covering her bed and brought it back to him. "Let me wrap you in this," she commanded, pulling him toward her. He nodded and let her drape it around him and tuck the edges tightly in while his eyes followed her every movement.

When she was done, he leaned forward toward the fire again and rested silently, wanting only to let the heat soak into him. Lindy watched his eyes close before she rose and went to the kitchen to make a mug of hot tea for him. When it was ready, she knelt beside him and offered him the steaming cup.

"Here, I made you some tea," she said. "You'll warm up faster if you drink it." The man opened his eyes and extended his left arm slowly outside the blanket to accept the cup. It shook wildly in his shivering grasp but he managed to raise it to his lips and take a long draught. His eyes closed as the warmth seeped down his throat and he moaned softly, but she couldn't tell if it was the comfort of the tea or the discomfort of his pain that caused his moaning.

"Good," he croaked hoarsely between sips. He drained the mug and handed it to her before drawing his arm back into the warmth of the blanket. Then he pulled the blanket tighter around him again and sat quietly, appearing to be on the verge of sleep.

Lindy put the cup down and set another log in the fire before sitting down next to the man. She gazed at him for a long time, trying to assess the situation. His bleeding had stopped and he seemed to be breathing well. The questions she wanted to ask him were coming fast and furious in her mind and she decided she couldn't wait any longer. "What's your name?"

His eyes opened slowly to return her gaze and it took him a moment to answer. "Gar… Gar…" He stopped, licked his lips and tried once more, fighting to control his shivering. "Gareth."

"Gareth," she repeated. *What an unusual name.* "Gareth, I'm Linda Anderson. Everyone calls me Lindy." She inched closer to him. "Do you mind if I take a look at your injury?"

The man shook his head slowly without speaking.

She pulled the blanket away from his neck until it fell down and draped across his back like a shawl, then rose on her knees to get a better look at the wound. A swollen, half-inch hole gaped from his white flesh; its jagged edges were darkened and puffy as though debris had somehow been ground into the skin. "Were you shot?" she asked, trying to keep the shock from her voice.

He nodded weakly without answering but continued to watch her. She could see he was struggling to keep his eyes focused on her as if he didn't trust her.

"Do you want to tell me what happened?"

Gareth's brown eyes flared for a moment, giving her the impression that he was afraid to answer. He reached behind him with his good arm and struggled to pull the blanket back up over his shoulder. When it was in place, he lowered his head to his chest without answering.

"Well then, can I call someone for you and let them know you're okay? I'm sure they'll be worried about you."

"There's no one you can call."

"What about your wife? Or your mother? Anyone?"

He shook his head again. "There is no one."

Lindy tucked the blanket around him again and shook her head at his elusiveness. She wondered what kind of trouble he could be in. The best thing for both of them, she decided, was to get help for him as quickly as possible. "I'm going to take you to the hospital, Gareth. The nearest one is in Timberlake, about thirty minutes away. I'll go warm the car up and then I'll be back for you."

"NO." His single word came out with surprising force.

Her eyes narrowed when she looked at him. He was obviously hiding something from her and it was beginning to worry her. "You need to have that taken care of; it looks infected," she insisted. *And I don't need a dead man on my family room floor.*

He shook his head back and forth before turning to look at the fire. His shivering had finally stopped and the blue tinge of his lips was beginning to fade. "I'm so tired. I just want to sleep. Please," he said, swinging his gaze back to her. "Just let me sleep for a few minutes."

She wanted to flat-out refuse him. There was no way of knowing if he was running from the police or in some other kind of trouble she didn't need to be involved with. Lord knew she'd had enough man trouble to last a lifetime. Still, she felt so sorry for him. And he did seem pretty helpless at the moment. How much harm could a wounded naked man do?

"Okay," she relented. "I'll let you sleep for a while but then I'm taking you to the hospital. No arguments."

He nodded weakly and sank down on the rug, curled in a tight ball like an exhausted dog. His eyes closed and Lindy watched for a moment, checking to make sure that his breathing was still even and steady. He looked so uncomfortable but she didn't know what else to do for him. As long as his bleeding had stopped, it wouldn't hurt to let him sleep for a few minutes.

"I'll get you a pillow," she said at last and left to retrieve one from the bedroom.

She walked back into the family room and looked at the sleeping man. The pillow tumbled from her grasp as a cry choked in her throat. She shoved the back of her hand against her mouth to keep from screaming.

He breathed deeply, evenly, his chest rising and falling in deep sleep. Thick, cinnamon-colored fur peeked out from beneath the blanket, its deep reddish tint glimmering in the firelight. Fur covered his shoulders, his neck, his head, and his muzzle. Where his hand had grasped the edge of the blanket, five long claws curved over the fabric.

It was not a man sleeping beneath the blanket, but a bear. Her eyes widened at the sight of the high rounded ears protruding from the top of his head and his long reddish-brown nose at the opposite end. Her gaze fell to his exposed shoulder, where a ragged bullet wound had matted his fur with dark blood.

"Oh my God," she said and took a step back.

Chapter Two

The hunters ran through the forest at full speed, damning the intense darkness that made running treacherous. Their breaths puffed out behind them in trails of white vapor that crystallized momentarily in the freezing air before drifting away, and their lungs ached from the cold and the exertion. They kept running, their hearts pounding in terror at the thought of the creature they had come to hunt but who was now hunting them.

"Do you see him?" Paul Roberts called out to the man behind him. He had his rifle clenched in one hand and his hat in the other as he tore through the thick vegetation. He desperately wanted to glance over his shoulder and see how much of a lead they had, but he didn't dare look back for fear of falling over some obstruction in his way. It would only take one momentary screw-up like that and he'd be a dead man. So he just kept running, his partner following behind him, while they crashed through the brush and swerved between trees trying to follow a trail that was barely visible in the darkness. He shoved an evergreen bough aside, ignoring its backlash and the sound of it whipping the man behind him in the face.

"Dammit," Billy Dixon muttered, swatting the branch out of his way. He would've given anything to be in the lead but Roberts was thirty pounds lighter and ten years younger than he was. His chubby hand flew to his cheek and massaged the red welt that was roaring to life. "I can't see shit," he yelled back between gasps.

"He was right on us a minute ago. He can't be far behind," Roberts groaned. "God, I hope we're on the right trail." His chest heaved with the effort of his running and cold seeped into his feet through his wet boots, but all he felt was the heat of his own panic surging in waves across his body. He'd hunted for twenty years and never known fear like this.

They kept to the trail as best they could, wary of the rotting logs and other forest debris that lay in their way. Earlier that afternoon, they had parked their truck at the trail's head and followed the path deep into the national forest in search of their prey. When the hunt was over, all they had to do was follow the trail back the same way they'd come. They figured it would be easy, but they hadn't counted on losing their way, or being hunted down by their own prey. Now they both realized that they'd only be safe if they'd been lucky and picked up the right path. Refuge couldn't come soon enough.

Somewhere in the darkness behind them, a deep growl rumbled. Dixon yelled to himself, willing his legs to speed up. Branches snapped and cracked but he couldn't tell if he was causing the noise or if it came from his pursuer. The noises jumbled together in his head and he just couldn't gauge how close the creature was to him. The growl came again, this time louder, and then he knew that it was coming closer. Another sound quickly raged into his ears, the thumping of his terrified heart.

"Son of a bitch, son of a bitch," Roberts muttered in a frenzied mantra. Even thirty paces ahead, he could tell that it was gaining ground and would soon be upon them. "Faster," he urged himself, but he didn't know how much faster his trembling legs could go.

The bear crashed through the underbrush, his massive paws trampling everything that lay in his way. Despite his huge bulk, he moved with the sureness and speed of a bear half his size.

Under his dense coat of jet-black fur, his muscles worked like a well-oiled machine. They rippled with strength, propelling him forward with ease. He inhaled the scent of the men just ahead of him, smelled the stink of their sweat. He could almost taste their fear.

Roberts bounded over a decaying birch trunk and landed face first in the clearing at the trail's head. He could just recognize the outline of the truck ahead of him in the darkness. "Thank you Jesus," he cried. He scrambled to his feet and ran the twenty yards to the driver's side door. For once, he was glad that he'd forgotten to lock it. Yanking the door open, he slid in and slammed it shut just as his partner burst out of the forest.

Dixon hadn't taken two steps into the clearing before the bear was on him. The animal charged him at full speed and knocked him to the ground with a loud *whomph*. The man cried out in terror from beneath the bear's steaming body as it straddled him between its powerful legs, its gleaming white canine teeth snapping in the air above his face and crashing together with snaps that reverberated through the crisp night air like gunshots. The man's screams mingled with the bear's furious roars until it became impossible to tell which sound came from which creature.

Roberts' hands shook uncontrollably as he struggled to get the key in the ignition. His fingers didn't want to work and the keys tumbled to the floorboard. Searching was nearly impossible in the darkness, but after a moment, his palm swept across the cold metal and he yanked the key back toward the ignition once more. Outside, the screams and growls rose in a terrifying crescendo as he finally got the key in and gunned the engine to life. He threw it into first gear, the tires spewed dirt and the truck jerked ahead.

Out of the corner of his eye, Dixon saw the truck pull out of sight and panic gripped him. *No, you son of a bitch, don't you leave me*, he whimpered. His left shoulder throbbed with screaming white heat where the bear's huge curved claws had slashed him and opened a three-inch gash in his flesh. The massive jaws slammed together inches from his face, splattering him with hot saliva and pulling his focus back to the gleaming black eyes that glared down at him with fury.

Dixon beat his fists furiously against the snapping black muzzle until shredded tatters of flesh hung from his palms. He kicked his legs at its body with what little leverage he was able to get, screaming all the while and unaware that he was even making a sound. The bear's deep-set eyes glared down at him from within its jet fur and Dixon knew with certainty what the bear was thinking. It wanted revenge.

A horn blasted from the darkness nearby, startling the bear. It lifted its massive head momentarily to look for the source of the sound, giving Dixon the diversion he needed. He flipped onto his stomach and crawled on his hands and knees to the passenger side of the idling truck. Roberts pushed the door open for him and he scrambled inside.

The men sat there for a long moment, too stunned to do anything but try to catch their breaths and stare out into the darkness. Finally Roberts looked at his partner and noticed the blood pouring from his slashed shoulder. He slipped off his heavy flannel jacket and tied the sleeve around the wound to stop the bleeding. "You're lucky the bastard didn't rip your face off," he said to Billy, his voice becoming high-pitched and shaky from his nerves.

Dixon nodded without replying. He had gone numb with the realization that the bear had almost killed him. Shivers swept through his body and he looked down to find that he had wet himself in his terror. "I want to get that son of a bitch," he muttered, his fury growing.

Roberts cranked the truck into gear and steered for the bear. In the play of the headlights, its dark fur glistened with a deep blue cast. Light reflected in its dark pupils, glowing eerily like the eyes of a phantom. The bear merely stood where it was and watched them before turning suddenly to bolt away.

The truck followed close behind, swerving through the clearing as the bear charged ahead with sharp left and right maneuvers. Shrubs crushed beneath the pickup as it sped over the rough ground, but Roberts didn't care what the branches did to the paint job. Twice he gunned the engine and edged the bumper up to smack the bear in the rear end and twice it bounded away with quickness astonishing for its bulk.

"Dammit!" Dixon yelled, watching the bear elude them again and again. "It's like the son of a bitch is playing tag with us.

The bear suddenly spun around and cut off to its right, disappearing into the darkness beyond the reach of the headlights.

"Don't lose him," Dixon cried.

Roberts gripped the wheel and gave it a hard jolt to the right, bringing the truck almost up on two wheels as it careened up behind the bear once again. "I don't intend to," he said.

The bear was running at full speed. In the glare of the headlights, the blue tint of its fur mingled with white wisps of steam rising from its heated body so that its outline shimmered like a ghost. Without slowing down a bit, it turned its head around and looked back at them.

Roberts laughed and pointed ahead of him out the windshield. "I got the bastard now." He saw that just ahead, the clearing abruptly ended at a massive granite cliff. As if it had understood the man's motion, the bear suddenly stopped in its tracks and looked around. Realizing that it was caught between the truck and the cliff, it turned and stood its ground, defiantly watching the truck approach. Breaths of white vapor rose from its panting mouth into the cold air and disappeared into the darkness.

Roberts gunned the accelerator and steered directly for the bear. "Kiss your shaggy ass good-bye," he laughed. The truck roared ahead at forty miles an hour, spewing dirt beneath its heavy tires.

The bruin's eyes were wide in the brightness of the headlights, but it stood immobile, just watching the truck bear down on it. An instant before impact, it bolted to its left and cleared the path of the truck. Roberts smashed his foot down on the brake, but it was too late. The men threw their hands in front of their faces and screamed as the truck smashed violently against a massive granite boulder that had been hidden in the darkness behind the bear.

The screech of tearing metal was deafening in the silence of the wilderness as the vehicle rebounded from the collision and rocked back and forth until it settled in place on the rocky ground. Smoke billowed from the smashed engine, drifting upwards in delicate swirls in the white of the headlights. The hood was a crumpled accordion of blue metal and every window was shattered. The headlights flickered once and went out, leaving everything in total darkness.

Roberts clutched his chest where the impact had thrown him into the steering wheel. Sharp pain throbbed inside him and he wondered if he'd broken some ribs, but he knew he'd live. He craned his aching neck to see how his friend had fared and breathed a sigh of relief to see him shaken but alive.

Dixon wiped the blood off his forehead and turned to stare at him, disbelief and shock on his face. It took him two tries to force the words out of his mouth. "Did that bear do what I think it did?"

Roberts nodded, too stunned to answer.

Dixon looked slowly around, searching for the bear in the darkness, but without the headlights it was impossible to see anything. He leaned his bleeding head back against the headrest and exhaled. "Shit, man, I can't believe this."

Roberts looked out the window, wincing at the pain throbbing in his neck. "I know. I can't believe that cinnamon bear got away from us after I got a shot in it. It couldn't have gone too far."

"But then to be outsmarted by that big black son of a bitch bear and wreck our truck..." Dixon groaned. "Paul, we screwed up. The boss is gonna be fuckin pissed at us."

Roberts nodded his agreement, too embarrassed by the sudden realization that he had also wet himself to answer.

Chapter Three

Gareth opened his eyes to find himself at the barrel end of a shotgun. A whimper escaped his throat and his eyes flared wide as they followed the gleaming length of cold metal up until it disappeared under the pink flesh of hands. The woman held the rifle butt to her shoulder, the barrel aimed right at him. She looked scared.

"Don't...don't shoot me," he whispered without moving.

Lindy lifted her eye away from the sight momentarily, allowing herself a better look at him. He stared back at her with sheer panic etched on his face. "What the hell are you?" she asked, her voice low and trembling. She didn't want him to know how scared she was, but she knew it was evident in her voice and probably on her face, too.

Gareth inched his good arm out from under the blanket and raised it before him.

"Don't move," she ordered. "Or I *will* shoot you."

He froze, able only to express his terror through his rapidly dilating pupils. Breaths came fast and shallow from his parted lips. "What did I do?" he asked, afraid to speak louder than a whisper.

Her eyebrows raised in response. "Are you kidding me? Answer me now. What are you?"

His heart began to pound in his chest and he felt a fresh trickle of warm blood seep from his shoulder, but he didn't dare turn his head to look at it. "I...I don't know what you mean." He couldn't figure out what she was talking about or why her demeanor had changed so dramatically.

Lindy waved the gun barrel in front of his face. Her hands shook so badly she couldn't hold it steady. "When I came back in here with a pillow, you weren't you. You were gone and there was a…" She stopped and dragged her hand across her eyes as if to clear away cobwebs, almost unable to spit the crazy words out. "There was a *bear* where you are."

Gareth's mouth tightened and he tipped his head back ever so slightly, but his eyes never left hers. He was silent for a long moment before he answered. "You must have been dreaming."

"Dreaming? No, I was wide awake," she retorted. She shook her head so hard that her blonde hair flipped in her face. It looked like she was having a hard time convincing herself of what she'd seen. "Who the hell are you, Gareth?" She spat out his name as though she questioned it, too.

"Huh," he said, exhaling a short breath of air that was meant to sound amused but only sounded panicky. "Do I look like a bear?" he asked, a hopeful smile growing on his face. He lowered his head to look down at himself. "Really, I'm not that hairy, do you think?"

Her eyes bored into him and she didn't laugh. "You were a bear when I first came back in the room and then I saw you change into a… into a… man. While I watched. One minute you were covered with fur. And then your fur started to…to sink into your skin, and your arms and legs became long and thin and then you were a man again. I never saw anything like it in my life. What the hell kind of monster are you?"

Gareth shook his head vehemently in denial. "What you're describing is just not possible. Listen to yourself, it's absurd. You must have fallen asleep and dreamed it. Sometimes dreams can seem so real."

"Don't lie to me," she hissed, shoving the shotgun hard against the flesh of his upper chest until the metal dented his skin. Blood spurted from his wound in a brilliant red gush and he recoiled with a yelp as his good hand flew protectively up to his shoulder.

"Don't kill me," he pleaded. Blood seeped out between his fingers and dripped in scarlet streaks down the side of his chest. When he looked up at her, his soft brown eyes were brimming with moisture from the pain.

Lindy gasped at what she'd done; hardly able to believe she could be so cruel. She laid the gun down and knelt beside him. "Oh God, I'm sorry. I didn't mean to hurt you." The harsh expression on her face faded with compassion at the sight of what she'd done to him. "Please forgive me, Gareth." Without waiting for an answer, she stood up and ran from the room, returning a moment later with a first aid kit and two towels.

Gareth had fallen backward and lay with his weight resting on the elbow of his good arm. He was shaking badly again, his chest jerking up and down in spasms of pain. His eyes were wide and he watched nervously while the woman took the wet cloth and raised it to his shoulder.

"Don't touch me," he cried, flinching back even farther.

Lindy looked at him and the fear in his eyes almost made her heart ache. She lowered the cloth and exhaled softly. "I'm sorry I hurt you. I promise I won't do it again."

He swallowed so hard the noise was clearly audible. "Then why did you raise your hand to me just now?"

"I need to stop the bleeding," she said. "You're already weak from blood loss; you don't need to lose any more. So if you'll move your hand, I'll help you. I promise you, I'm not going to hurt you."

Gareth hesitated, afraid not to do as she ordered. He was still reeling from the pain and he cringed at the thought of her touching him, but he forced himself to slowly lower his hand. Blood had stained his palm and fingers scarlet and she wiped the towel across his hand to soak it up.

She dabbed the cloth gently against his shoulder, watching his reaction to gauge his pain, and then used firmer pressure to stop the flow of blood coming from the wound. She glanced up and caught him wincing, but he didn't make a sound. She felt like a complete jerk for hurting him. After a few minutes the flow stopped and she wiped the wound carefully to clean it as best she could. When the hole was clean, she pressed a bandage over the skin.

"You still need to go to the hospital."

He shook his head slowly, his brown eyes gazing steadily into her blue ones. "I can't."

"You need to go."

A soft sigh escaped his lips before he shook his head once more. "Didn't the bullet come out my back?"

She leaned to his side to take a look at the back of the wound. Just as he'd said, another hole marked the bullet's exit site. "Yes, it came out."

He nodded his acknowledgment. "Then I don't need to go."

"You need stitches to close up the wounds."

"I'll be fine."

Lindy stared at him from the corner of her eye, agitated by his stubbornness.

Gareth's mouth pulled down in a frown. He could see she was still upset and he didn't want to make her mad or scared again, but he didn't know what to do. "You don't understand. I can't go to a hospital. Ever," he said at last.

She sat back, setting the first aid supplies on the floor beside her, and drew her knees up to her chest to look at him. He seemed recovered from his exposure to the cold, but the wound was shiny and red with infection. "Look, I'm sorry I pulled a gun on you. That was a terrible thing to do after you've just been shot, but you've got to admit, Gareth, that something here isn't kosher. I mean, why are you naked? How did you get shot and end up on my porch? And how the *hell* did you turn into a bear?"

Gareth closed his eyes as the breath rushed from his throat in a great quivering sigh. This was one of the few things he had ever feared in his life, and now he faced the situation alone with no one to help him. It was one thing to deny the shift as a myth or a dream, but she had *seen* it. How could he deny that?

"I… I really can't explain it," he mumbled.

Lindy sat for a moment just looking at him. Then she stood up and walked across the room to a table near the dining room wall. She took the cordless phone off its holder and raised it to her head. "I have to call the Sheriff then."

A panicked look flooded across his face. "No, you can't," he cried, struggling to rise to his feet. It was only a moment until the room swam before his eyes in a dizzying circle and he tumbled sideways, coming to rest lying partially across the sofa. He groaned at the pain shooting through his shoulder and back.

Lindy set the phone down and rushed to his side to help him. Putting her arm gently around his slender waist, she guided him onto the couch and straightened his legs out on the cushions. When he was as comfortable as possible, she sat beside him, her blue eyes steeled onto his. "Okay, so you don't want me to take you to the hospital and you don't want me to call the Sheriff. You won't let me call anyone to come for you and you won't tell me what happened to you. Yet I've let you into my home and tried to make you comfortable." She continued to stare directly into his eyes, wanting him to understand that she wasn't joking. "I think it's time you were honest with me."

He turned his head away to avoid the heat of her stare. Fear was raging through him again and he knew she could see the sweat beginning to bead on his forehead.

Lindy's heart pounded at the sight of his suffering. It wasn't just his physical pain that got to her, but the obvious mental anguish he was going through. She wondered if he was telling her the truth, that he really didn't have anyone to come for him. Maybe there was no one that cared about him. "Tell you what," she said, unable to stop the pity from overwhelming her hesitancy. "I'm willing to let you stay here for a while and I'll take care of you myself, but you need to be honest with me about who… or *what* you are." She leaned closer and swept his copper hair gently from his forehead. He suddenly looked so boyish and helpless. She bent low over him and gazed into his eyes. "I promise you, whatever your secret is, I'll keep it safe."

His eyes narrowed to return her gaze. "Humans never keep their promises."

A shudder ran through her at his words. Why did he speak as if they were different species? She sucked in a deep breath and forced her fear away. "That's the deal, take it or leave it."

Gareth turned his head to look into the fire. There were so many things to fear here, most of all the woman sitting beside him. He couldn't let her involve the police, that was an absolute. No one else must ever be involved in this disaster. But he knew he was too weak to make it home, and he wasn't sure that the others even knew where he was. So there was nothing he could do—she had made the choice for him.

He turned his head back until his eyes met hers and he opened his mouth, ready to tell her the truth.

Chapter Four

The bruin stood at the edge of the forest and stared across the open yard to thc small cabin. Yellow lights burned inside and flooded through the windows to spill out into the darkness. A shadow crossed before the window, passed out of view, then crossed at the window again. The bear watched warily, his deep-set black eyes discerning that it was a woman who moved back and forth inside.

He shook his shaggy head and snorted angrily, hoping that he was mistaken. But he knew he wasn't. The blood trail was heavy and vivid as it wound through the forest and continued into the yard before him. Even from this distance, he could see a pool of dark blood caked on the stairs leading up to the house and he knew that Gareth was inside. *Inside*. The thought of it made him shudder.

His imagination ran wild and he tried to keep the horrible thoughts away, but he couldn't. He knew how humans acted, knew what cruel things they were capable of. And he knew that in his present condition, Gareth was incapable of protecting himself from anyone. They could do anything to him and he would be helpless to protect himself.

A plan began to formulate in his mind. He gazed at the cabin, noting every window and door, trying to figure out where Gareth might be inside of it. Did more than one human live here? So far, he had only seen the one pass before the window, but he knew that where there was one human, there were usually others.

He swung his head to look at the others waiting nearby. Four bears stood in the shadows at the edge of the tree line, their eyes focused on the big boar. At his unspoken signal, they turned in unison and lumbered back into the woods. Then he shifted his great black bulk to take one last look at the house.

Marin growled deeply to himself at how quickly things had turned bad. Then he wheeled angrily around and disappeared into the forest without making a sound.

Chapter Five

Gareth looked ridiculous in her baby blue terrycloth bathrobe, but it was the only thing she had that would do a decent job covering him. If he was going to be staying for a while, the robe was better than having him lay there naked on the couch, although she had to admit that there were definitely worse things in life than that for a single woman.

She handed him another cup of tea and settled into the chair near the couch to hear his explanation. His wound had been bandaged, she'd fed him a sandwich and helped him get cleaned up and comfortable on the sofa. There was nothing left to do but hear his answers to all her questions.

He took a long sip of the hot tea, letting it sit in his mouth for a moment before swallowing it as though it was the most delectable thing in the world. Every so often, his skin rippled visibly with a violent shiver that surged through his body. The wound had become more swollen and full of pus and Lindy knew that he would need a strong antibiotic if he was going to recover.

Gareth tucked the robe tighter beneath his legs before pulling the blanket close around his neck. Even under all the fabric, his shudders were apparent. He stared at the woman for a long time, not speaking, just hoping that she wouldn't hold him to their agreement.

"You can start any time now," she said.

His heart sank. It was just as they'd warned him: humans never kept their word, except when it benefited them to do so. But he knew he didn't have a choice. He didn't want to die. Softly he cleared his throat and fixed his eyes on hers, willing her to have compassion and understanding.

Lindy melted beneath his gaze. The color of his eyes reminded her of the honey she bought at the farmer's market each summer, a dark gold syrup full of sweetness. His eyes were liquid, beautiful. She blinked and tore her gaze away. It was almost as if he was hypnotizing her with his eyes and it scared her. She was in control of the situation, or at least she hoped so. "I'm waiting," she prompted.

Gareth raised his hand to gently probe his bandaged shoulder. He could feel the heat growing inside, the infection spreading, and it scared him. He knew he needed her help. After a moment he lowered his hand to his lap and let his gaze linger there. "Have you ever heard the word 'shapeshifter'?" he asked at last. His voice was so soft it was barely audible.

The question caught her off guard and it took her a minute to respond. "Sure," she said. "Anyone who grew up in the Northwoods has heard all kinds of stories about weird creatures like Wendigos and shapeshifters who supposedly lived in the forest. There must be a hundred of those old legends and Indian tales. My sisters and I grew up hearing them, but I stopped believing in them the same time I gave up Santa Claus and the Tooth Fairy."

He nodded slowly, wisps of cinnamon tinted hair drifting down around his face. The fine strands framed his face more beautifully than any artist could have painted him. "It's easier to believe that some things *aren't* real, especially when they threaten the foundation of our reality."

Lindy snorted softly. "What? Are you saying that Santa Claus is real?"

He raised his head to stare directly into her eyes. "No, I'm saying that shapeshifters are real."

She shifted in the chair; suddenly uncomfortable with the direction the conversation was headed. "Let me get this straight. You're saying that there are real live spirits out there that are part human and part animal?"

"Basically, yes."

"Uh-huh. And are you saying that you're one of those spirits?"

Tipping his head to one side, Gareth stared into the air for a moment before flicking his gaze back to her. "I'm not a spirit, like a ghostly spirit. My body is flesh and blood, as you've seen, but my inner spirit can manifest in two different ways. That's what shapeshifters do; we change our form to adapt to different situations."

"Uh-huh." She nodded, hearing him but not believing him. "So you're like a werewolf then. Sort of a… werebear?" She brought her hand to her mouth to stifle the giggle trying to escape her lips.

"Not exactly," he said, ignoring the ridicule. "Were-creatures are humans that assume animal form. We're bears that can assume human form, but we're not human."

Her eyes grew wide in feigned shock. "We? You mean there are more of you?"

Gareth turned his head away to stare into the fire. She obviously didn't believe him so what was the point in continuing? "I've said enough."

Lindy rose and stretched tiredly before taking the empty cup from his hand. "More tea?" she asked, relegating his explanation to the dark corner of her mind where she kept her ex-husband's sorry explanation for his affair. She figured if nothing else, at least her guest was entertaining.

He looked up at her with a blank look on his face. "Why don't you believe me?"

"I believe you," she said, trying to force a smile that wasn't too contemptuous. "Just like I believe that the Sandman sprinkles sand in my eyes at night to help me fall asleep."

Gareth smiled and gazed at her with those soft honey eyes. "You asked me for the truth and I gave it to you. I guess it's your choice whether to believe me or not. And yes, I would like more tea."

"Sure, no problem." Lindy shrugged and went to the kitchen to make them both more tea. She put her hands down on the counter and lowered her chin to her chest, feeling concerned about her safety again. *I have a madman on my couch who's probably going to kill me in my sleep*, she thought, suddenly wishing that her ex-husband was here to protect her. Then she laughed quietly and shook her head. No, that would only be trading one lunatic for another. She forced the thoughts away while she refilled the mugs and walked back to the family room.

The high-pitched scream echoed through the house and it took her a moment to realize that it had come from her own throat. Tea splashed out of both mugs and splattered on the floor around her feet. She couldn't tear her gaze from the couch, from the bear sitting there in a baby blue bathrobe.

The bear turned its head to watch her come in the room and gazed at her with its honey colored eyes before its mouth parted slightly. It snuffled softly and one shaggy, cinnamon colored paw rose to wave at her as if beckoning her over.

Lindy couldn't move. Her feet were frozen in place, her legs leaden and unable to move forward or backward even an inch. She knew her mouth was open but she didn't have the strength to shut it. "Oh…my…God," she sputtered.

The bear slid its hind legs off the couch and set them down on the floor, then lowered its front legs down beside them, holding the injured one up cautiously. Its shaggy head was aimed right at her to keep her in sight. Arching its back gently, the bear rose and stood up on its hind legs. Instantly, the long cinnamon fur sucked inside its body and disappeared beneath smooth white skin. The bear's thick muscled limbs grew long and slim and its furred chest grew smooth and hairless. The elongated brown muzzle shrank into a nose on a face that now belonged to the man she knew as Gareth.

Exhaustion lined his face and he fell back down on the sofa with a groan, clutching his injured shoulder with his good hand. Shudders washed over him from the exertion.

She didn't know how long she stood there before the lead left her legs. Finally Lindy walked over to the chair and sank down in it, both mugs still in her hands. Half the tea had slopped out of them. Her mouth was open so far her jaw ached. "Holy…shit…" was all she could mumble.

Gareth closed his eyes and laid his head back against the armrest. His chest rose and fell with ragged breaths that sounded painful to take.

"Are you okay?" she asked. His struggle to breathe was beginning to worry her.

"I think so," he whispered. "It just takes a lot of energy to shift form, especially when we're injured."

Lindy set the cups down and knelt on the floor beside him. The sweat beading on his forehead glistened in the firelight. "Why did you do it? Why did you change your form like that?"

He opened his eyes and looked at her without lifting his head. "Because I told you I'd explain, and we always keep our word. Besides, I figure I owe it to you for not calling the Sheriff."

She took a tissue from the box on the end table and ran it gently across his forehead, mopping up the sweat. His skin was flushed with red and she swept her fingers over his face, trying to discern if he had a fever.

His eyes widened at the feel of her hand on him. He'd never been so close to a human before, had certainly never been touched by one like this before, and he was surprised by how good it felt. Her skin was warm and her touch very gentle, a dramatic change from the force she'd used to shove the gun into his chest. But it occurred to him then that maybe she was as afraid of him as he was of her. Now that she had calmed down, he knew that she was actually very kind.

"I can't believe this," she said. "I really thought… I don't know what the hell I thought. I don't know what to think even now." She just kept shaking her head back and forth and shoving the blonde strands away from her face.

He nodded weakly. "That's why we keep our existence secret. It's just easier for everyone. And remember, you promised you won't make me go to the hospital."

She nodded and swallowed down the lump in her throat.

"I remember. You kept your word and I'll keep mine. But I'd still like to know how you got shot." She laid her hands in her lap and waited beside him, hoping that he'd tell her.

Gareth gazed silently at her, his brown eyes burning into hers. He wasn't thinking about her question, but about something he couldn't shake from his mind. "You touched my face."

She looked away and stared at the wall. "I'm sorry. I guess I shouldn't have done that," she said softly, unsure how to respond. She had no clue how to act with him, how to treat him.

Gareth shook his head at her misunderstanding. "No, I liked it when you touched my face like that. I've never been touched by a human before. I was always told that humans used their hands to hurt others, so I thought that when you touched me, it would hurt. But it didn't. It felt…nice. It made me feel calmer."

She was struck with a sudden realization. "I hurt you before, with the gun, and now you're still afraid of me, aren't you?"

"Wouldn't you be in my situation?"

The truth of his words was so obvious that it hit her like a brick and she felt compassion well up inside her for the man. She raised her hand toward his cheek and he flinched. "It's all right," she said, "I give you my word that I'm not going to hurt you." He took a deep breath and when he had relaxed, she resumed her soft strokes along the side of his face. His skin felt so soft, so human, that she couldn't stop chastising herself for hurting him with the gun. "Please don't be afraid of me, Gareth. I'll keep my word and you'll be safe here while you recover. I promise you that."

He gazed into her eyes, wanting to believe her. Needing to believe. "You really promise?" He sounded strangely innocent and naïve for a man his age.

She smiled and nodded, continuing to stroke her hand across his cheeks and over his flushed forehead. "Promise. Now will you please tell me how you were wounded?"

A long sigh came from his throat, revealing his relief at her promise and yet betraying a hint of hesitation. "My clan has lived in this forest for… well, forever. We keep to ourselves to safeguard our secret and we rarely venture outside the boundaries of our territory. We prefer to avoid contact with humans, as you can imagine."

She laughed softly. "Yeah, I see why. Your transformation, or whatever it's called, scared the hell out of me."

Gareth's expression was solemn as he shook his head no. "It's not that we care whether humans are frightened or not, but because what humans fear, they always try to hurt."

Lindy ran her fingertips around the bottom of his chin before sweeping them back up the right side of his face. His skin was as soft and fine as a young boy's and he seemed to be relaxing more and more beneath her touch. "Yes, it's a very unfortunate habit of ours."

"Not unfortunate, Lindy, deadly. Over the last four or five generations, as humans have moved deeper into our territory, they've indiscriminately killed my people. Bear hunting has become a popular *sport*, as humans call it."

She pursed her lips together while she considered his words. "But they don't know what you are. They don't realize that you're human, too."

Gareth gazed into the fire and sighed. "We're not human. Not really."

"You look human. You feel human."

His eyes flicked back to hers and pulled her gaze to him. "But I'm not human. Doesn't that knowledge make you afraid of me, afraid to touch me? You have no idea how I might react or what I'm capable of."

Her eyes widened a bit at the idea of it. "I wasn't afraid until you mentioned it. Are you trying to scare me, Gareth?"

"I'm just asking for your honesty as you've asked for mine."

Her fear eased again and she smiled. "I can appreciate that." She brushed the hair away from his eyes again to look at his copper colored brows. His hair was such a strange color, but it was attractive on him. She looked straight into his eyes and took in a breath. "I think that if you had wanted to hurt me, you'd have done it by now. Just as I could have killed you if I'd wanted to."

He considered her words for a moment, and then nodded in agreement, all the while rolling the side of his face against her soft palm. "I think we have a truce then, you and I."

"So who shot you? Who would do such a cruel thing?"

Her question sent his thoughts back to that awful moment and his face contorted with the pain of the memory. "There are always hunters... poachers... who ignore their own laws and hunt animals where and when it's forbidden."

"Yeah, I know hunting is prohibited in the national forest," she agreed, nodding toward the kitchen and the vast wilderness that lay beyond the house.

"But it doesn't stop them. It never stops them. They came after me this afternoon when I was feeding." His mouth wrinkled in a grimace. "I'm often the target because of my unusual color."

She remembered the long strands of cinnamon tinted fur that had poked from beneath the robe moments ago. "Your fur is a beautiful color. So unusual for a bear."

Gareth grunted in disgust. "Yes, so beautiful that many have tried to hang my hide on their wall."

The idea of it sent a shudder down her spine. She abhorred hunting. "So one of the poachers shot you. How did you escape?"

He changed position on the couch and reached up to touch his shoulder again. It throbbed in searing pulses that shot down his arm and ribs, making him slightly nauseous. "We never travel alone. There were five others with me, including our guardian. As soon as we heard the first shot and I knew I'd been hit, I ran while the others chased the humans to keep them from finishing me off. I know I ran for a long time but I don't remember much of anything else but the pain."

Lindy rose and sank into the chair opposite him. It was

almost too hard to hear his story, to think about the agony he must have been in as he fled from his attackers, but she wanted to know everything. She wanted to do everything she could to help him. "How did you end up here… and why weren't you a bear when I found you?"

"It's difficult to explain," he sighed, tucking the blanket tighter around his legs to ward off the cold that continued to seep into him. "The gunshot hurt so bad I couldn't think straight. I just ran without knowing or caring where I was going, just wanting to get away from the hunters. I really don't have any recollection of how I got here, but I do remember shifting."

"Shifting?"

"That's what we call it… shifting between bear skin and human skin. Under normal conditions we have no trouble controlling where and when we shift. But under stress or because of injury, we can lose control."

She nodded, understanding his meaning. "Like when you fell asleep on my rug."

He looked at her with obvious regret on his face. "Believe me, I would never have chosen to do that. Exposing our secret to you is one of the scariest things I've ever done in my life."

Lindy smiled, certain that he meant it. "I believe you, Gareth."

He licked his lips and let out a long tired sigh. "I've told you everything you've asked. So what do we do now?" he said. The softness of his eyes shimmered seductively in the firelight.

"Well," Lindy said, swallowing hard. "We get you well. And then we get you back home."

Chapter Six

"Dr. Dean, thank you for working me in on such short notice."

Lindy stepped inside the office and sat in a chair near the stainless steel exam table. The smell of urine and cleaning solution permeated the air of the veterinary clinic. The bright overhead light glistened off the glass jars of cotton balls and gauze forming a neat line on the countertop. On the wall to her right, a color poster of dog breeds was framed behind glass.

The doctor smiled politely from the other side of the table, looking quite handsome in his clean white lab coat. He was a tall man with well-chiseled features and dark brown eyes that penetrated hers. "Margaret said you had an emergency?"

"Yes." She fidgeted on the chair, feeling foolish and very unsure what to say. But she needed the medicine and didn't know of any other way to get it. "I know this is going to sound strange, but I need an antibiotic. For a bear."

Dean's eyebrows raised beneath his crop of sandy blond hair. "Did you say a bear?"

"Yes, that's right."

A smile flickered across his face and his index fingers came to rest on the edge of the table. "You're right, it is a strange request. May I ask how you came to need medicine for a bear?"

She felt a flush rise to her cheeks. "I'd rather not go into it, if you don't mind."

"I really need to know."

"I really can't tell you."

The easy smile that lit his attractive face faded, replaced by a stern look of warning. "Do you understand that I could lose my license for dispensing prescription medication for fraudulent purposes?"

"I'm not lying to you," Lindy said, squirming beneath his heated glare. She wondered how someone so good-looking could become so quickly frightening. It was clear that he wasn't going to make it easy on her. "Look, I found the bear in my yard. I think it's been shot and I'm just trying to help it, okay?"

"No, it's not okay," he said gruffly. "Citizens are not legally allowed to house or care for wildlife, especially dangerous animals that can cause you harm. You should have contacted the conservation police or myself immediately to have someone come and pick it up."

She exhaled defensively. "This bear is just a cub. I'm not afraid of it hurting me."

Dean walked around the table until he stood directly in front of her with his back resting against its metal edge. "Why didn't you bring it here with you, then? Don't you think it would receive more appropriate care here in my clinic?"

"Because it's heavy. And it's resting in my laundry room."

"Uh-huh."

Lindy stood up until she and the vet were face to face. Anger burned inside her, anger at herself for telling this growing pack of lies and at him for making it necessary. "You know, I'm just trying to be a good citizen. I found this animal suffering in my yard and I cared enough to do something to try and help it. But you're treating me like some criminal. Maybe I should have just let it die out there."

His expression softened a bit and he raised his hands before him. "Calm down. I'm not saying you're a criminal, just that you did the wrong thing."

She sighed and pulled her coat tighter around herself. "When I get home, I'll call the conservation police and have them pick it up. But until they arrive, can I at least start treating the poor little thing? He looks so miserable. It just breaks my heart to think he might be suffering."

Dean gazed into her eyes, trying to read her face. He hesitated for a long moment before walking to a cupboard behind the table. "Tell you what. I'll give you some of these antibiotic pills to get him started until the DNR picks him up." He handed her a tiny bottle with several white pills inside. "You can wrap a pill in a piece of lunchmeat or cheese and give it to him that way. But be careful, you don't want him to bite you. Even a cub can do some serious damage."

"Thank you, Doctor," she said. *Thanks for your generosity. And you can bet your sweet ass I won't be calling the DNR to my house.* She smiled and turned to go out the door.

"By the way, Mrs. Anderson, where do you live that a bear found its way into your yard?"

She stopped in the doorway and swung around to look at him. "I live on Otter Lake right next to the national forest. I see bears quite often when they come down to the lake for a drink."

He nodded without answering and watched as she left. When she was gone, he walked to his office and reached for the phone. He smiled to himself, pleased that he had been less help to her than she had been to him.

Chapter Seven

"Thundermaker, you in there?"

It took a few minutes for the door to open and a gnarled hand to beckon them inside. The two men stepped across the threshold into darkness as the door creaked closed behind them. Except for the light coming weakly through a cobweb-filled window, the room was totally dark. They blinked again and again and stumbled forward, trying to get their eyes adjusted to the darkness.

"Jesus, don't you pay your electric bill?" Dixon muttered.

The old man ignored the comment and wobbled past him to sink into an old chair whose stuffing had long ago flown south. When he was comfortable, he raised his head to face them. "You come here to insult me?" he asked.

Roberts shot his partner a look of warning and took a seat near the old man. "Sorry Jack, you know what an asshole Billy is."

A sparkle gleamed in the old man's one remaining eye before he chuckled softly. "Some things never change, eh? So why have you come?"

Dixon looked around the dim room. The trading post was in complete disrepair, little more than a collapsing hulk. *Shame*, he thought. It had made Jack Thundermaker a comfortable living over the years. He wondered how many tourists had passed through its doors in search of the perfect Indian trinket to take home as a souvenir. He could see that even now, twenty years after the store had closed, a few handmade baskets and toy birch bark canoes lined the dirty shelves. He wondered where all the money had gone so that Jack now lived in squalor and darkness.

He forced his eyes back to the Indian sitting in front of him. The old guy always gave him the creeps. "Here, we brought you some tobacco," he said, removing a small package from his pocket.

Jack took the gift in his wrinkled hand and leaned back in the chair again. "You've come to ask something of me," he said, nodding because he already knew the answer.

Roberts pulled the baseball cap off his head and rested it in his lap for his fingers to play with. "Yeah, we want to ask you about something."

"What?"

"Shapeshifters. Specifically bear shapeshifters," Dixon blurted out.

Roberts shot him another warning glance to shut him up, but it was too late. A chuckle had already escaped from Jack's mouth.

A smile appeared on the old Indian's face, breaking his aged skin into a hundred wrinkles. So that was it. Someone had finally decided to question the old legend. "That…" he said, fingering the package in his hand, "that will cost you more than tobacco."

Roberts shifted uncomfortably on his chair. "How much more?"

The old man laid his head back against the seat cushion and thought. His eye closed and he was quiet for so long that the men wondered if he had fallen asleep.

Dixon leaned forward to nudge him when the old man's eye popped open and he jerked back into his chair with a jolt. "Shit, don't do that, man, it creeps me out."

Jack merely smiled and rested the tobacco in his lap. "It's an unusual thing you want to know about—a secret thing. Secrets are very valuable."

"How valuable, Jack?" Roberts asked.

Jack ran his arthritic hand over the single wisp of snow-white hair remaining on his head. "Ten thousand dollars valuable. And a Playboy magazine." One eyebrow rose suggestively.

"Ten thou… " Dixon started to gasp. "Why so much?"

"Because the knowledge is worth that much."

Roberts flipped his cap between his fingers, unaware of his booted foot tapping nervously on the bare wood floor. He'd been prepared for this but it still made him swallow hard. "Okay. You've got it, Jack," he said at last. "I'll bring the check over tomorrow."

"Cash. No checks," Jack said.

"Right." As long as they got what they wanted, Roberts wasn't going to argue.

The old man nodded slowly. "This information isn't for you, then. Someone else wants it. Someone sent you here to get it."

Roberts struggled to contain his shock. *Damn, the man was ancient but still sharp as a tack. Did Jack know that he didn't have that kind of money to blow?* "Yeah, that's right," he admitted. "We're here on someone else's behalf."

A broad grin filled Jack's face, revealing dark shadows where many of his teeth had fallen out. "I should've asked for more."

"A deal's a deal," Dixon said gruffly. It would have been quicker and easier just to beat the information out of the old geezer than to go through all this butt-kissing.

"Who sent you?"

Roberts shook his head. Jack was pushing the limit now. "Can't tell you that, Jack."

"Then what do you want to know?"

Roberts sucked his lower lip for a moment. "How do you catch a shapeshifter? And once you catch it, how can you keep it from changing form?"

Concern clouded the old man's face at his words. He shook his head in warning, sending the white hair drifting down over the hole where his other eye had been. "Some things are best left alone. The Bear People should be left alone."

"Bear People?"

Jack nodded solemnly. "In the forest. That *is* who you're talking about, isn't it?"

"No," Dixon retorted. *It was none of Jack's damned business.*

"Shut up, will you?" Roberts said, raising his eyebrow at his partner. He looked back at Jack and knew that the old man already knew who they were referring to, so why bullshit him? "Yes, that's who I'm talking about. But it's nothing, Jack. I just want to know, that's all."

The grin returned to Jack's face as a chuckle slid from his throat. His voice sounded as old as his face looked. "Whatever you say. It's your fanny."

"So what can you tell me, Jack? Tell me everything you know about them."

Jack leaned back and closed his eye again, letting his memory slip back eighty years. The words and stories of the elders came back as clearly as if they'd been spoken yesterday. "The Ojibwa tell of a time when there was no line between dreaming and waking, or between people and animals. All creatures lived in peace and spoke each other's languages. Some animals learned human tongue and some humans knew animal speak."

"But over time, things changed and a boundary formed between them. People forgot that they were friends with the animals; they forgot how to speak their language. Humans no longer treated animals with respect or honor. They killed without gratitude or compassion, without caring."

"The bears did not want to die at mans' hand. They decided to change so that they could fool the people who would hurt them. They learned to control their energy and change form—to trade their fur for human skin in order to survive."

"They became the Bearwalkers and though they spent most of their lives in their true bear form, they could stand up and walk among humans, passing for human, and no one would even know."

Dixon swallowed the lump in his throat and scratched

absently at his neck. "What happened to them?"

"They went away. Into the forest, as far from people as they could go."

"How do you catch one?" Roberts asked.

Jack sighed softly and sucked on his lower lip for a moment. "I have never heard of a Bearwalker captured." His eye opened to peer at Roberts. "But I have heard of men killed making the attempt."

"But supposing that one was somehow caught, how would you stop it from changing form?"

Jack shook his head as though he was talking to a slow-learning child. "What is the difference between a man and a bear?"

Dixon slapped his hand roughly against his knee. He wanted to get on with things, not waste his time talking to some senile old man. "We don't have time for riddles, Chief."

Roberts exhaled disgustedly, ready to smack Dixon if he didn't shut his damn mouth. "What is the difference, Jack?"

"A man stands on two legs and a bear stands on four."

Roberts nodded without understanding. "So…"

"If you want to keep the bear a bear, you must keep his paws on the ground. If you want to keep the bear a man, you must allow only his feet on the ground. He must stand upright as a man."

"I get it," Roberts said, his eyes widening as he visualized it. "I understand. So tell me, how dangerous are these Bear People?"

Jack threw his head back and laughed. "Tell you what. You make sure and bring my money tomorrow before you go chase after them."

Roberts opened his mouth to ask another question but stopped abruptly at the rise of Jack's hand in front of him. The old man rose from his chair and ushered them to the door, tired of their endless questions.

"And don't forget the Playboy," he called after them, still cackling.

Jack watched out the grimy window while the men got in

their car and drove away down his driveway, leaving a swirling tornado of gravel dust drifting behind them. Then he turned and padded back across the room to his chair and sank down in it.

"You hear that, Johnny?" he asked.

A young man stepped through the dark doorway of the adjacent room and sat in the chair across from him. He was a stocky man with the same dark eyes and ruddy complexion as his uncle. His long straight hair fell softly around his shoulders. "Yeah, I heard. They're both assholes."

Jack chuckled and nodded his agreement. Then he reached his gnarled fingers inside the front of his shabby flannel shirt and withdrew a tattered string. When he pulled it out into the dim light, Johnny could see that the string encircled his neck. At the end of it, a circular piece of wood dangled.

"You know what this is?" Jack asked.

"I can't even see it," Johnny complained. He scooted closer and took the wood from his uncle's shaking fingers. Holding it up to his face, he saw that one side was carved with a simple figure that went from the uppermost edge of the wood to the lowest edge. He ran his fingertips softly against the grooves gouged into the surface, straining to make out its detail. "It's a bear."

Jack nodded solemnly and pulled the wood back into his hand, handling it carefully as though it were a piece of gold. "It's a medallion."

"It's not our totem," Johnny said. "So what's the deal?"

"Do you remember all the stories I taught you about the time when the Earth was young and people treated the animals like brothers?"

Johnny nodded. He'd practically memorized the stories he'd heard over and over in his youth.

"And you know that the bears changed and became the Bearwalkers and moved deep into the forest."

The young man snorted his laughter softly and shook his head. "I just heard you tell them the story, Uncle. They're fairy tales, folklore."

Jack swung the medallion out in front of him again. "This is real, Nephew. And so are the Bear People."

Johnny swallowed hard and stared at the wooden circle swinging in the darkness before him. All his life he'd heard the tale and wondered if it was true, but as he grew to adulthood and felt himself slipping away from the tribe, his doubt has solidified. Now it melted away like candle wax near a flame. He knew his uncle wasn't senile or crazy. "What are you saying?" he said so softly it was almost a whisper.

"I wear the bear medallion because it marks me. It reminds me of a promise my father made, and his father before him, and his before him. And like them, it marks me as a Protector."

Johnny swallowed again, almost afraid to ask. "Of what?"

That toothless grin spread across Jack's weathered face again. "The Bear People."

Johnny leaned back and looked up at the dingy ceiling, trying to make sense of things that seemed absurd. Bears turning into people. People protecting bears that turned into people. He wondered if his poor uncle had finally lost his mind, after all. It certainly seemed that Jack believed what he was saying.

Jack saw the turmoil on the young man's face and reached out to touch his hand. He couldn't blame him for being confused. That was the way of these things. But the heart knew when truth was spoken and Johnny's heart would come to accept this truth. He just needed time.

"So what does a Protector do?" Johnny asked.

"When the Bear People first changed their energy, they needed help to survive. Our tribe has always lived near them here in the Northwoods, we saw them struggling and trying to adapt. We've always respected the bears and they respected us, so we offered them our help. We protected them from outsiders who moved in to claim what they thought should be theirs. My father was the last man to actually speak to a bear person; this is his medallion. It's worn by every Protector to identify himself to the bears. It's like a badge of honor."

Johnny's dark eyes were huge with fascination and he

leaned farther forward as Jack's story went on. "But *you* never spoke to them?"

Jack shook his head, and for a moment, an expression of sadness settled over his face. "By the time I was a lad, the Bear People had withdrawn deeper into the forest and into their own seclusion. They were so angry they wanted nothing more to do with any human, so my father came back to us and never saw them again. But he told me their story and honored me with his medallion so that if the time came, I would be prepared to wear it and the Protectors would fulfill their promise once again. I think it's time to put it on."

Johnny leaned back and sighed, looking from his uncle to the medallion and back to his uncle. "But I don't understand. You told those men what they wanted to know. You *sold* them information that puts the Bear People in danger. That's not protecting them."

Jack clenched the wood in his palm. "You're right, Johnny, I did. I had to. If they were willing to pay me that much money without blinking, it means someone wanted that information badly. I know Billy Dixon, and I know that he would have forced the information out of me and then killed me without a second thought. And if you had tried to help me, he would have killed you, too." He stopped and took a long quivering breath that betrayed regret. "I should have passed this medallion on to you a long time ago when my own son died. But I didn't. Then a few minutes ago I realized that I had to live long enough to make you understand your obligation. If you refuse, there will be no one left to help the Bearwalkers. *Ever.*" He opened his hand and held the wood out to Johnny. "This is yours now."

The medallion lingered there on his open palm as one minute stretched into two. Johnny just stared at it, afraid to touch it, afraid to take it. It carried a heavy burden and he wasn't sure he was ready for it.

"My arm is getting tired, boy," Jack complained. "You must take it. This is how your life is meant to be. You must help the Bear People."

Johnny reached out and took it hesitantly in his trembling fingers. He looked at the carving, trying to imagine everything that its many wearers had seen. His great-uncle had died before he was born so he didn't have the luxury of asking him what it meant to be a protector. He knew he was on his own. He looked slowly up at his uncle and shrugged. "Even if I agree to it, I don't know what to do, how to start."

Jack smiled his toothless smile again and nodded while he took the string and slipped it over his nephew's head until the medallion lay flat against the young man's chest. "We'll work together. You're young and strong, but I have the knowledge. By helping you, it may not be too late for me to meet the Bear People. I've dreamed of it all my life."

"But how will we find out what Dixon and Roberts are going to do with the information?" Johnny protested. "They won't tell me just because I ask them, you know."

A sly smile crossed Jack's face. "My father always said, 'If you want to catch a fox, you need to run with the foxes.' And my father caught a lot of foxes." He leaned back and folded his bony fingers across his stomach. "I think you should buy our fox, Paul Roberts, a few drinks and have a nice conversation. Liquored lips are loose lips."

Johnny chuckled, remembering more than one Saturday night that he'd spent drinking with Roberts in the bar. "Yeah, that'll work. I don't think there's anything he likes more than his whiskey."

Jack nodded and laid his head back to rest. "Then bring on the firewater."

Chapter Eight

Gareth wandered around the house and snooped. Wonders were everywhere; enticements the likes of which he had never even dreamed existed. The clan had always taught him that humans were lazy, loathsome creatures, but he was finding the opposite to be true. Humans were smart and ingenious and surprisingly fascinating creatures.

He peeked out the window to watch for Lindy's car. She had gone to town on an errand with the promise to return shortly, but he hoped she would take her time. Her absence gave him the opportunity to explore her strange and curious world without fear of being discovered. He wasn't sure how she'd react to him snooping through her personal belongings, but he couldn't help it. He'd been in her home for several days already, and with each hour that passed, he became more charmed and enchanted by her and her human belongings. After all, personal belongings were not something that Bear People even had.

His favorite discovery so far was the thing she called a refrigerator. What a marvelous invention was this big metal box stuffed with cold food of all sorts. He tasted a smorgasbord of food inside, from the funny red liquid called ketchup to the sour things labeled pickles, which he hated and spit out. Then he helped himself to an entire bag of grapes and a package of bread before heading over to the sink. Running the water full force, he stuck his head in the cold stream and drank his fill.

Water was never taken for granted in his world. It was always an effort to find fresh, clean water, especially with the humans polluting more of their water sources all the time. But here, all he had to do was turn the metal handle and lower his mouth to the cool clear liquid splashing from the faucet. He bent over and looked up inside the metal spout, trying to figure out how she got the water in there in the first place, but it was a mystery that he couldn't solve.

Popping grapes into his mouth, Gareth strolled into her bedroom and sank down on the bed. It was soft and bouncy, infinitely more comfortable than the earthen dens the clan used. He lowered his face to her pillow and sniffed curiously, fascinated by its human smell. The scent of female brought a growl of arousal to his throat and he wondered what it would be like to mate with a human. To mate with her. It had never before crossed his mind that mating possibilities existed outside of the she-bears of his clan. Not that he hadn't always been perfectly content with them; they were satisfactory at meeting his needs. But Bear People never mated in human skin and the thought of it was suddenly hard to push from his mind. He remembered the soft play of Lindy's fingers on his face, the warmth of her arms against his back. He gazed down at the bathrobe he wore, the one she'd loaned him to cover his nudity. *What did she think when she saw me naked?* he wondered.

Then the absurdity of it all struck him. *What are you thinking?* he asked himself. Since the time he was a cub just learning the ways of the world, it was forbidden to even think of mating outside the clan. He knew he had no business thinking about such things. And why would she even consider such a thing as mating with someone who wasn't even human?

He exhaled slowly and forced himself to stand up. Why did he even have thoughts like these when he knew that once he returned to the clan he would never see her again? Besides, he was well aware that the Guardian would never allow any kind of relationship between his kind and humans. Pushing the disturbing thoughts out of his mind, he determined to finish his exploration of her house. He glanced around the room, noticing a picture of Lindy with three other females. Her sisters. They all looked similar, all blonde and very pretty. He decided any of them would be good to mate with.

Stop it, Gareth, he warned himself.

He walked to the closet and opened the door. Hangars of clothes hung from a bar on the wall, while a row of shoes lined the carpeted floor beneath them. Sweeping his good arm through the clothes, he sniffed deeply, inhaling the intoxicating scent of female. He sifted through the clothes, searching carefully until his suspicions were confirmed. There was no male scent here at all. *She was unmated.*

Gareth closed the door and walked out of the room. There was one other bedroom in the small cabin, the one she'd given him to use during his recovery, but it was also empty of any clues that she shared her home with anyone. The only other room was the bathroom and he avoided that at all costs. She had shown him how to operate the toilet, but it was just so unnatural to relieve one's self in a big *bowl* that he had always ignored her funny looks and excused himself to go outside.

Returning to the family room, he whirled around to look again at all the strange things humans had. There was the box that brought colorful images to life and another box that emitted a bothersome noise she had called music. But what fascinated him most were the little things scattered around that she called *decorations.*

There were bear decorations everywhere. Statues of bears sat on the mantle above the fireplace. The bottom of the table lamp was a carved bear emerging from a log. A piece of colorful fabric cut to resemble a bear hung on the dining room wall. Even the socks she wore at night to keep her feet warm had little bears woven into them. When he'd asked her why they were everywhere in her house, she had merely shrugged with a smile and said, "I like bears."

Outside, a car door slammed and he walked to the door to look out. Lindy's face appeared at the glass as he opened the door to let her in. He jumped back with a scream.

"What's wrong, Gareth?" she asked, dumping bags of groceries on the kitchen table.

He had wedged himself against the wall as far from the door as he could go, his eyes huge. "Wo… wolf…" he stuttered.

Lindy followed his gaze to the doorway where a large dog stood eyeing him warily. The fur on the dog's back stood erect and a low growl escaped his throat between bared fangs. She laughed softly. "That's just Gunther. He's harmless."

Gareth didn't move, hardly daring to breathe. He was petrified. "Lindy… why do you have a wolf in your house?"

The dog was a large black and tan German shepherd with bright eyes that oozed intelligence and, at the moment, alarm. Lindy bent down beside him and rubbed the thick fur at his throat, wondering why he was so agitated. "What is it, baby?"

The growl continued to roll from Gunther's throat and his eyes didn't move off the man across the room. Wanting only to lunge at him, the muscles of his haunches went taut and his eyes widened until the whites showed around his brown irises.

"I don't know why he's acting like this. He's really a sweet dog."

Gareth groaned. "He knows what I am, Lindy. He can smell the bear in me and dogs instinctively hate bears. Why did you bring him here? He scares me."

She rubbed the dog's ears while she cocked her head to look at the man. "He's my dog, Gareth. He belonged to us when we lived in New York and my husband, well, my ex-husband, has finally sent him back to me. I picked him up at the airport on the way back here." She looked from the man to the dog and back to the man again. "He's a well-trained dog and I promise he won't hurt you."

From the look in Gareth's eyes, it was clear that he didn't believe her. His good hand clutched his injured shoulder protectively, anticipating an attack. He had seen them attack too many times when hunters brought their wolves with them to hunt his kind.

"Watch," Lindy said, trying to persuade him. She walked across the room and stood next to Gareth. Raising her hands to her mouth, she let out a sharp whistle. Gunther scrambled to his feet and lunged across the room until he was a few feet from Gareth. "Sit!" she quickly ordered. The dog slid to a stop on the tile floor and plopped his rump down, but his eyes never left the man. Lindy bent down and wrapped her arms around the dog's neck while she spoke in a calm voice. "Gunth, this is Gareth. It's okay. He's okay." Then she craned her neck sideways to talk to Gareth. "Say hi to him, Gareth."

He inhaled sharply. "Hi." It was all he could do to force the word out.

"Oh, that was a friendly hi," she laughed. "Here, let's try this. Stay Gunther," she commanded. She stood up beside Gareth again and slipped her arm behind his back to pull him closer to her. His muscles were tense and twitching but he let his body slide against hers until their sides touched. She gazed down at the dog while her hand raised to caress the side of Gareth's face. "See Gunth? It's all right."

The dog watched for a moment. Then finally convinced that his mistress was safe and the intruder meant no harm, Gunther sank down on the floor with his huge head resting on his outstretched paws. A whine accompanied the slow roll of his eyes as they focused on Lindy.

"See, everything is fine," she assured Gareth, easing herself away from him. But instead of letting go, he wrapped his arm around her back and held on.

He gazed into her blue eyes, noticing for the first time how they matched the color of the spring sky. They were radiant. No one he'd ever met had eyes that color and he didn't want to stop looking at them. He pulled her closer, surprised by how good she felt against him, and he wondered if she knew that her held her for enjoyment rather than out of fear of the dog.

"Do you want me to put him in another room?"

Gareth shook his head to tear his gaze away from her

eyes. "What?" His thoughts were suddenly confused by the enticing scent of her human femininity. How could his clan have been so wrong about humans?

Ever since she had taken him in on that cold night, she had disproved everything he had been taught. The clan had told him that humans were vicious and ruthless, that they showed no mercy or compassion. Lindy was nothing of the sort; in fact, she had treated him with nothing but kindness. They said humans were greedy and selfish, yet she had shared her food, medicine and her home with him. Humans were supposedly dirty and lazy, but the clean, sweet smell of her made him want to be closer to her. Nothing seemed assured anymore because everything they had taught him was wrong.

"I'm sorry. What did you say?" he asked at last.

"I asked if you want me to put him in another room."

Gareth's face registered surprise at her question. "You'd do that for me? I mean, he is your wolf and I'm just a…a bear."

The look on his face was so sweetly innocent that for a moment, she was struck by the overwhelming urge to kiss him. But the reality of getting that close, of actually putting her lips on lips that belonged to a bear… it was just too creepy. She laughed nervously, ashamed of herself for even thinking such crazy thoughts. "Gareth, I'll do whatever I can to make you feel comfortable here, even if it means locking my dog away from you."

He looked down at the dog, who had his eyes closed and seemed to be sound asleep. Reluctantly releasing his hold on Lindy, Gareth shook his head. "If you say I'll be okay, I'll take your word for it."

A broad smile lit her face as she helped him step around Gunther. "I think you're starting to trust me."

"You haven't given me any reason not to," he said, returning his gaze to her bright blue eyes. "Besides, how can I not trust someone who likes bears so much?"

When the food and supplies were put away, they sat together on the couch before a warm fire. Though spring was advancing and buds were beginning to open on the deciduous trees in the yard, the temperature still fell low enough at night to make a fire welcome.

Gareth had changed into a pair of gray sweatpants and had a blue flannel shirt draped over his shoulders. "Thanks again for the use of your robe, but I have to admit that I feel less silly in pants," he laughed. "Thank you for getting them for me."

Lindy raised an eyebrow at him and smiled. "You're welcome. But I must say, you looked pretty cute in my robe."

"Yeah, but my clan would've thought I'd lost my mind if they'd seen me in it."

She nodded, trying to picture the scene in her mind. "I suppose they would." She got up and added another log to the fire. When she sat beside him again, her lips were drawn tightly together in thought. "What are they like?"

"Who?"

"Your clan."

Gareth smiled and his eyes lit up as though he was seeing them appear right in front of him. "They're wonderful. The clan is like a community, you know, with some older and some younger than me. We're fairly evenly split between he-bears and she-bears. And everyone helps take care of everyone else. We're like a big family."

"They sound wonderful. Do you have something like marriage as humans do?"

He laughed softly and shook his head. "No." Then he stopped for a moment and reconsidered his answer. "Well, some bears mate for life, but most don't."

They were silent for a moment before she rose and brought over the first aid kit. "It's time to change your bandage."

He nodded and slipped the shirt off his shoulders, noticing how her eyes flicked down to look at his bare chest as she sat beside him. A warm flush of desire swept through him and he hoped that she would run her soft fingers across his chest, but she merely removed the bandage and began rubbing in a cleansing ointment.

"When did you come here?" he asked, forcing himself to think about something else. "This cabin has been vacant for years."

Her fingers worked the ointment gently into the front of his wound while she spoke. "After I married Allan, we decided to move to New York because he wanted to try his hand at playwriting. He'd been writing stories for years and was a talented guy, so he did pretty well. During the six years that we were married, he became one of New York's top playwrights. He even tried his hand at directing and producing plays. But when he started directing actresses in our bed, well, that was the last straw."

Gareth's face screwed up with confusion. "I don't understand. What did he do wrong?"

Lindy finished the front bandage and began removing the one on his back. "He cheated on me. You know, he had sex with another woman."

"Oh, I understand," Gareth said, though he really didn't. Most of the bears in his clan mated indiscriminately, though the thought of having a permanent mate the way humans often did was intriguing.

"Anyway, I got a bundle as part of the divorce settlement. There was no way I was staying in New York where he was, and since all my family was back here, I decided to come home. I wanted to find a place that was really quiet and private and I was lucky to find this cabin."

He nodded appreciatively. "And lucky for me that you were here."

She taped the bandage in place on his back and leaned back to gaze at him. Those glorious honey-colored eyes focused on her and made her want to hug him tightly. There was a boyishness about the man that was so attractive she couldn't help but smile. Whatever fear she had once had of him was long gone, replaced by utter fascination. "I'm so glad I met you Gareth. You've certainly made my life… interesting."

Gareth tried to read the expression on her face and swallowed hard. "Interesting good or interesting bad?" He wasn't sure he wanted to know.

She reached out and stroked the side of his neck gently. "Good," she said. "Very good. I've enjoyed having you here so much that I'll hate to see you go."

He forced a smile and gazed at the fire, swallowing the lump that had formed in his throat. Despite the warnings from his clan to stay away from humans, he wanted so very much to tell her the thought on his own mind: *I'll hate to leave you, too.* But he clamped his lips tightly together and remained silent.

Chapter Nine

Marin called the clan together for an emergency meeting and now all sixteen bears gathered around him as he sat on a large granite boulder at the edge of the meadow. The spring night was cool and clear, brightened by a canopy of silver stars sparkling overhead. In their midst, the moon shone brightly, bathing the big bear in a glow that made his jet fur glisten a deep dark blue.

He growled to convene the meeting and sixteen pairs of eyes immediately focused on him. His voice was loud and forceful, demanding their attention. "Bear kin," he said, using bear-speak, the language of their kind. "It's been many years since we've faced the perils now threatening us. We face not one, but three dangers."

A murmur of concerned growls and whines rose from the circle around him as the sixteen bears wondered what he had to tell them. They knew that whatever it was, it wasn't good.

"Our first priority is to retrieve our kin Gareth from the human who holds him hostage."

A roar of assent came from a large brown bruin lying below Marin at the base of the boulder. The force of his voice testified to the strength of his muscular, chocolate-colored body, but the grizzled fur on his head attested to his great age. "Aye," Thoren growled, rising to a sit. The old boar had seen many battles and had earned his standing as a respected elder of the clan. "But how?"

"I've just returned from her cabin and discovered that she has brought in a *wolf* as her guard." At the mention of the word, gasps drifted from the bears' mouths. If there was one creature they hated as much as humans, it was the wolf. The humans had used the snarling animals to hunt them for years, and they were well aware of the canines' tenacity and viciousness. Marin waited for their shock to pass before continuing. "All of the he-bears will travel together to the human's cabin. When we arrive, I will lure the wolf away, giving you the opportunity to force your way into the building and free Gareth."

"I will lead the attack on the human," Thoren said.

Marin nodded, his dark eyes gleaming in the moonlight. "Once you're inside the building, do as you must to secure Gareth. Bring our kin safely home."

"I will," Thoren vowed.

"Two," Marin continued, his strong voice booming in the quiet of the forest. He commanded the attention of all things, even the frogs at the nearby pond, which ceased their croaking in fear. "Gareth's attackers have escaped from forest home. Despite my best effort to catch them that night, they were able to reach their vehicle and elude me." His voice lowered in shame at his failure and he paused for a moment.

"You did your best, Marin," Lilea said, her voice soft and lush with desire for the great Guardian bruin. She was stretched out on the cool grass below him where she could watch every move his handsome body made. She loved the way the moonlight glistened on his fur and lit up his penetrating dark eyes.

"But my best wasn't good enough, was it!" he roared self-consciously in response. Though in truth, five he-bears were responsible for letting the humans escape, as Guardian, he took responsibility for the failure and bore its burden squarely on his shoulders. But he wasn't accustomed to failure and it wasn't a burden he carried well. His expression didn't soften when he looked down at Lilea. Though he hadn't meant to respond so angrily, he was too proud to apologize to her as she cowered and inched away.

Thoren swiped a massive paw across his nose to shoo away a bothersome moth. "The hunters will return, Marin. They always do. And when they do, we won't fail."

"*I* won't fail," Marin growled.

A small black cub scampered away from his mother and stood on his hind legs to look up at Marin. He gazed adoringly at his idol, wanting only to grow as strong and intelligent as Marin. And as handsome. "What's the third thing, Guardian?" he asked.

Marin looked down at the cub with the notched ear and grunted. He had little patience for the young, but Notch was particularly endearing. He reminded Marin of himself as a cub. "The last problem is the human woman. We have no way of knowing if she's forced any information from Gareth or what her connections are with other humans who wish to harm us. After Gareth is safely back with the clan, we must ensure that she doesn't threaten our safety again."

"I can help," Notch volunteered. "I'll bite her." He snapped his tiny jaws together, trying to act fierce, but only garnered chuckles from the rest of the clan.

Marin nodded his appreciation and swatted playfully at the cub. "It will require more than that," he said sternly.

"Marin?" Thoren prompted, anticipating his response.

Marin nodded his huge black head in answer to the unspoken question. "We must do more than bite the human woman. Tomorrow we will kill her."

Chapter Ten

Lindy walked along the shore of the lake and looked out at the dark water. The ice had gone out and the surface of the lake was still choppy with bits of floating ice that looked like miniature icebergs. The ground crunched beneath her feet with every step she took and even though the daytime air was beginning to warm, it still had the cold bite to it that sank right down to her bones.

She stopped and turned to look back at her cabin. From the outside it looked ordinary, just a small, 1930's hewn-log cabin that needed some serious updating. Who would have thought that something so unbelievable waited within it?

Shapeshifters. Just the mention of the word sent shivers up her spine. They were the stuff of folklore and Indian legend, not the human-looking person lying in the bed in her guest room. She wanted to believe that he was making it all up, that he *was* a human being, but she just couldn't. She had seen him shift, seen the bear on her rug and on her couch, and she knew that he was telling the truth. Shapeshifters were real. She looked beyond the cabin into the dark woods that stretched out from the rear of her property. They were out there, though Gareth wouldn't tell her how many. Maybe there were hundreds, maybe a dozen. All she knew was that every time she saw a bear now, she would wonder if it would rise up and walk away on two legs like herself.

It was so strange how the stories of her childhood were coming to life. She couldn't count the number of times that she and her sisters had sat around a glowing campfire, eating sticky s'mores while their father held a flashlight beneath his chin and told the spooky tale of the shapeshifters. He warned them never to go into the woods alone at night or the creatures would get them. *If only you knew how right you were, Dad*, she thought.

She began to wonder what other mythical creatures might live out there in the dense forest. The wilderness of the great Northwoods was so vast that some parts of it still hadn't been thoroughly mapped. Anything could be lurking out there and humans could be totally unaware of their presence. If the Bear People were there as Gareth said, why not Wendigos and witches? Were the other creatures evil or good? Would they, too, find their way to her door?

She thought back to the night she'd found Gareth and remembered how scared he was. She could still see the look on his face when she'd pointed the gun at him, the terror in his eyes when she pushed the rifle barrel against his chest. Even now, she felt so bad about hurting him that she wanted to cry. For being one of those scary mythical creatures of the forest, he was certainly sweet and kind and non-threatening in any way.

And soon he would be leaving. Just when she was starting to feel comfortable having him around, he was going. There were so many questions she wanted to ask him and now she would never have the chance. Even worse than that, there were so many things she wanted to tell him and show him about humankind, and she wouldn't have a chance to do that, either. It felt like a once-in-a-lifetime opportunity was slipping out of her grasp.

She turned back to the lake and looked across its surface to the forest edging the distant shore. Were they there, watching and waiting for him to return? Did they wonder if he was safe in her home, or did they fear what she might do to him? He'd said that they avoided humans, didn't trust them, didn't like them, and she wondered if they would like her if they met her?

A thought had been playing in her mind for days now. Was it possible? Could Gareth arrange for her to meet his clan? Would he even agree to it? And if he did, would she have the courage to follow through with it? She knew she had to decide quickly whether to ask him or not. His wound was healing well and his strength had returned. He was ready to go home.

All she had to decide was whether or not she wanted to go with him.

Chapter Eleven

Jack shuffled across the dusty floor of the trading post and stopped at the edge of his bed. He turned around slowly, hating how unsteady he'd become. He bent over, using one arm for support, and lowered his failing body down on the mattress. Though it was older than he could remember and had lost most of its padding, he was grateful for the little comfort that it offered. It took him three tries to raise his legs up and straighten them out on the bed, and when he was done, he panted for a moment to catch his breath.

Closing his eyes, he let his body relax and grow still. Life was so unfair, he thought, to trap a good mind in a body that was falling apart. He sensed that death would soon be coming, and almost welcomed its release. Only one regret stood in the way, the one thing that he'd dreamed of all his life and had absolutely no control over. More than anything, he'd wanted to meet the Bear People.

He let his mind slip back over the years until he saw himself as a young boy. The picture in his mind was as clear as if he had two good eyes and they were both focused on the scene. He was standing at the edge of the forest, waiting for his father to come back. As was his father's custom, he had left the day of the full moon and walked the path that led to the deepest, wildest part of the forest. It was a day's journey to the meadow where the clan spent their lives, where they hid from those who wanted only to hurt them and take their home.

It was a journey his father had made every month for

more years than the boy could count, and it always began with the man taking the wooden medallion from around his neck and holding it up before his son's face. "It is time," he would say. "Time to check on our friends and see if they're well. Remember that someday it will be you who walks this path." Then, with a pat to the boy's head, he would turn and disappear into the woods.

Jack would sit and watch the figure of his father grow smaller until it disappeared in the shadows of the trees, wishing that he could go with him. But of course he couldn't. So he let his imagination create wild images of the Bearwalkers he himself had never seen. He thought perhaps that they might dress in buckskin and play with arrows as he did, and eat rabbit and wild rice and tell stories around the fire at night. He carried these childish ideas with him for several years before he understood that they weren't people like himself at all, but bears. They walked on four paws and ate from the ground and had no fire.

When finally his father came home, he would set the boy in his lap and tell him all that had happened. Once he had helped heal the wounded nose of a cub that had tangled with a porcupine and lost the fight. Another time he had agreed to guide a party of white hunters in search of the clan and then purposely led them astray, taking them as far from the Bearwalkers as possible before slipping away from the furious men.

"This," he told his son afterwards, "this is what Protectors do for our bear friends."

But on this particular day, his father had walked slowly out of the forest with his eyes cast down on the ground. His shoulders were slumped and his expression was sullen. The boy knew immediately that something was wrong.

"What is it, Father? What happened?"

His father lowered the quiver of arrows from his back and laid it on the ground beside his bow. Then he sat down and slowly lifted the string from around his neck. Taking the medallion in his hand, he laid it on the ground before him and stared at it. "Everything has changed," he murmured.

The boy looked at him with surprise on his small face, knowing that somehow his father had changed on the inside, but he was unable to figure out exactly how. He sat down beside the man and waited for him to speak.

Finally his Father looked up at him, and when he did, the boy could see a sadness in his eyes that he had never seen before. The man swept his fingers softly over the wooden circle while he spoke.

"I went to the Bear People as was my custom. All these years I have gone and they welcomed me into their midst, but no more. Instead of greeting me, they bared their teeth and slashed their claws at me. I could not believe that they would threaten me so. 'Brothers, why do you treat me with anger?' I asked."

The boy's eyes had grown large and he leaned closer to his father with each word the man spoke.

"The Guardian came forward and shifted into human skin to speak to me. I have never seen his eyes so full of anger and hatred. 'We no longer need your help, human,' he said." Father cocked his head and his brow furrowed in thought while he considered what had happened. "The Guardian called me *human* the way we would scorn an enemy. I did not understand and so I asked why I was not needed. He drew close to me and looked down into my eyes with fury. 'We have had enough dealings with humans to last forever,' was all he would say to me. I asked him to explain but he refused. Then he warned me never to return and he took his bear form again."

The boy sat quietly considering his father's words, wanting to comfort him but not knowing how. He picked the medallion up out of the dirt and placed the string around his own neck. The cord was so long that the wooden circle reached down to his navel. "Were you a good Protector?" he asked innocently.

His father looked over at him and nodded solemnly. "I was. As was my father and his father before him. I don't know why the bond between our kinds has been broken, but

I must honor their wishes. Perhaps someday they will open their eyes and see their need for us. Until then, we will keep this safe." He nodded toward the medallion. "Perhaps someday you will be the next to speak to them again."

But that day had never come. The Bearwalkers moved elsewhere in the forest and never spoke to another human again. And every full moon, his father had taken the medallion from the deerskin pouch where he kept it and slipped it around his neck, reliving the times he had spent with the clan. The day his father died, he had been wearing it, and Jack had taken it gently from his neck one last time and returned it to the pouch. There it had remained until recently, until Jack realized that he was dying and that his dream would never be fulfilled.

Then the miracle happened. The two white men had come to him for information and he'd realized that harm was being planned for the Bear People. Everything his father had taught him about the Protectors had come roaring back and he knew that the time had come to re-establish the bond between humans and Bearwalkers. Jack knew that with the wisdom of his ancestors and the strength of his nephew, he could fulfill the role that had been denied him. And maybe, just maybe, he would get his wish after all.

Chapter Twelve

"How do you feel?" Lindy asked, removing both bandages from his shoulder. The wound had healed considerably, leaving a bright pink circle of new flesh front and back. There was no sign of infection and little discomfort.

Gareth hunched his shoulder up to swing his right arm in a circle through the air. The limb moved smoothly and without hesitation, bringing a smile to his face. "It's still sore but I think I'll have full use of my arm." He nodded approvingly.

She ran her fingertips gently over the healed circle before letting them drift down across his chest. His skin was warm and soft to her touch and it occurred to her how much she missed having a man in her life. Gareth was amazing, this creature that seemed so appealingly human, yet wasn't. She wondered if the rest of his clan was as beautiful as he was. She swept her fingertips in small circles on his chest once more and when she looked up at his face, she realized he was staring intently at her. Embarrassment flamed her cheeks and she pulled her hand away and looked down at her feet. "I'm sorry," she said.

"I like when you touch me," he said, his voice almost as quiet as a whisper. "Are you sorry for giving me pleasure?"

"It's just that… it's just not right, that's all."

Gareth raised her chin with one finger until they looked eye to eye. He couldn't admit that he had lied when she'd asked him how he felt. Physically, he felt well enough. But emotionally—that was a different matter. Just the thought of leaving made his stomach churn and his chest ache. No matter how many times he reminded himself that bears and humans didn't mix, he couldn't face the thought of never seeing her again. The human world, at least her part of it, wasn't a bad place to be at all.

"It doesn't feel wrong."

She pushed her arms against her sides, knowing that if she didn't, she'd be wrapping them around him. She forced a smile to her face. "It's not that it feels wrong to me, either, Gareth. But you yourself told me that Bear People don't mingle with humans. And if that's the case, if that's really how you feel, then it's wrong of me to touch you the way I would touch a human man."

A frustrated sigh rushed from his lips and he swung his head away momentarily. "I don't know how or when it came to be that we couldn't associate with humans, but I think it's foolish. I know that the elders were trying to keep us safe, but to forbid us to have contact with all humans...well, it makes me angry." He turned back and fixed his gaze on the brilliant blue of her eyes. "The elders were wrong, Lindy. They always warned us that the only thing humans wanted was to see us dead. They told us that humans were heartless murderers. And some humans are like that. The ones who shot me certainly are. But you're not. You're not like that at all. And it's unfair to banish people like you from our lives just because of the ones that we do need to avoid. Do you understand what I'm saying?"

She nodded and brought one hand to her face, wanting to hide her misty eyes from him. "I do. And I wish that we could be friends. There's nothing I'd like more than to see you again, maybe even meet your clan. But I'm sure they would never accept it."

He pulled her hand away so he could look at her face. The emotion she was feeling had reddened her cheeks and brought moisture to her eyes, making them even bluer. He'd never seen anything lovelier. "I want to see you again, Lindy. I'm willing to stand up to my clan until they give you a chance.

I owe you at least that much."

"You don't owe me anything," she said.

"After everything you've done for me? I would have died if not for your care. I wish I could repay you." He stopped and took a deep breath, aching inside for her to touch him again, but she didn't. She remained silent and unmoving before him and he knew he hadn't convinced her. "It's best that I go, then," he murmured. "I'll miss you." He ran his finger under her chin, then turned and started out the door.

She grabbed his hand. "Do you mind if I walk with you for a while?"

His solemn face brightened and he cupped her hand in both of his. "I'd be glad if you joined me."

She grabbed her coat and threw it on, then slipped out the back door with him. "Stay Gunther," she ordered. The dog gazed forlornly out the window while his mistress walked away toward the forest.

She slipped her hand back in his and they crossed the yard to enter the pines. Though the sun was bright, the dense woods were thick and dark and the air was filled with the crispness of spring. A raven cried from the top of a massive pine, its sharp call echoing high above them. "It's spooky in here," she shuddered, tightening her grip on his hand. She felt his fingers lock securely over hers.

Gareth's gaze was focused on the sunlight filtering through the pine boughs, at the golden rays falling in broken streams to illuminate the forest floor. Tall fiddlehead ferns had begun to unfold in the warming air and lined their way as they moved deeper into the wild greenery. "This is my home," he told her. "There's nothing to be afraid of here." When he turned to look at her, the sunlight reflected from his brown eyes in a luminescent glow and her fear left her, filling her instead with a sense of peace she hadn't felt in a long time.

Gareth led the way through stands of towering pines so tall that their crowns were lost to her sight. The forest was perfumed with the scent of spring flowers blooming around their feet and a thick mat of decaying needles padded their steps like the softest carpet. The needles were brown and fragrant and lay scattered in geometric patterns like pick-up sticks. She'd walked in the forest many times before, but she'd never seen it the way she saw it now with him.

"They're beautiful," she said, pointing to a small patch of trillium glowing in a spotlight of sunshine several yards away.

Gareth couldn't restrain the grin that lit his face. *Now she sees the beauty of this place*, he thought. "I'll get one for you," he offered, releasing her hand to step away and retrieve a flower. He walked between the trees and pushed aside small bushes until he stood at the edge of the circle of flowers. He bent to pluck one when her scream pierced the air.

"Lindy?" he said, pivoting around to look back at her.

She stood immobile, staring at the forest straight ahead of her. A sound was coming from the shadows in the underbrush, coming loud and fast, and then he saw that the sound came from the throat of a huge black bear. The animal moved so fast its paws were a black blur under its massive body, and its jaws snapped open and shut, spewing flecks of foamy spittle as it ran. Its deep-set eyes had only one thing in sight. Her.

"NO!" Gareth screamed. He ran to her as fast as he could, knowing he would arrive too late, and watched helplessly while the bear charged her and knocked her down. Lindy crashed to the ground and rolled in the bear's grasp in a deafening whirl of human screams and ursine roars. Her body disappeared beneath a mass of blue-tinted ebony fur.

He dashed forward and lunged at the snarling animal, trying to place his own body between it and Lindy. They were thrashing furiously at each other and Lindy had no chance of winning the fight. "No Marin!" he cried, grabbing a handful of fur on the bear's shoulder. He could feel the bear's powerful shoulder muscles move smoothly beneath his grasp with each swipe of its paw and he strained to pull the huge animal back but it wouldn't budge.

The bruin had her pinned on her back between its huge front legs. Heat streamed off its panting body, radiating on her sweating face until she thought she would pass out. The bear's breath was hot on her neck, her face only inches from its long white canines. Its curved claws slashed by her head as she struggled beneath it, trying to beat it away with blows from her fists.

"Marin, no!" Gareth screamed again, his voice barely audible over the bear's roars. "Please." He still held the dark fur in his grip, afraid to let go. He yanked the long strands until his fingers trembled from the exertion, but Marin was too powerful for him to pull back alone.

Then, as if hearing Gareth's plea for the first time, the bear snorted and swung its shaggy head to look at him. Saliva dripped from its panting mouth in foamy white splotches.

"She knows everything and I trust her. She saved my life, Marin. I trust her." He withdrew his hand from the bear's shoulder and let it fall against his own side, clenched into a fist. "Please stand up, Marin. Please. Talk to me."

Lindy watched in terror as the bruin dropped its head to stare into her eyes again. She knew it wanted to kill her, could almost *see* the deadly determination in its eyes. It huffed in her face, deep panted exhalations from the adrenaline coursing through its body, and stood immobile for a long time, just watching her, daring her to move. The ebony fur of its chest began to move closer to her face, making her recoil deeper into the litter of the forest floor when suddenly the bear backed up and arched away from her. In one fluid movement, its thick forelimbs lifted off the ground, slimming and lengthening to become muscular human arms. The furred hind legs stretched into smooth, powerful human legs. The long, tooth-filled muzzle shortened into a human face that looked down at her. What had been dark fur was now smooth olive skin. With his legs straddling her, the man towered above her and glared down with hate on his face.

Gareth reached down and grasped Lindy's hand to help her to her feet. She was shaking so badly her legs would hardly hold her and her teeth were chattering together loudly. He pulled her into his arms to calm her trembling and felt her heart racing against his bare chest in hard pulses. She couldn't speak, but could only stare in shock at the tall naked man glaring back at her from the spot where the bear had stood a moment before. He wondered if she was in shock.

"It's okay, Lindy," he said, running his arm up and down across her quivering back to soothe her. "This is Marin, our Guardian." He saw Marin's eyes following the movement of his hand on Lindy's body and he felt like he was melting from the heat of his disapproving stare. A lump formed in his throat at the thought of the trouble he was in.

"How badly are you hurt?" Marin asked him, ignoring the woman. His voice was deep and stern and rumbled from his throat when he swept his gaze over Gareth's body to assess his condition.

Gareth knew instinctively that Marin was questioning not only the damage done by the hunters but any harm that had been inflicted by Lindy, as well. "I'm healed, thanks to her good care." He swung his healing shoulder toward him as evidence.

The Guardian lowered his gaze to examine the wound before resuming his glare at the woman. He saw that she had stopped trembling in the safety of Gareth's arms and was now sweeping her gaze across his own body. Her eyes were wide at the sight of him.

Lindy tried to look away but she couldn't. The imposing man standing before her was well over six feet tall and like Gareth, was hairless except for his head and between his legs. His face was framed by ragged tufts of black hair so shaggy it could have been barbered by a child. The darkness of his hair matched the black depths of his eyes and fell haphazardly over them so that when he looked at her, he appeared to be peering through a tangled curtain of black. She wanted to run her fingers through that mess and sweep the hair out of his eyes. They were just too beautiful to cover.

Marin followed her gaze and as if reading her mind, raised one huge hand to his forehead to sweep the hair away. She realized then that it wasn't just his eyes that were beautiful.

His face was long and angular; still vaguely bear shaped, with high cheekbones and a square chin. His mouth was full and strong, melding with his other features to form a face that was rugged and wildly handsome. She couldn't take her eyes off him.

Marin stood immobile and watched her look at him, not the least bit embarrassed by his nudity. His eyes followed hers as they lowered from his face, traveled across the width of his broad shoulders, following down the sleek curves of his muscular chest and flat stomach. Lindy didn't even notice that he was watching her. She couldn't force her gaze away from his body. She'd seen plenty of men in her life, but never one that oozed raw sexuality the way this man did.

She felt Gareth's arms pull her tighter against him and couldn't help comparing the two men. Unlike Gareth's slight, lithe body, Marin had brute, muscular strength. Gareth's limbs were lean, while Marin bulged with well-developed power. And where Gareth was normally endowed, Marin was doubly blessed.

Gareth stood awkwardly between them. Her fascination with the Guardian was becoming dangerously obvious and he suddenly whirled her completely around until she faced him. Jealousy surged through him at the thought of her looking at Marin, at how she looked at him, filling him with surprising rage that he fought to keep under control. He groped for an explanation to keep her from looking at him further. "Don't ever stare at a bear unless you're challenging him," he whispered at last, at the same time squeezing her upper arm in warning until she nodded in understanding.

A rustling in the bushes caught their attention and they turned in unison to see five bears charge out of the forest toward them. Lindy recoiled in terror, drawing deeper into Gareth's embrace again. He held her tight, pleased that she found comfort in his arms, but suddenly very frightened by their situation. His heart began to race in time with hers. The animals came closer until he could see that they were charging in together for an attack.

The snarling bears circled around them, drawing closer and closer in a tightening noose until Marin raised his hand in an order to await his signal.

A shiver rippled down Lindy's back and she was struck by a raging pang of nausea. She gripped her arms tightly across her stomach to keep from getting sick. "Why do I have the terrible feeling they're going to kill me?" she whispered to Gareth, her voice shaking uncontrollably.

Gareth looked at her with fear on his own face. "Because they are."

Chapter Thirteen

Marin led the way back through the woods, followed by Lindy clenched in Gareth's grasp and the five bears trailing behind them. No one spoke, and other than the raven calling from high above, the forest was eerily silent.

Two hours passed before the thick forest gave way to a huge green meadow. Tall wild grasses waved in the gentle spring breeze, rustling soft whispers over the warming earth. Tiny flowers bloomed everywhere and released their sweet scent in the warmth of the afternoon sun. It was the most beautiful place Lindy had ever seen.

A flat granite boulder jutted from the edge of the meadow and towered over the grasses. Behind it, a huge cliff rose straight up toward the sky, its upper edge obscured by the crowns of ancient pines growing in front of it. When they neared the rock, Marin forced himself roughly between Gareth and Lindy. He grabbed her shoulder with one hand.

"Sit," he ordered, pushing her down at the base of the boulder while his fingertips dug into the tender flesh of her shoulder to assert his authority. "And you," he nodded to Gareth, "will address the clan."

Gareth nodded solemnly and walked around the boulder to stand on the opposite side from Lindy. Marin mounted the rock; his muscular arm rose to shield his face from the sun, and called the clan forth. "Kin, come forward to welcome Gareth home."

Bears appeared from everywhere. Large brown bears

the color of dark, rich chocolate, bigger black bears with gleaming ebony fur, small black cubs that tumbled playfully with every step they took. One huge black bruin bore a white, star-shaped patch of fur on his chest; another smaller ebony bear had the grizzled muzzle of great age.

Lindy watched amazed at the bears' advance. They loped from the forest and rose on hind legs from the meadow grasses, all coming together to gather around the rock where Marin stood. She could tell that the bears were of all ages, some very old and some newly born, and each one had its own unique appearance. She had grown up seeing black bears and never realized how different one could be from the next.

When they were settled, Marin looked down at Gareth with stern eyes. "Stand down and address your kin," he ordered.

Lindy looked over at Gareth, her forehead wrinkled with fear and confusion. Sweat was beading on her forehead and he knew it wasn't from the sun's warmth.

"Stand down means to shift into bear skin," he explained. "He wants me to speak in our language."

"But then I won't know what you're saying," she groaned.

"Silence!" Marin commanded, glaring down at her again. "You will not speak unless I tell you to do so." *How typically human, always wanting things their way*, he thought to himself.

Gareth turned to look up at Marin, a frown forming on his face. "It's only fair that she be allowed to hear what's spoken about her. If we were on trial, none of us would want any less."

Lindy looked up at Marin to see his response, but quickly looked away when he shot her a look that was pure hatred. A low growl slipped from his throat as he raised his face to the sun, thinking. He'd already determined that he would have to reprimand Gareth for contesting his order.

There was utter silence from the clan. No one dared to speak until Marin asked for them to do so. He'd been their Guardian for many years and had always advised them wisely and guarded them well. They respected his authority and knew better than to challenge it.

"Very well," he relented. "Stand tall," he called out to the clan.

As one, every bear arched its back and pulled its body away from the ground to stand up on two legs. Fur withdrew inside skin, exposing bare arms and legs where furry limbs had touched the ground a moment before. Bear faces became human faces and suddenly men, women and children stood in a semi-circle around the rock.

Lindy exhaled loudly, unaware that she'd been holding her breath. It was utterly miraculous seeing these creatures change before her eyes. Never in her wildest dreams had she dared to imagine that they really existed, that nature could have created such wonders. But she knew that the old stories were true. The subject of the tales she had heard around the campfire had come to life. A smile lit her face as she looked from each one of the Bear People to the next.

Her smile did not go unnoticed. Lilea glanced at Thoren, who stood nearby, to see if he saw what she did. He had a strange look on his wizened face and he nodded in response but didn't speak.

Marin cleared his throat, forcing their attention on him. "We celebrate the return of our bear kin—and the capture of his kidnapper."

"But I…" Lindy started to protest until one harsh look from Gareth made her words die in her throat.

"Tell us what happened," Marin ordered.

Gareth gazed out at his bear kin and pointed to his right shoulder. "Some of you were with me when I was shot by the poachers. I remember how you pursued them and how grateful I was that you denied them the chance to finish what they started. I ran blindly, unable to think clearly because of the pain. No one was with me when my strength gave out and I fell, knowing that death was near. Then this human…" he swept his arm back to point at Lindy, "saved me."

Whispered gasps drifted up from the Bear People. They

had never heard of such a thing. Humans were only capable of hurting and killing them; it was unbelievable that a human would rescue one of them.

"Her name is Lindy. She didn't hold me against my will as a kidnapper would, but welcomed me as a guest in her home. She gave me food and shelter, she cared for my injury. Not once did she force me to do something I didn't want to do, or to stay when I didn't want to stay. I was treated with kindness and respect. Without her help, I wouldn't be standing here before you now."

Lindy turned to peek up at Marin, hoping to see compassion on his face. Instead his expression was harsh and unmoved. Just the sight of his angry face made her shudder. *How much authority does he wield over this clan*, she wondered. *And will Gareth's testimony even matter in the end*?

"My kin, you know that I would never betray our family to the humans or knowingly endanger us in any way. But when I was injured, I couldn't control myself and I shifted in her presence, unintentionally revealing our secret. When I realized what I had done, I didn't know what to expect from her or what harm she would do to me."

A collective tremor rippled through the crowd of bears as each one imagined in his own mind how Gareth must have felt when he realized what had happened in front of the human woman. It was forbidden to shift in the presence of anyone other than a clan member. They knew they would have been terrified.

"But I had nothing to fear. Trust me when I tell you that she has a good heart. If she had wanted to do me harm, she had many opportunities to do so. And yet, here I stand, unharmed and healed. I've come to understand that what we've been taught about humans is not true about *every* human; that some are kind and compassionate just as we are. That this woman is not like others we've encountered. I know in my heart that she would never harm us. So I ask you to consider my plea and spare her life."

Spare my life? Sweat beaded on the back of her neck at

the thought of what they might do to her. Marin looked more than eager to rip her apart and chew her up in little pieces. The memory roared back into her mind of his huge clawed paws slashing into the ground on each side of her head and the thought of it sent waves of nausea washing through her. The sweat trickled down her back and plastered her shirt to her clammy skin.

"Are you finished?" Marin asked Gareth.

He shot a peek over at Lindy and nodded. "I've said what needs to be said."

"Then it's time that we vote. What will it be?" Marin called out, obviously anxious to get on with the dirty work. "Aye to remove the threat?" The phrase was less a question than a statement of presumption.

One by one, the Bear People voiced their votes as Marin called on them, and one after another, ayes were tallied against her. Gareth couldn't believe it. It was as though they hadn't heard a word he'd said. He lowered his head, devastated by the direction of the voting. Marin nodded toward Lilea, requesting her decision. Only she and Thoren had yet to vote. She opened her mouth to speak.

"Wait!" Lindy cried out, ignoring Marin's scowl. She stood up in front of the boulder and looked at the clan, her gaze searching all the eyes focused on her. "I'd like to speak. If this vote is to decide whether I live or die, then I at least want to have my say. *Please.*" She turned and stared up at Marin, challenging him to deny her what was only fair. She knew she had nothing to lose.

The corner of his mouth rose slightly at her impertinence. *Humans! The foul creatures never knew when to keep their mouths shut. But what would it hurt to let her speak? After all, it would be the last chance she ever got.* His eyes narrowed as he looked down at her. "Then speak."

A shudder tremored through her and all she could think of was running away as quickly as she could. But she knew there was no way she could escape them. They would outrun her easily and kill her anyway. Instead, she took a deep breath and fought to keep her voice calm. "Gareth has explained to me how you feel about humans, about the hunters who trespass in your home and kill bears without knowing or caring who or what you are. I understand this and I condemn those of my kind who treat you so badly. But if you kill me, you're doing the same thing that those outlaw humans do. You're judging me as though I were one of the poachers, though I've never harmed a bear or any animal. I offered sanctuary to Gareth and I will offer it again to any of your clan who need a safe haven in times of danger. I can help you. I *will* help you. But don't you see? By voting to kill me, you're becoming the very thing you hate. And you're losing a friend."

There was silence while the Bear People considered her plea. Most of them had never heard a human speak more than a few words and they were surprised that she spoke so passionately to them. Marin didn't like it one bit; there should be nothing to consider. But he knew he had to ask. "Does anyone wish to change his vote?"

Lindy held her breath and looked imploringly from one face to another, but there was silence.

"The vote stands," Marin said with a touch of satisfaction in his voice. "It seems that we are all in agreement that humans are good for only one thing. *Trouble.*"

Gareth walked over to Lindy and boldly took her hand, causing a gasp of shock to arise from the clan. "No they're not," he retorted, visibly angered. "I've given testimony to show that this one is different. If you vote to kill her, you're calling me a liar. And I will not live among those who doubt my word." He stood defiant before them, his fingers clenching hers forcefully.

Lindy squeezed his hand, gratefully acknowledging the sacrifice he was willing to make on her behalf. But hope had left her and she just felt numb inside.

Marin scowled at Gareth's inappropriate behavior and shook his head. Such foolishness. He'd have to give the young he-bear a good talking to when this was all over. "The vote will continue. Lilea?"

The she-bear looked from Marin to Gareth and then to Lindy, trying to read their hearts. She knew that Marin spoke the truth, as he always did. Humans were trouble; there was no doubt about that. But could Gareth be right, too? Could there be a human that didn't want to hurt them?" She gazed into the woman's blue eyes, remembering her smile of delight when she'd watched the bears shift. That wasn't the face of someone with evil intentions. And Gareth had admitted that she could easily have hurt him if she had so chosen. But she hadn't, she had taken care of him and restored him to health, and because of that she deserved to be given a chance.

"Nay," she said.

Marin's eyes flared open and he cocked his head low and to one side, not believing what he'd heard. "Repeat your vote."

"I said nay. I will not condone her murder." Lilea lifted her head high, looking defiant.

"Nor will I," added Thoren from beside her. The old he-bear rarely disagreed with the Guardian, but on this occasion, he thought Marin was wrong. "This woman offers us sanctuary and I believe it would be a wise precaution on our part to have a safe haven away from forest home."

The bears looked from one to another, momentarily confused. This was the first time that they could ever remember sparing a human's life.

Gareth pulled Lindy close against him to speak quietly in her ear. "The vote must be unanimous to kill. You're spared."

Relief flooded through her and she wanted to sweep him into her arms and hug him, but she knew better than to do such a thing in front of his kin. Instead she stood silently with her head bent down in humility.

Marin jumped down from the rock and stood before them, his displeasure clear in his expression. Then he swung around and thrust his face toward Gareth's. "If any member of this clan dies for your mistake, you will pay."

For the first time in his life, Gareth wasn't intimidated by the Guardian. "I'm not mistaken, Marin. You are." He stood there for a moment, and then quickly pulled Lindy away before he said something that Marin would make him regret.

"Wait," she said, laying her hand on Gareth's arm. She turned away and walked over to where Lilea and Thoren stood together watching. She smiled and held her hand over her heart, wanting them to know how deeply grateful she was. "Thank you. I appreciate what both of you did for me."

Thoren nodded, his brown eyes flashing warmly beneath a mop of grizzled gray and brown hair. He looked old enough to be Gareth's grandfather. He seemed suddenly embarrassed, and clearing his throat softly, he stepped away to talk to the other he-bears.

Lindy and Lilea stood together. Lilea was petite and lovely, her long ebony hair shining in the afternoon sun. Her brown eyes were so dark they seemed almost black and they sparkled when she gazed at the human woman. She moved her face closer to Lindy and peered deeply into her eyes. She had never seen eyes that were blue.

"I'm sorry for staring," she said shyly. "I've just never been this close to a human before."

Lindy smiled and nodded. "Please don't apologize, I understand completely. That's how I felt when I met Gareth." She paused and exhaled softly, still reeling from what had just happened. "How can I ever thank you for what you did?"

The she-bear returned her smile. "Thanks are never needed for doing what's right."

Despite Lilea's assurance, Lindy wasn't so confident. She nodded over her shoulder toward Marin, who had remained by the boulder to watch them. "I admire your courage for standing up to him. He's so frightening."

Lilea's eyes swept past her to settle on Marin, a flicker of emotion surging within their dark depths to betray her desire for the Guardian. A knowing smile broke across her pretty face. "He acts meaner than he really is," she murmured. "But he doesn't scare me."

Lindy saw the longing on Lilea's face and turned around to look at Marin again, trying to see in him what Lilea obviously saw. She had to admit that he was handsome with that rugged face and firm jaw jutting out determinedly. His arms were crossed over his chest, causing his biceps to protrude, and the tops of his powerful pectoral muscles thrust up behind his thick forearms. He stood with his legs open in a wide stance, a masculine display of his power and authority. Every time he shifted position, the muscles of his huge thighs bulged prominently. Every part of him boasted confidence and strength.

Her eyes fell to the mound between his thighs and lingered on his masculinity. It was impressive, to be sure. She felt her face grow flushed and she looked up to find his gaze fully upon her. He didn't flinch, but seemed rather to enjoy her embarrassment while he obviously felt none. She knew that he was forcing her to back down and look away.

She turned back to Lilea and smiled, understanding the woman's attraction to Marin a bit better. "Well, thank you again." Then rejoining Gareth, she let him lead her away and take her home.

Chapter Fourteen

Marin climbed back on the rock and watched his kin stand down and resume their feeding. He began to arch his back to shift into bear skin too, then changing his mind, he rose back up and stood straight to look over the grasses waving in the meadow. He could just make out their figures as Gareth and Lindy disappeared into the forest in the direction of the human's home.

This was worse than anything that had ever happened to the clan. In all his years as Guardian, he had never had as bad a feeling as he had now. He couldn't count the number of times that he'd had to rescue his kin from hunters or free them from the cruel steel traps that humans hid in the forest. Even now, he could hear their haunting cries as they begged for release from snares or called for help after being shot. He had borne the pain of helping them over and over and never felt the terror that he felt now.

From the time that they were born, cubs were taught to never trust a human. Above everything else, the safety of the clan was paramount. They knew that humans couldn't understand their shapeshifting ability or why they had adapted themselves to use it. History had taught them that if humans knew about their unique abilities, they would try to conquer the Bear People and use them to their own advantage. It was that way with humans. They always took what they wanted.

Marin was born of the Guardian bloodline. His father and all his grandsires before him had been the Guardians of the clan. It was their responsibility to protect the Bear People from anything or anyone that tried to hurt them, and sometimes it even meant protecting them from themselves. Marin had devoted his life to his kin and risked his own safety many times to do so. Yet no matter how many times he did, one of them would inevitably put himself in danger once again and Marin would be forced to rescue him.

Not that he minded. There was no position in the clan that garnered more respect than his. He loved the way everyone looked at him when he walked by, loved the admiration in their eyes when they gazed at his powerful body. No one in the clan was stronger than him. Or smarter. No one was more desired by the she-bears than he was.

But despite all the advantages, there were times when he thought he would give it all up to live a normal life. He spent every minute doting over his kin; never taking his eyes off them for fear that someone would get hurt. He'd spent many sleepless nights worrying over injured yearlings and searching for lost cubs, and it took its toll on him. But nothing in the past compared to what he was facing now.

Leave it to Gareth to bring a human to forest home. The young man had always been a thorn in Marin's side. He had a good heart and a good mind, but tended to think more with the former than the latter. Once, as a yearling, he had strayed beyond the boundary of the forest and followed a human child into a city park. Marin had been forced to sneak into the humans' habitat and guide the cub out, barely making it out safely. And now this.

Marin couldn't fault Gareth for shifting in the human's presence, though. He knew that it was sometimes beyond their control when they were injured or scared. But it was what the young he-bear had done *after that* that concerned him. Gareth should have done what was expected of him to keep the clan safe. He should have done what Marin had instructed all of them to do in an emergency: kill the human. Then there would be no doubt that the damage was contained and the situation was over.

But Gareth hadn't killed her. He had done the worst possible thing and brought her into their midst, betraying not only his kin but their home to her, as well. And as if that wasn't bad enough, the clan had been foolish enough to agree with it. He shook his head at the thought of them allowing her to go free. The memory of Gareth taking the human's hand into his own was enough to make him sick.

But despite his warning, the clan had voted and he was overruled. He was powerless to undo the damage Gareth had caused. Now all he could do was keep a vigilant eye on the clan and prepare himself for what assuredly was to come. The human would betray them and once again, he would be forced to risk his life.

Marin sank down on the rock and let his head droop to his chest. He loved his kin but sometimes they were almost too much trouble. Why didn't they listen to him? Why hadn't they taken his warning to heart? If he lost even one of the clan, he would be heartsick. And it would be Gareth's fault. He took a deep breath and tried to force the foreboding feelings away. But he knew the first impression he'd had standing outside the human's cabin was correct. Things had taken a very bad turn indeed.

Chapter Fifteen

Lindy arranged the logs in the fireplace and set them ablaze. Then she sank on the couch, relieved to be safe at home again, and covered her eyes with her hands, unable to hold back the tears as the impact of what almost happened finally sank in. Her body began to tremble and she sobbed uncontrollably.

Gareth sat beside her and watched helplessly. He had never seen someone cry before and had no idea what to do. But he knew how shaken she was by what had happened and he was willing to do anything to comfort her. Or anything to feel her arms around him again.

"I'm sorry," he murmured over and over. "I didn't know they were coming here to rescue me or I would never have let you come with me." How could he tell her the awful truth—that they weren't just coming to rescue him, but were coming for *both* of them?

Blonde hair fell across her eyes, hiding her face from him. The one thing that brought her some comfort was knowing that it wasn't his fault and that he couldn't have known what his clan was planning for her. She was sure of that. And the way he'd protected her, stood up to his own kin to help her only made her appreciate him more.

"I know," she said, wiping her tears on the back of her hand. "I'm not mad at you, Gareth. Jeez, you saved my life. You saved me from them." She looked up at him through the wet strands and smiled, forcing herself to control the fear tremoring through her. Her stomach was still in knots.

His heart melted at the sight of her terror. He inched closer until he could slip his arm behind her shoulder and then pulled her closer to him. He hated the way his kin had treated her and made her so frightened; they had been as cruel to her as some humans were to them. But he didn't know how to make it better for her, so he just sat silently and held her.

They watched the fire for a long time, both of them content to be together away from the pressure of Marin and the clan. Gunther laid on the floor at Lindy's feet, snoring softly in the warm glow of the flames, oblivious to his mistress's distress.

Finally Lindy shook her head and groaned. There was one horrible thought she couldn't shake, no matter how hard she tried. The image of it played over and over in her mind until she thought she would scream. "I know what Marin would have done to me. He wanted to rip me to shreds. There were a few times when his jaws came so close to my head that I could feel his breath on my cheek. I was so scared, Gareth. What kind of a leader is he anyway? Why would he do something that evil? He's horrible."

Gareth smiled and rubbed his fingers across the top of her shoulder, wishing that her skin wasn't hidden beneath the fabric of her shirt. He wanted to see what lay beneath the cloth and run his fingers over the curves of her chest as she had done to him. All he could think about was touching that soft white skin. "He's not evil and he's not our leader. Marin is our Guardian and what he did is exactly what he's supposed to do—guard us. He protects our clan."

She snorted softly with a toss of her head and shoved her damp hair off her cheek. "Some protector. He didn't do a very good job protecting you that day, did he?"

Gareth took her chin in his fingers and tilted her head toward him. The look on his face was dead serious. "Don't ever let him hear you say that or he *will* kill you, Lindy. I guarantee it. Marin is an excellent Guardian and he's risked his life many times to save me, but even he isn't infallible. We're helpless against the power and accuracy of a rifle."

Lindy nodded and pulled away from his grasp. "I just don't understand why he hates me so much. I never did anything to him. I never hurt any of you."

A sigh escaped Gareth's lips, revealing the division in his feelings. He owed his life to Marin several times over and would never stop being grateful for that, but at the same time, he couldn't deny that the Guardian could be too harsh and judgmental, and always refused to admit when he was wrong. He had his way of doing things and he expected the clan to comply.

"It's a complicated thing, Lindy," he sighed again. "It's not that Marin hates you, in particular. He's sworn to protect the clan from anyone that could hurt us, and that *anyone* is always a human. All his life he's seen the worst in humankind and never the best. He's never known a human who hasn't tried to hurt us, so he doesn't know any better. Honestly, I don't think he believes there *could* be a good human. But I'll try my best to change that."

Crossing her arms over her chest, she laid her head against the back of the sofa and pictured the Guardian, remembering how smug he'd acted. "Well, I have no respect for a man who tries to kill an innocent woman."

Gareth swung his head to look at her, stunned by the irony of her statement. If only she knew how true those words were, and how that very thing had wounded Marin so badly. But what had happened to the Guardian so long ago was not for him to share. He would leave it to Marin to explain, if and when he ever chose to do so.

"Thank God I'll never have to see him again," she said, her voice full of relief.

"Then you'll never see me again, either." Gareth hung his head and closed his eyes, wounded by the thought of it. He couldn't let that happen.

"Why not? Can't you come here to visit me without Marin tagging along like a big brother?"

Looking sidelong at her from beneath his lowered eyelids, Gareth shook his head slowly back and forth. "He would never allow it. It's not safe for me here, or any place where humans are near. The only way I can see you again is if you visit me at forest home, if I bring you there so Marin can keep an eye on you. It's the only way he would ever accept it." *If he ever accepts it*, he thought.

She exhaled slowly, considering his words. It was clear from his behavior that Gareth wanted to keep in contact with her. She owed him so much that the thought of disappointing him made her ache inside. But it was more than that, she realized. It wasn't just his need, but her own that she wanted to satisfy. She was fascinated by the Bear People. There was so much she wanted to know about them. The thought that she could be among them, learning from them and maybe even teaching them about the goodness of her own species, was tantalizing.

"How can I make the clan like me?" she asked, thinking that if she couldn't win the Guardian over, perhaps she could appeal to the others. Maybe there was some way to earn their trust.

"You can't make them like you any more than you can force them to accept you," he said softly, trying not to sound too harsh. "All you can do is prove to them that what you said is true and that you're worthy of their friendship. They need to unlearn what they've always been taught about humans. It will take time, but I'll help you."

She laid her hand over his and squeezed it softly. "Any suggestions on how to begin?"

Gareth's mood brightened and he thought for a moment, then stood and left the room. When he returned, his hands were full of food—fruit, jelly, a jar of honey. One eyebrow raised above a broad grin.

"Did you know that the way to a bear's heart is through his stomach?"

CHAPTER SIXTEEN

Notch tumbled down the small hill, rolling end over end until he came to rest on his plump rear end with a thud. "Look, Mama, I'm a rolling stone," he giggled.

Lena looked up from her feeding and eyed her cub, assuring herself that he was safe before lowering her mouth back to the log in search of the black ants swarming along the bark. As long as he was in view, she was comfortable giving him room to run and play.

Notch climbed back up the hill and somersaulted down again, squealing with delight each time his head bumped the soft earth. This was his first spring and everything he discovered was new and exciting. Each day brought wonderful adventures and challenges and he took full advantage of every opportunity to get in trouble. Like any child, he drove his mother crazy.

At the bottom of the hill, he rolled on his back over the green grass, loving its soft tickle against his fur. He raised his soft dark eyes skyward and found a face looking back down at him.

"Hi Gareth," he giggled. "You're upside-down."

Gareth laughed and scooped the cub up into his arms, inhaling his young scent that smelled of milk and grass. "Good morning, Notch."

The cub nuzzled the man with his small black nose. "I'm glad you're back. I was worried about you."

"I'm glad to be back, too. I have a good friend who helped

me come back home."

Notch nodded solemnly. "The lady."

"That's right. And she's brought you a surprise. Would you like to see it?"

"Yeah!" Notch wriggled in his arms until he was set back down on the ground. "What is it? Tell me!"

"Just a minute." Gareth stepped away and disappeared behind a nearby bush before reappearing with Lindy at his side. She held a large oblong basket in her hands and smiled at him.

"Hi Notch," she said.

He drew back with a frightened hiss and turned to run to his mother when Gareth held out his hand, imploring him to stop. "Don't be afraid, little one. Lindy won't hurt you, I promise. Remember what I said the other day, about what good care she took of me? She's a nice human, a friendly human. And look what she's brought you."

Notch had frozen in place halfway up the hill. This posed quite the dilemma, he decided. Mama had taught him to run at the first scent of humans, but Gareth's friend carried a very big basket and he would give anything to see what was in it. Curiosity won out over caution. He descended the hill and stood beside the man. "What is it?" he asked, his small round eyes growing large with interest.

Lindy set the basket down, reached inside and brought out a clear jar. She unscrewed the lid and handed it to Gareth, who waved it in front of the cub's nose.

Notch's eyes became as large as full moons in his tiny head and his nose twitched uncontrollably at the delectable scent. Honey! Sweet, rich, golden honey. "Yum," he whined.

"Let's go ask your mother," Gareth said, drawing Lindy and the cub to his side. They crested the top of the hill and came face to face with the sow.

"Good morning, Lena," Gareth nodded as the cub ran to her and hid between her front paws.

She raised her mouth from the log and her eyes widened with surprise, but she nodded politely in acknowledgment.

"Does she understand you when you speak English?" Lindy asked.

"Yes," Gareth said, nodding. He held out the jar of honey before him until she caught a whiff of it. Her chocolate brown eyes widened even more at the offering but she hesitated, her eyes rolling from Gareth to Lindy and back to the man. She was closer to the human than she really cared to get.

"It's all right. It's a thank you gift...from both of us," he said, swinging his head to indicate Lindy.

The she-bear peered curiously at Lindy for a moment, thinking to herself that the woman didn't look too frightening, then she lowered her head to her cub and snuffled softly to him, checking to ensure that he hadn't been harmed. When she saw that he was fine, she gazed at the honey-filled jar. It smelled delectable. One swipe of her paw sent the jar to its side, releasing a molten flow of golden honey. Notch scrambled forward and stuck his tongue deep in it, but his mother was reluctant to share. After all, honey was a precious commodity and this was her first sampling of the year. She swatted Notch away and stuck her mouth in where his had been.

Gareth smiled and took Lindy's hand to lead her away. Lena's acceptance of the gift was a good sign, but he knew it may not go so well with all of the clan members. But he was optimistic. They had a full basket of treats to distribute: juicy apples and peaches, bread and sweet rolls, jars of honey and jelly. It was a feast big enough to treat the entire clan and he hoped that they would accept it as a message of Lindy's desire to be friends.

They made their way through the meadow where the trial had occurred the day before, moving from one bear to another and offering their food. For many of the bears, their reluctance to accept the gifts was momentary and with Gareth's assurance of their safety, they were easily convinced. For others, it was a more difficult decision and Gareth had to do a lot of convincing. But before the afternoon was half over, every bear was stretched out in the warm grass with his or her chosen treat. If they had any reluctance to have this human in their midst, it was overcome by Gareth's promise that he was keeping a vigilant eye on her. Only Marin remained perched on the boulder, warily watching the others while he denied the gifts offered to him.

While Lindy played at the hill with Notch, Gareth approached the rock and nodded to the Guardian. "You haven't taken a gift, Marin. There's a jar of honey for you."

The bear merely yawned and plopped his rear end down on the soft moss covering the boulder.

Gareth looked over his shoulder at Lindy and when he turned back to Marin, exasperation was plain on his face. "Would you please stand tall, Marin?" His tone was almost begging. "Please stand up so I can talk to you in man-speak."

The bear blinked lazily and swatted away a fly, knowing full well what Gareth wanted to ask. He really didn't want to hear it, but not wanting to be rude to his kin, he panted out a growling sigh and arched his back to stand up; raising his bulky body upright until his front paws rose off the boulder. His rear legs straightened and lengthened, growing into two muscled, olive-skinned legs that supported a well developed upper body. When he looked down at Gareth, Marin peered from two human eyes.

"What is it, Gareth?" he asked, sitting down on the rock again. He leaned back on his arms with his long legs stretched out before him.

"I wish you'd take the gift Lindy brought you. It would mean a lot to her."

Marin harrumphed condescendingly. "You mean the bribe? Sorry, I'm not so easily bought."

Gareth rested his hands on his hips and shook his head, wondering if this was a lost cause. Marin was difficult to convince when his mind was open, let alone when he already had it made up about something. But he knew that if he was going to have any chance to continue seeing Lindy, he had to try. "It's not a bribe. It's a thank you, or in your case, a peace offering." A look of frustration swept across his face. "You know, she's trying her best to prove to the clan that they made the right decision about her."

Marin just stared at him. "And you know that I think the clan was wrong."

"I guess time will tell," Gareth retorted. They stared at each other in silence for a few moments, neither ready to back down. Then realizing that nothing would be gained by an impasse, Gareth took a step closer and looked into Marin's hardened eyes. "Guardian, I rarely ask a favor of you. But I'm asking you now, as my bear kin, will you please make an effort to be civil to her? I'm not asking you to become friends with her, or even to like her. All I'm asking is that you not treat her like a criminal. She saved my life. If that means *anything* to you, please do this for me." With a nod of respect, he wheeled around and walked away.

Marin grunted to himself, annoyed yet impressed by the younger man's words. Gareth knew just how to get to him, how to throw the one thing in his face that he couldn't deny. The woman *had* saved his life and restored his health. He sat on the rock a while longer, weighing the idea in his mind. It had been a long, cold winter and the fruit the woman had brought did look succulent. But he had never taken anything from a human and the thought of taking even a single piece of fruit from one now was almost beyond comprehension.

His sight fell upon Gareth and Lindy sitting together in the meadow. The young man gazed wistfully into her eyes while he ate, more delighted by her presence than the food. In the afternoon light, her hair shimmered as golden as the sun itself. And her eyes... Marin had never seen such a glorious color in eyes before. They looked like the clear summer sky. He couldn't deny that she was a beautiful woman, her tall, lithe body so opposite the small, golden-skinned she-bears of his clan. His gaze drifted across her body, falling from the curve of her chest to the long legs that she had folded beneath herself. Her pale skin looked as inviting as the soft drifts of snow that he had jumped into as a cub. He wondered how her skin would look lying next to his own deeply tanned skin...

He shook his head to drive the thought away. *Fool.* That

was exactly why he stayed away from the she -bears. Females were too great a temptation, and temptation meant putting the clan at risk. That, he would not do. Still, sometimes the loneliness was more than he could take, and his dreams would fill with memories of the sensual nights so long ago that he had shared with someone else.

A soft, slow growl rolled from his throat. What harm would it do to be cordial to her? It wasn't her fault that she'd been born human, and she was putting forth an effort to thank the clan. At least she knew how to show proper gratitude. He thought about Gareth's testimony, about how she'd given him food and shelter and taken care of his wound. In his mind, he could see her slim fingers cleaning the blood from Gareth's shoulder and hear her talking calmly to soothe him.

For just a moment, an unexpected twinge of jealousy rushed through him. Why had Gareth been the one to meet this human woman and experience something no one else ever had, to actually be *inside* her home and discover what her life was like? He was mystified by how quickly Gareth had fallen for her when he'd only been with her for a few days. What had she done to make him want her so? Would she someday invite others into her home? Would she invite him?

Marin sighed and looked away to gather his thoughts. He knew he was traveling dangerous ground with thoughts like these. Humans and bears were not meant to interact; this had been a law of the clan for as long as the Bear People had existed. They had chosen this way of life for good reason—to stay alive. It was foolish of him to entertain thoughts of any kind of relationship with a human now. He among all of them should know better.

Still, Gareth was right. He rarely asked for a favor. It would take a stone cold heart to deny him the one thing he asked, and Marin wasn't sure his heart was quite that cold. Yet.

Exhaling deeply, he slipped off the rock and walked across the meadow to the place where the couple sat.

"I will speak to her," he said grudgingly to Gareth, indicating his desire to speak to her alone. The younger man rose with a nod of thanks and walked away, leaving the two of them staring at each other.

After an awkward moment of silence, Marin sat down facing her and gazed into the basket at her side. Two peaches, a jar of honey and a frosted sweet roll remained.

"Take them, they're for you," Lindy offered, struggling to keep the tremor from her voice.

Marin looked up at her with surprise on his face. "All of them?"

She nodded and pushed the basket closer to him. "You're the Guardian. You need to keep up your strength."

A tiny smile appeared on his face at her acknowledgment of his position, and he took the food and placed it on the ground by his side. He raised his gaze to look at her face again, to stare at the liquid blue softness of her eyes.

She returned his gaze, suddenly full of questions she wanted to ask him but knowing better than to do so. Then she looked away again and sat silent, heeding Gareth's warning to let he-bears initiate conversation. While the seconds dragged by, she fought to keep her gaze on the basket or on her own hands folded nervously in her lap. Anywhere but on his handsome naked body.

Marin watched her eyes flick back and forth in her struggle to keep from gawking at him and he chuckled softly. Her gaze rose immediately to meet his, her eyes instantly full of anger at him for enjoying her embarrassment. "Does the sight of my body bother you?" he asked at last. His voice was deep and slow, seeping out of his throat like thick, rich syrup.

One eyebrow arched above her clear blue eyes. "I'm just not accustomed to your clan's nudity. All the men I know wear pants."

A grin broke across his face. How delightful it was to make her squirm. "*Human* men, you mean." He stretched his arms out behind him and leaned back, letting the sunlight glisten off his muscular chest and bringing his manhood into even clearer view. "Clothes are so confining," he laughed.

Two can play this game, Marin, she thought, returning

the smile. "Well, if it doesn't bother you then I won't let it bother me." She mimicked his position and settled her focus on every glorious inch of him. Why not enjoy the view if he was so intent on providing it?

They sat for a moment quietly eyeing each other. Marin was perfectly content to wait and test the limits of her patience. He raised a peach to his mouth and took a bite, ignoring the trickle of sweet juice that fell from his chin.

Lindy watched the juice drop onto his chest and roll across his burnished skin. With every bite he took and each movement of his arm, his well-developed muscles rippled, directing the juice into the valley between his pectorals. The moisture glistened golden in the light like flecks of pure gold in a shallow stream. She watched the drop roll slowly down across his taut stomach and inch toward the hair of his groin. Heat rushed through her and she felt her lower body tighten with arousal. She quickly looked away.

Marin noticed each subtle movement her body made, from the flutter of her eyelashes to the trembling of her thighs as she became aroused. A sudden thought raged through his mind: *could it be that she desires me*? He wasn't sure if he was flattered or disgusted by the idea of it. He knew that he could have his choice among any of the she-bears and if he rejected all of them, why would he even think sexual thoughts about a human female? Still, the possibility of such a forbidden thing was intriguing.

He exhaled softly and wiped the juice away with his hand, deciding he'd tormented her enough. "You like him."

"What?" Lindy lifted her head to look at him, surprised that he had spoken again.

"Gareth. You like him."

She wasn't sure if he was implying friendship or something more, so she decided to play it safe with a vague answer. "Yes I do," she said simply.

"Why did you help him?"

"He needed help."

Marin narrowed his eyes and leaned forward. "But you

knew what he was."

She shook her head, sending tendrils of glistening blonde swaying attractively around her face. She felt like a criminal being questioned by the police. "Not until after he was in my house. When I found him, he was in human form."

"Would you have done differently if you had known before that?"

Lindy thought about it for a minute. "If I had found an injured bear in my yard, no, I wouldn't have brought it into my house. But I would have called a vet and gotten some help for it. I can't *not* help something that's injured, whether it's a person or a bear or a dog. I'm just that way."

A low hum slipped from Marin's throat. *At least she was honest.* He leaned closer and stared into her eyes. "You shouldn't be here."

"I know," she admitted, realizing that she was starting to tremble as his dark eyes bored into hers. She wished Gareth had stayed nearby in case she needed help.

"Then why are you here?"

She took two deep breaths to calm her nerves before answering. "Because I wanted to meet the Bear People. Gareth told me so much about them that I just wanted to meet them for myself. And…" she paused, wondering whether to continue with the thought or not. "And because I don't want to lose contact with Gareth."

The corner of Marin's mouth rose just enough to look like a sneer. "He's fond of you. Too fond."

She felt a blush rise to her cheeks. "I think he's grateful to me for taking care of him."

"He's naive and easily enchanted by the wrong things."

Lindy narrowed her eyes to return his stare. Was Marin insulting her? "You make it sound like I'm deceiving him in some way. I am not taking advantage of him, if that's what you're implying."

"Aren't you?"

"NO," she retorted. "Gareth is a grown man who can make his own decisions. I like him and if the feeling is mutual, that's fine with me."

Marin rose to his knees and rested his hands on the tops of his thighs to lean closer to her. His dark hair tumbled down around his face like an ominous cloud covering the sun. "You would do well to remember that he is not a man. He is a bear and he is not for you." His voice had become gruff and intimidating.

"Is that your advice for me, Marin?" she asked, her anger rising. Who did he think he was to tell her who she could or couldn't care about?

His eyes narrowed as he stood to leave and he glared down at her. "No human, it's not my *advice*. It's my warning."

Chapter Seventeen

Clan life was thrown into chaos by the presence of the human woman among them. While some of the bears welcomed her with curious amusement the way a human welcomes a strange new pet into his home, other bears thought it outrageous that Gareth had even dared to bring the enemy into their territory. But either way, Lindy was the center of attention and a great fascination to all of them.

The clan was split fairly evenly in their opinions. Most of the he-bears felt the way Marin did, that Gareth was a fool to even entertain the notion of a relationship with a human. They all knew that bears and humans weren't meant to mix, yet the taboo of it was somehow enticing. And while Gareth had never come right out and admitted that he was attracted to her, it was embarrassingly obvious how he felt. When they were together, he never took his eyes off her. He behaved as though he didn't trust the others to be near her without hurting or scaring her, but they began to wonder if that was truly the reason or if he simply feared that they might want to steal his prize away from him. Judging by some of their comments, it could have been either way.

On one occasion, Gareth had overheard the he-bears discussing the woman. One of them in particular, an overweight, middle-aged bruin called Arlin, had expressed a lewd interest in her that immediately perked up the ears of the other he-bears. Gareth wasn't surprised, knowing that Arlin had trouble maintaining much of a relationship with any of the she-bears.

The other males poked fun at him, calling him 'sexually challenged' for his inability to attract the females. From the way Arlin talked, maybe he thought he'd have a better chance of mating with Lindy. He seemed to be giving the idea a lot of thought.

He had been stretched out on his back letting the sun warm his furry belly when he made the comments that worried Gareth. "I've heard that humans mate from the front," he had drawled with a gravelly voice. "Now how do you suppose that works?"

The others turned to stare at him with quizzical expressions as though the thought had never occurred to them. They knew it just wasn't done that way.

Arlin continued, oblivious to their stares. "How would she do that down on all fours?" he asked, trying to work out the mechanics of it. "I don't get it."

The he-bears were silent, except for Marin, who lounged nearby and burst out laughing. "Did it ever occur to you that you might have to shift to do it?" he asked.

Arlin thought for a moment, unable to visualize mating in man skin. "But once I've stood tall, do I stand up or lay down to do it?"

Everyone snickered as they considered the possibilities.

"I think you'd have to stand up to get the job done," a young bruin named Shara said.

"No, no," Thoren disagreed strongly. "It would be done best lying down."

Arlin was becoming more and more confused. "But if I lay down, is she on me or am I on her?"

Now they were all equally confused, but no one was willing to admit that he just didn't know. Any way they pictured it, it seemed awkward and ridiculous.

"Well, all I know," said Arlin, "is that I'd love to rest my head on those chest pads of hers." Murmurs of agreement rose up around him.

Marin hummed thoughtfully. "They do look tempting. I wonder if they're as soft as they look."

The others nodded, picturing the way Lindy's breasts moved when she walked.

"Gareth," Shara called to the cinnamon bear that grazed near Marin at the edge of the group. "Did you get a look at those things when she had you there?"

Gareth raised his head from the grass and tried to keep the anger from showing on his face. If they suspected how jealous he was of their fascination with Lindy's body, they'd never stop harassing him. He finished chewing and forced himself to speak calmly. "Sorry guys, I never got the chance."

Arlin rolled over and rested his head on his paws. "So what really happened all those days you were there, Gareth?"

All eyes swiveled to focus on Gareth and hear his answer. Every ear perked up.

"What do you mean 'what happened'? What do you think happened? I was shot in the shoulder and she took care of me." He shook his head at the stupidity of his question.

Thoren snorted raucously. "Yes, but what *part* of you did she take care of?" The others roared with laughter.

Gareth took a step toward him with his head lifted defensively high. "What do you mean by that?"

Arlin interrupted with his own explanation. "Oh come on, Gareth, add it all up. She's female. You're male. She's used to seeing males in clothes. You had no clothes on. She had you trapped in that building—alone. You said she touched you when she cared for your wound. We just want to know the details. Anything could have happened."

"But *nothing* happened," he protested.

"*Nothing?*" Thoren repeated.

Gareth shook his head. "You guys make it sound like some spring mating ritual went on in there, but it didn't. I was hurt; she took care of my wound, end of story."

"I bet you *wish* that something had happened," Arlin drawled. "Just to be able to say that you did it with a human."

"Of course not," Gareth lied, speaking a little too forcefully. "Who would wish such a thing?"

Marin swung his head to look him in the eye. "Who

wouldn't?" he replied before he could stop himself. Then his eyes flared with embarrassment and he rolled on his side, unable to believe that he'd just said what he did. He, above all of them, had no business thinking such thoughts.

Everyone was quiet for a moment while they contemplated Marin's shocking admission. Each of them suddenly realized that despite how they condemned her for being human, and cursed her kind for the trouble they'd caused the Bear People for so long, they couldn't deny that Lindy had at least one asset they could all agree on. She was sexually alluring.

Gareth chuffed and stalked away, knowing he'd have to keep a careful eye on her. And, apparently, on Arlin and Marin, too.

Chapter Eighteen

Marin grazed in the meadow, enjoying the tender green shoots that grew in the cool soil. But even while he ate, he swung his head from side to side, surveying the scene around him. He had an uneasy feeling in his gut, a slight burning sensation he got whenever a human entered forest home, and he knew immediately what was happening.

He lifted his head up to peer over the tops of the tall grasses and saw the problem. Gareth was approaching the meadow. He was walking on two legs in man skin and his hand was firmly clenched around the human woman's hand. Marin snorted disgustedly and spit his food out of his mouth. He'd lost his appetite.

Great, he whined to himself. Now he couldn't even enjoy a meal without needing to keep an eye on the troublemakers. He ambled over to the boulder and climbed on top to take his usual perch. He could see everything from this vantage point: the meadow, the trails leading into the forest and much of the forest itself. It was from this very spot that many of the Guardians before him had watched over their kin here in the place they called forest home.

Gareth led the woman across the meadow and motioned for her to sit in the shade of an old hickory tree. The woman carried her basket of food, but Marin could see that what she had brought this day was not for everyone to share. She reached in and pulled out a blue blanket, which she spread out under the tree. Then she and Gareth sat down on it side by side.

Marin watched the bizarre couple amusedly. The human pulled her food out of the basket and set it on the ground before them. She pulled some red grapes off a bunch and fed them to Gareth one by one. He must have said something funny to her because she laughed. The wind carried the sound across the meadow and Marin thought it sounded like the bubbling of the stream that wound through the forest. It was a pleasant sound that he liked very much.

Then Gareth picked a grape and tossed it to the woman, who tried to catch it in her mouth and missed. He tried again and she missed again, and she laughed harder each time. Soon Gareth was laughing with her until they both fell to their backs on the blanket.

Marin stretched up, trying to peer over the grass to see what they were doing. They were so involved in their own fun that they hadn't even seen him. He felt a pang of anger roar to life in his chest. Gareth had no business being with a human, let alone having *fun* with her. They were rolling around on the ground and behaving like cubs instead of the adults that they were. It was sickening.

A disturbing thought flickered to life in his mind. Maybe it wasn't anger he was feeling as much as jealousy. He shook his head and tried to push the ridiculous idea away, but he couldn't. He sank down on the boulder so he couldn't see them any longer, but the sound of their laughter still carried to him on the breeze. He wanted to cover his ears and drown out the sound. He couldn't stand it.

His heart began to pound in his chest at the thought of them laying together in the cool shade. His thoughts drifted back to a different time when it was he who lay under that very tree and rolled in the grass with the one he loved. He could still see her eyes, the way the sunlight caused glimmers of gold to sparkle amid the brown. And when she spoke, her voice was rich and full of life, just as she was.

Marin closed his eyes and forced the memory away. Even now, it hurt too much to think about it. To think about her. No matter how hard he tried, he couldn't forget her, and so he accepted the unrelenting memories as his punishment for failing her the way he did. And now, when he heard Lindy's voice drifting on the breeze, he was reminded of it all again and all the hurt came rushing back as though it had never left.

Marin, old bear, you're a bigger fool than Gareth, he berated himself. He pushed his body up and gazed over at the couple again. They still laid together, only quietly now because the woman had a book in her hands and was reading to him. Marin could tell by the look on Gareth's face that he was enjoying every moment of it. He sighed and forced himself to admit that she didn't seem to be much of the threat that he had feared. She wasn't aggressive or mean, and she'd done nothing to discredit what she'd told the clan about herself and her good intentions.

But then he reminded himself that humans were devious and self-serving. They'd proven that to him time and time again. Though he didn't know it for a fact, he suspected that even human females would kill his people without a second thought. He knew better than to let his guard down. He never wanted his clan to be hurt the way he had been, and he knew he'd need to keep a careful eye on her. *It's not jealousy you're feeling,* he reassured himself. *It's a warning. Be careful, Marin. Don't let yourself fall under her spell, too.*

Chapter Nineteen

For several weeks, Lindy had been bringing food to the clan in an attempt to get to know them better. Gareth told her that he'd noticed a change in the way they talked about her, as though they were beginning to feel more comfortable in her presence. She wanted to believe him, but she wasn't sure if he was telling the truth or just trying to make her feel better. She knew that he would do anything to ensure her continued visits to him.

After she'd distributed the food on one unusually warm spring afternoon, Gareth grabbed her hand and nearly threw her off balance in his excitement. "We're going to the waterfall. I want you to come with me, Lindy."

She put her hand on his arm to steady herself and smiled. "There's a waterfall in the forest?" she asked. "I never knew there was one in this area."

"It's somewhat of a secret, a special place where the clan goes once in a while."

Marin, who had shifted to man skin and was standing nearby watching as usual, shot him a look of warning. "Use your head, boy," he growled.

Gareth stared back, his eyes blazing a challenge. He'd wanted to take her to the falls for some time and was in no mood to be reprimanded in front of her. "Are you forbidding me to bring her with, Marin? I didn't know the falls were ours alone to enjoy."

Marin was silent for a moment while he debated whether

to force the issue or back down. Gareth was young and strong and more attracted to the woman every day. If he was pushed, he might do something foolish or reckless that the clan could ill afford. Besides, what harm would it do to allow the woman to come with? "Very well," he sighed, his eyelids flicking down for a split second in deference to the younger man. "Do as you will. But know that I don't approve."

A smile lit Gareth's face and he nodded his thanks to the Guardian before turning his attention back to Lindy. "Then it's settled. You can come with me to the waterfall. I want to show you how beautiful it is."

"I appreciate your offer," she answered slowly, needing time to think. She truly liked Gareth and enjoyed spending time with him. He was a wonderful man full of energy and enthusiasm; with him, she felt like she was seeing nature for the very first time. But Marin… He hadn't spoken to her since the day of his warning and now he'd made it very clear that he didn't want her to go with them. Gareth had no fear of the Guardian, but she couldn't help being terrified of him. "Maybe it would be best if I stayed here today," she said.

Disappointment clouded Gareth's face for a moment before he fixed his gaze on Marin again. "This is exactly what you wanted, isn't it?" he said angrily. "You want her to keep her distance from the clan…from me. Just because you aren't bear enough to have a female of your own doesn't mean you can deprive me of mine. Or is it that you want *mine*?"

Marin's eyes widened more with each angry step he took toward Gareth. "Watch your tongue, cub," he roared. "You'd best be prepared to defend such accusations if you choose to make them." When he stopped moving, he stood only inches away from Gareth. "And I would think hard and well before making them if I were you."

"Then why are you so hard on me, Marin? Maybe you should search your heart to find the truth behind your own actions. Maybe what you really want is not to protect me from her but to protect her from *me* because you want her for yourself." His voice was exploding was anger.

"Watch your place, Gareth," Marin threatened, his face growing red with fury.

"And you remember that I am not a cub to order about as you wish."

Marin lowered his face down to Gareth's level and stared into his eyes. "I am your elder and your Guardian. Do you wish to challenge me?"

Lindy's heart pounded harder in her chest with each response the men gave each other. She could see the fury building. Without thinking about her own safety, she slipped between them and placed one hand against each man's chest to push them apart. "Stop it, both of you," she ordered, her voice trembling at the realization of what she was doing. She felt their rage, their thumping hearts pulsing against her palms. Gareth's chest was slick with sweat, but Marin's was cool and dry and she knew immediately that he was in complete control, as he always was. If they fought, Gareth would undoubtedly be badly injured.

"Gareth, this isn't worth fighting about," she said. "Please don't argue with him. Maybe I can go another time."

The men continued to glare at each other, neither of them willing to back down. A bead of sweat trickled down her palm and forearm from Gareth's chest. Lindy turned and gazed at him, pleading with her eyes for him to give up and let Marin have his way. She nodded twice, reinforcing her request. He took an audible breath and lowered his head the tiniest bit before looking her in the eye.

"I don't want to wait for another time, Lindy. Will you come with me or not?" His voice was soft and imploring and almost broke her heart.

Lindy gazed into those pleading, honey-colored eyes and swallowed hard. She was forcing him to back down before Marin, knowing that it was a blow to his ego. But she had to do it to keep him from getting hurt. How could she embarrass him further by refusing him again? She decided that she would just have to risk Marin's wrath. "Yes, I'd love to go with you," she said, trying to hide her hesitation. For just a second, his eyes peered around her to flaunt his victory in Marin's face, and then he looked back at her and grinned. "So glad you see it my way."

A growl rolled from Marin's throat but he forced himself to hold his ground and watch while Gareth took her hand and led her toward the forest. Anger surged inside of him, lodging like a lump in his chest. He became aware of his fists clenching at his sides and quickly flattened his palms against his thighs. The problem, he decided, was that he didn't know who he was more furious with: Gareth, for challenging his authority, or Lindy, for siding with Gareth. Then a third possibility flickered through his mind. Was Gareth right? Was he trying to keep Lindy from the younger man because he wanted her for himself?

That's idiotic, he thought. *I find nothing desirable about this woman. This human woman*, he reminded himself. Watching them for a moment longer, he saw Gareth's arm slip around her shoulder before they disappeared among the trees and he realized that his fists were clenched again.

The path that led them deeper into the forest was little more than a deer trail. Too narrow for them to walk side by side, Gareth led the way, never letting go of Lindy's hand as she followed behind him. The trampled vegetation padded their feet from the ground and they made no sound when they walked. The forest was oddly silent without a single bird calling or insect buzzing.

"I've never heard it so still," she commented, scanning the trees for animal life. Not a bird or squirrel could be seen. The woods seemed completely deserted.

Gareth slowed his pace and turned back to look at her. The expression on his face was kind, almost pitiable. "They're afraid of you. They've been seeing you with me and they don't understand what you're doing here. They don't know if you're going to hurt them—or me. But then, this is the way it's been ever since the pale people came here." His comment was matter-of-fact, as though that was just the unfortunate way of the world now.

Lindy was confused and shook her head. "The pale people?"

"White humans. Like yourself."

She didn't need to ask for an explanation because it suddenly became clear. He was referring to her people, the settlers and immigrants and developers who claimed the land for themselves and took and took until there was nothing left to take. Then they moved on, leaving the land destroyed and barren. The thought of it overwhelmed her. "Is that how they see us?"

Gareth merely smiled and nodded toward the path. "It's not much farther now."

She pulled her hand out of his and rested it on her hip, unwilling to go on until he answered the question that had bothered her for some time. Now that there was no one around, she figured this was as good a time to ask as any. "Gareth, why are you doing this?"

"Doing what?"

"Pursuing this friendship with me. It's obvious that the clan has serious reservations about our relationship and just now, you made me realize that even the animals in this forest are afraid of me. So why are you putting yourself in this miserable position just to see me?"

He swung slowly around and when they were face to face, he placed his hands gently on her shoulders. He breathed deeply, realizing that he wasn't ready to divulge his true feelings for her. Instead he smiled and massaged his fingers softly against her shoulders. "How could I not be friends with the one who saved my life?"

It didn't satisfy her. "Gratitude doesn't necessitate friendship. I think Marin is grateful that I saved your life but he certainly isn't rushing to be friends with me. He views me as nothing more than a threat, and it seems to me that the clan usually follows his lead."

The corner of his mouth rose in a barely perceptible smirk of contempt. "Marin has a heart of stone. He trusts no one and cares for no one. He never apologizes to anyone or expresses gratitude. He's the perfect Guardian."

"You sound like you don't care for him much."

Gareth's fingertips dug into her shoulders before he realized what he was doing and eased his grip. "He does what he thinks is best for us, but sometimes I get so tired of his rules. It's fine for us to be cautious, but at the same time, it limits the experiences we can enjoy. Just once I'd like to go somewhere else or do something new. I want to have *fun*, Lindy. Meeting you has opened up a whole new world for me, opened my eyes to new possibilities. Is that wrong? Is it foolish like he constantly tells me?"

Lindy raised her hands and let them rest on Gareth's outstretched arms before she chuckled softly. "Not at all. In fact, you sound like any normal young person. You just want to enjoy life."

"Yes," he agreed. "And I want my life to include you. If Marin doesn't like it, too bad. That's his problem. But I won't let him deny me that pleasure." He swung his arms down and picked up her hand to lead her along the path again.

"Why did you make that remark about Marin wanting me for himself?"

Her words stopped him cold in his tracks and his mouth dropped open. He quickly looked away to regain his composure and took his time before answering. "Marin…" he said, stopping to choose his words carefully. "Marin will protect us at any cost and wouldn't even think twice about taking away something that he thought was harmful to us. Including you. But I spoke out of anger when I challenged him. As I said, he has a heart of stone and he has no interest in females, she-bears or otherwise."

Lindy watched his eyes search her face. "Then I guess we'd better just stay out of his way," she said, noting with interest the long tense breath of air he released after she'd answered.

They broke out of the forest and stepped into a large clearing. A wide stream spread out before them, its clear water mirroring the blue sky above. Large flat rocks scattered about its depths, their pink and gray granite speckles posing a pleasing contrast against the blue. Where the water rushed over and around the rock, it gurgled merrily as though singing to itself. She followed the stream to where it disappeared in mid air and a gasp of delight slipped from her lips.

Where the stream seemed to vanish, a cliff of rock rose up and under the flow. The water fell in an iridescent cascade, tumbling and crashing to land fifteen feet below in a large shimmering pool. Sparkles of foaming water glistened in the air before misting down into the swirls below. The roar of the crashing water was matched in intensity by the roars of delight coming from the pool.

She gazed down at the water, a huge smile lighting her face, and took a count. Fourteen bears frolicked in the blue depths like huge shaggy dogs. Water flew from their brown and black fur while they rolled and dove, splashing each other with a glee she thought only humans experienced. She could tell they were having fun.

Gareth picked up her hand and pulled her close. "Shall we join them?"

Lindy swung her head to look at him, her mouth open in protest. "Join them? No…no, Gareth, I couldn't."

His voice came back calm and reassuring. "They won't hurt you, you know."

"It's not that," she said, trying to smile despite her nervousness. "I'm not afraid of them when you're here with me. It's just that…I don't belong here. I feel out of place."

"You belong wherever I belong, Lindy." His eyes melted into hers, wanting her to believe. "Come on." He led her to a path that circled around the falls and they emerged a moment later at the side of the pool.

Fourteen shaggy heads rose out of the water and turned simultaneously to look at them.

"Greetings, kin," he yelled over the noise of the pouring cascade. "How's the water?"

For a moment, the only sound was the crash of the falls. Then a lone roar rose above it and echoed back to shore.

A grin broke across Gareth's face. "He says the water is cool today."

"I can't believe you understood that," she said, her jaw lowered in amazement

Gareth laughed heartily. "Duh, I speak bear, you know."

A red flush crept up her cheeks until her own laugh surpassed his. "I forgot. Sometimes I still can't believe you are what you are."

He laughed again and pulled her closer to the pool's edge. "Can you swim?"

Panic filled her eyes. "Yes, but I… I don't have a swimming suit on."

The word was unknown to him and his brow wrinkled with puzzlement. "A what?"

"A swimming suit. You know, clothes to wear in the water."

His head shook with another hearty laugh. "You don't need to wear anything." The thought of seeing her naked made his heart race and his breaths come faster.

"Yes I do." She surprised herself with the speed at which her words came, embarrassingly fast.

Gareth shrugged his shoulders and sighed, disappointed that she was resisting. "We're all naked. No one here cares if you have a swimming suit or not."

"I care." She felt like a prude but she couldn't stand the thought of being nude in front of fourteen pairs of eyes, even if they were *bears'* eyes. "I'm sorry Gareth, but I just don't feel comfortable. Besides, the water must be freezing. Remember, they've all got fur coats on in there."

He squeezed her hand reassuringly, trying to hide his frustration, and scrambled to come up with a solution that would be acceptable to her. "You can wear your clothes in if you'd be more comfortable," he offered. "But don't leave over this, please. I want you to stay."

Lindy watched the bears romping in the water and suddenly felt a childish yearning to join in. It had been so long since she'd had any *fun* and she realized that she couldn't remember the last time she'd even been tempted to do something crazy. The last few years of her marriage had been utterly miserable and she was long overdue for some joy. Gareth was giving her an opportunity that she had no good reason to pass up. "Are you sure it's okay?" she asked.

He nodded vigorously, delighted with her decision. Then his head drooped and he gazed at her from the corner of his eye. "Would you be upset—would you mind if I return to bear skin? I still tire so easily in human form."

She swallowed down her surprise at his request, not wanting him to know that she was uncomfortable with that, too. She chided herself for being such a baby. "No, Gareth, you go right ahead."

Every time she saw the shift, it took her breath away. As Gareth arched his back and reached his arms toward the ground, she watched amazed while fur sprouted from every inch of his body in long cinnamon colored strands. His hands and feet lengthened into thick, flat paws with curved claws. The lithe muscles of his limbs swelled and thickened into powerful legs; his face lengthened into a long muzzle tipped with a brown nose. He panted in several deep breaths, allowing his pink tongue to probe out from between long canine teeth. A muffled snort chuffed from deep in his throat, signaling that it was over. He swung his shaggy head and gazed at her with round eyes the color of deep, rich honey before his lips parted in a bear smile. With a great grunt of effort, he heaved his body off the shore and plunged into the water.

Lindy watched spellbound, fascinated that such miraculous creatures could exist, let alone allow her to be among them. She had her invitation; there was no need to wait further. She slipped off her shoes and socks and eased into the pool. Waves of tumbling blue splashed up around her, washing her legs with foam. The cold made her breath catch in her throat, but she didn't mind. She was barely in up to her knees when a dark shadow crashed against her side, knocking her off balance and throwing her completely under water.

She came to the surface sputtering and coughing and

looked around. A small bear, his dark brown fur beaded with glistening water droplets, bobbed near her, frozen in fear. He was only a yearling full of mischievous enthusiasm, and he looked at her the way a child facing discipline looks at a strict parent.

The fear on his small face melted her heart and she burst into a laugh at his prank. Relief flooded into his eyes, his mouth rose at the corners in a childish grin and he plunged beneath the surface to splash her again.

The other bears had stopped their play momentarily to monitor the scene. Protecting their young was paramount in the clan, especially from the humans who constantly threatened their home and lives. As soon as they saw the human woman react without malice and play harmlessly with the cub, their worries eased and they resumed their own activities. It helped that Gareth swam nearby keeping a close eye on her. If there was any trouble, they knew that he would assume responsibility for her actions.

Gradually the other adults swam by to nudge her gently with their muzzles or give her a push with their huge paws. Lindy wondered if they were testing her in some way, pushing her to watch her reaction. She could only guess what they would do if she showed any aggression. But they merely watched her from beneath the wet strands of fur draping their eyes and then swam away.

Undaunted, she submerged beneath the churning surface and felt her cares glide away. It felt so good to be free of the anger and grief she'd felt so often since her divorce. It was wonderful to be surrounded by life again. She popped to the surface and almost bumped into Gareth. Her eyes widened at the surprise of seeing his furry face right in front of her and she burst into a giggle. He snorted in response and lapped his tongue into the air.

There were definite drawbacks in attempting to communicate with an animal, she decided. Her mind whirled with all the things she wanted to say to him, all the questions she still wanted to ask him. She wondered if she would ever be able to learn bear-speak or if she would be forever shut out of his life in that respect. For now, all she could do was gaze into his glistening eyes and smile, hoping that he understood the joy he'd given her.

He swam away with the little brown yearling, leaving her free to do what she wished. Suddenly realizing how cold she was, she climbed back up on shore to take a rest and stretch out on the sun-warmed grasses growing around the waterfall pool. A warm breeze drifted from over the water and tickled her cold skin until it tingled. She closed her eyes and tipped her head back, soaking up the heat of the spring sun.

For a while, the sounds of the bears' play mingled with the murmur of the moving water and she drifted in sleep, utterly relaxed. When she finally opened her eyes again, the bears still played in the water, spraying each other with giant shakes of their furred bodies. Only one individual stood alone and her eyes were drawn immediately to him.

Marin stood in waist deep water beneath the falls, his olive-hued human skin vividly contrasting with the dark fur of his bear kin. An unexpected shudder of desire rippled through her at the sight of him and she wondered why he had chosen not to shift like the others. But she was glad he hadn't. The falling water beat down on his broad, bare shoulders, sending sunlit sparkles flying off his body like iridescent fireworks. His muscled chest glistened in the sun and even from this distance she could see the taut muscles contract. She remembered how good his chest felt against her hand when she'd broken up the fight, and how her hand slipped over the curve of his pectoral. The thought of it made her shiver. He raised his arms to sweep the dark hair out of his face, making his biceps pump with each movement. And he was looking right at her, just watching her watch him.

He's putting on a damn show for me, she thought. *Why else would he be in man skin when everyone else had assumed bear form*? She thought back to all the other times she'd seen him guarding the clan. He'd almost always been in bear skin then. It seemed absurd that he would want her to watch him, that he would care whether or not she *liked* to look at him. Or was it the other way around, she wondered. *Does he like to look at me? Is he attracted to me*? She recalled Gareth's words about Marin wanting her for himself and wondered if he had been completely honest with her. After all, she knew that Gareth was attracted to her and he had a lot to lose if she suddenly decided she liked Marin better.

But the way Marin treated her betrayed absolutely no hint of attraction or interest. In fact, his treatment of her suggested just the opposite. It seemed he had little inclination to bother with a human who could only cause him trouble, except when he made it a point to be rude and abrupt with her. He seemed to enjoy that greatly. Could it be that he was trying to show how physically intimidating he was?

"Well, it's working, Marin," she whispered to herself, her eyes falling again on that hard, lean stomach glistening in the water. "You've definitely got my attention."

Chapter Twenty

Marin watched Gareth take Lindy by the hand and follow the rest of the clan into the forest. They disappeared in the deep emerald shade among the trees, leaving him alone at the waterfall. This was his favorite time, the few minutes of solitude that he allowed himself. Every waking moment was spent with the clan, watching over them, protecting them, until at times he thought his mind would shatter from the stress. But for the last seven years, he'd broken his own rules and granted himself these few precious moments to be alone.

He dove under the water and emerged in the middle of the pool. The water was still cold and invigorating despite the sun beating warmly on his shoulders. He shook his head to rid the water from his ears, sending glistening droplets flying in a circle around him. Water trickled down his chest, playing lightly across his skin, and he looked down to follow its iridescent path.

The water trickled over his bulging pectorals, skirting around his nipples that had grown hard from the chill. The drops fell lower to his taut, rippling abdomen and disappeared in the flare of his lean hips. *Not bad for a forty-year-old he-bear*, he thought, knowing that he was in the best shape of his life. Yet despite his strength, he knew that something was lacking in him, that there was some deficit he couldn't name. He just felt that he was somehow incomplete, but he didn't know how to fix himself.

He forced the thought from his mind and walked from

the water to lie on the warm grass. The breeze drifted softly over him, teasing his skin like the play of fingertips, and he realized that he was laying in the exact spot the woman had rested in. The vision of her laying there, her golden hair sparkling in the sunlight, her wet clothes accentuating her feminine human curves, filled his mind, making his skin tingle. He loved the way her blue eyes locked on his body and his groin tightened with the thought of her watching him, at the realization that he had *wanted* her to watch him.

He growled softly in warning to himself. The human would bring trouble to the clan, as he had affirmed during his argument with Gareth. Her presence among them would only stir up thoughts that the he-bears had no business thinking. But how could he convince Gareth of that? The young he-bear was naïve and undoubtedly entranced by the exotic possibility of sex with a human. As Guardian, he would have to put an end to this nonsense immediately. He just couldn't admit that he would have to purge the thought from his own mind first.

The sun disappeared behind a cloud, casting him into a shadow. He knew he had dawdled long enough and needed to get back to the clan. Forcing his fantasies away, he stood up to stretch when he heard something click behind him. Cold metal pressed against the muscle of his back.

"Don't even breathe or I'll shoot, you son-of-a-bitch," the man warned.

Marin's breath caught in his throat. He recognized that voice, the whining human speech that he'd heard the day Gareth was shot. It sent a shiver down his spine. He took a slow breath to steady himself. "You're a lousy shot," he muttered.

Dixon jammed the gun barrel deeper into Marin's flesh. "Yeah, I almost cried when that pretty red bear got away, but I won't make that mistake again. We'll get our bear rug back, don't worry. But for now, put your hands behind your back."

Marin's mind raced but he didn't move. "What do you want with me?"

Roberts stepped around his partner to face Marin and cast his glance up and down the man's body. "You always walk around nude?"

"I take my clothes off when I swim."

"I don't see any clothes lying around here," Dixon snorted. "But then I guess they're not all that comfortable when you're a *bear* now, right?

"Shut up," his partner warned. Didn't he ever keep his big mouth shut?

So they know, Marin thought. If there was any chance of feigning ignorance, it would be pointless now. He quickly assessed the situation and knew he only had two choices: outsmart them or outfight them. Either way, he had to escape. "You didn't answer my question," he said.

"I'm not going to, asshole," Dixon retorted. "You're not in charge here. Unless you want me to beat your face in, you'd better put your damn hands behind your back."

Marin looked at Roberts, appraising the man who seemed the more intelligent of the two hunters. "No one will believe you when you tell them what I am," he said. "Or at least what you think I am," he added with a sarcastic laugh.

"We know what you are, bear-man. And when the time is right, you'll show them the truth," he answered curtly.

"When the time is right? I'm not so sure the genius behind me even knows how to tell time," Marin laughed.

"Shut up!" Dixon yelled, swinging the gun up to slam it against Marin's temple.

"NO!" Roberts screamed, but he was too late. Marin had already swung around and had his hands on the gun barrel. The two men struggled, each with his hands yanking the weapon in a tug of war that Marin was easily winning. Roberts quickly drew the pistol from the holster under his jean jacket and placed the barrel against Marin's head. "Stop. Now."

Marin felt the hard metal poking into his skull and lowered his hands to his sides. His hope sank. One gun he could overcome, but two?

"Put your damn hands behind you," Dixon ordered once

more, pissed off that he'd been suckered in so easily.

Marin fought to control his anger. How could he have let this happen? But of course he knew the answer. It was because he'd been daydreaming about the human that he let his guard down. He had no one to blame for this but himself. *Think*, he urged himself. He had to stall. "Don't you think you should make sure you're getting what you think you're getting?" he asked.

Roberts laughed. "I suppose you want to change into a bear and show us?" He shook his head. "No thanks. No, we're taking you in human form, so put your hands behind you like the nice man said."

"I'll go peacefully," Marin offered, desperate to keep his arms free. "There's no need for restraints."

Dixon snorted and dug the barrel of his rifle roughly into Marin's back again. "You must think we're stupid if you think we'll believe that. First chance, you'll be bent over sprouting hair and growing fangs.

Utter dejection flooded through Marin in a wave so violent he thought he would be sick. So they not only knew what he was, but they knew how to keep him from shifting. If his arms were pinned behind him, he'd be stuck in man skin and the advantage he had with his bear strength would be lost. Suddenly everything changed. He realized that now his goal was just to stay alive long enough for the clan to find him. This time, they would have to come to his rescue.

Roberts stuck the pistol back inside his jacket and slipped a pair of handcuffs out of his pocket. Grabbing Marin's wrists, he jerked them roughly behind his back and locked the metal rings around them. He clicked them tight with a laugh and pushed Marin forward. "Try to get out of those," he smirked.

Marin felt like a boulder was crushing his chest. He couldn't breathe, couldn't move. He felt the human's hand on his arm, pushing him, forcing him ahead, but his body didn't want to cooperate. All the strength went out of him and his legs felt as though they would cave in beneath him. He'd never felt the kind of paralyzing fear that was assaulting him now.

"How...how did you find me?" he mumbled.

Dixon thrust his chubby face in front of Marin and laughed. "Let's just say, a friend told us."

Marin closed his eyes and his head sank low to his chest. He knew it. It was just as he'd predicted. She had betrayed them even as they opened their lives to her, shared their world with her. But this time, it wasn't his kin who would pay the price for a human's betrayal. He would.

"I said move!" Roberts yelled, giving his back a rough shove.

Marin stumbled forward with his captors on each side of him. He didn't say a word, couldn't. Never had he imagined that he would be in this predicament. For the second time in his life, he felt total panic grip him. He couldn't imagine what they wanted him for, but he had the terrible feeling that whatever it was, he would be better off dead.

Chapter Twenty-One

Gunther's bark drifted through the splashing and Lindy pulled the curtain aside to stick her head out of the shower. She stared down at the dog, who paced before the tub with his ears twitching.

"Good grief, Gunth. What's the matter with you?" She stepped back under the water for a moment until she realized what had alerted him in the first place.

Someone was pounding on the front door. Gunther dashed out of the bathroom toward the door, barking furiously. *Who the hell could that be*? Lindy muttered under her breath. Quickly toweling dry, she slipped on her bathrobe and walked into the family room to peek out the picture window. Even with Gunther to guard her, she wasn't about to open the door for anyone.

She could see the front porch from the window. Light from the motion detector flooded down from above, illuminating Gareth. He was in human form, his arms crossed over his chest to ward off the cold, but it wasn't helping. His teeth were chattering. Six of his bear kin waited at the bottom of the steps, pawing anxiously at the ground.

Lindy ran to the door and flung it open. "Gareth, get in here before you freeze," she said, reaching out to pull him inside.

He stepped into the room, rubbing his upper arms furiously. This far north, even late spring evenings were bitterly cold and the air still crackled with frost. "I didn't think you'd ever answer the door," he complained.

"I'm sorry. I was in the shower and didn't hear you" she replied.

"I wouldn't have come, but we need your help," he said apologetically.

Her eyes widened with his words as she pulled the afghan off the back of the couch and draped it around him. Grabbing his arms, she pulled him closer and stared into his eyes. They were flared open with concern. "What's wrong? Why do you need my help?"

His face contorted in an expression of panic as he pulled the coverlet tighter around himself. Lindy hadn't seen that look since the day she'd found him on her back porch and it scared her.

"It's Marin. He's missing."

Her heart skipped a beat. "Marin is what?" She didn't believe what she'd heard, but from the look on his face she knew it was the truth.

"He didn't come back from the waterfall this afternoon."

Lindy walked around the couch and sank down on the cushion. She pictured Marin at the waterfall, remembered how confident and strong he looked. How defiant. She was sure there must be a practical reason for his absence. There couldn't be anything wrong. "Maybe he just wants some time alone. Maybe he went somewhere," she said.

Gareth shook his head and sat down beside her. He was so upset he didn't even notice Gunther sniffing at his feet. "No, something's wrong. Marin has always taken some time for himself after we all leave the pool. It's his way of relaxing and getting away from us for a while. But even by the time I brought you back here and then returned to forest home, he hadn't come back. He was still gone when we left to come here and get you."

"He's a grown man. Bear," she corrected herself. "He can take care of himself."

Gareth just shook his head, his honey eyes glazed with panic.

Lindy scooted nearer him. "What is it, Gareth? What do you think happened to him?"

When he looked at her, she realized how much he cared for the Guardian. He'd never shown any outward affection for Marin, but she could see that his concern ran deep for the he-bear who was his friend and kin. "We think he's been taken by hunters. Possibly the same ones who tried to kill me."

She shivered, whether it was from the cold or the thought of hunters taking Marin, she didn't know. "Why do you think it's them?"

He reached over and grabbed her hands, squeezing them tight to comfort himself. "The day I was shot, Marin was with me. He took off after the hunters. He told us later that they had him cornered at the cliff but he escaped by making them crash their machine. They were so angry. There was no doubt in our minds that they would come after him, or me, or both of us again."

Lindy squeezed his hands in return and sighed. "Even if they did take him, wouldn't they still be in the forest? Can't you follow their scent?"

Gareth leaned against the armrest and tipped his head back in despair. His hands slipped out of hers and fell limply to his sides. "We can track them but what good will it do us if they have guns? How many of us will be killed in the fight to save him? After all, look what they did to me." His head drooped low on his chest as though he was ready to cry.

She moved beside him and slipped her arms around his shoulders to bring him nearer. For the first time, she noticed a faint scent about him. It was his bear scent, a pleasant woodsy smell. It hit her then how much she missed him, missed all of the clan, when they were separated. "What can I do?"

He looked up and stared into her eyes gratefully, hoping that what he was about to ask wouldn't scare her. The feel of her arms around him gave him hope and courage. "We talked about it and we want you to come with us now to look for him. We want you to bring your gun."

Lindy recoiled at his request. She wasn't a good shot and

kept the gun more for show than anything. There was no doubt in her mind—if the hunters had guns, she'd be the one to end up getting shot. Her heart raced in her chest as she scrambled for an excuse. "Isn't there someone else you can get to help you, Gareth? Is there another clan nearby who can help you search?"

He shook his head vehemently. "No, we're the only ones here. We have to find him and we need to do it soon. The longer we wait, the farther away they'll get."

"But it's almost pitch black outside. How can you even see where you're going? I wouldn't be able to see where I was going." Her voice was strained and high, almost whiney, and she knew she sounded like a coward.

Gareth turned toward her and took her hands in his own again, leaning forward until his eyes were only inches from hers. "Do you remember the day Marin put you on trial, Lindy? You said you'd offer us sanctuary. You were offering your help to us. Well, we don't need the use of your home. We need you. And we need your gun. Please help us. Please help Marin."

She exhaled slowly and closed her eyes, trying to fight the panic rising in her chest. Damn him for asking this of her. He knew how Marin felt about her, and how scared she was of him. She would gladly search for anyone in the clan. But Marin? Why did it have to be him? She felt a soft warmth against her cheek and opened her eyes. Gareth was staring at her, waiting, caressing her face gently. She could see the tenderness in his eyes, how his kindness flowed out through the golden brown. She could see how badly he needed her to do this for him.

"Tell me what to do," she sighed.

His mouth lifted slightly with relief. "It's freezing outside, so you'll need to dress warmly. Bring some food, water, medicine, a blanket. If we don't find him tonight we'll search tomorrow and the next day until we do find him, so bring something to sleep in that will keep you warm. I don't know, Lindy, bring whatever you can think of that might help us. Bring your damn gun."

Lindy stood up and walked over to the window. The motion sensor light had gone off, leaving the world dark. Light from the family room was seeping through the window into the darkness outside, illuminating the frost that was beginning to etch the glass in soft lacy patterns. It was so cold. She didn't want to go. "I'm bringing Gunther with me, too," she said at last.

Gareth cocked his head to look at her from the corner of his eye. "We don't need your wolf along, Lindy. The others wouldn't like it."

She looked down at him with her hands perched on her hips. How could she tell him that the gun was virtually useless in her hands and that Gunther might be her best protection? Biting her lower lip, Lindy forced a smile. "Gunth is *my* Guardian. I'm not going without him. The clan will just have to deal with it."

Gareth swallowed hard and nodded. "I'll do my best to explain it to them, then." He stood up beside her and dropped the afghan back on the couch. "Let's get packing."

Chapter Twenty-Two

"Where are you taking me?" Marin asked again. He didn't expect an answer but he figured it was worth asking. The older of the two kidnappers, the one called 'Dixon', obviously wasn't too bright and had messed up once before. Marin figured he was likely to do so again and any information he let slip out might be valuable. But Dixon was also the one with the short temper and he cautioned himself not to push the man too far.

It wasn't Dixon who answered him, but Roberts. "What's it worth to you to know?"

Marin glanced sidelong at him, studying him warily. "Are you willing to negotiate with me?"

Roberts barked out a deep hearty laugh that oozed with sarcasm. "Sure, I'll swap information with you, bear man. What can it hurt?"

Marin looked back at the path before them while he considered the offer. He trusted no one and despite how tempting the offer seemed, he would never trust any human. Especially poachers like these two who had already demonstrated their willingness to shoot his kind.

The path they followed was an overgrown trail that wandered through the vast forest. He'd passed it many times before on his way to the cliff and knew that it continued eastward to an abandoned farmstead at the edge of the national forest. He'd never gone near the old farmhouse but had seen it from a distance several times. It was several hours' walk in man-steps and he shuddered at the thought that it could be their destination.

Two concerns weighed on his mind. The first was that he'd never been inside a human's building so he had no idea what to expect. He couldn't imagine what dangers might lie within and he didn't know if he'd be able to escape if they did take him inside. Would more humans be inside waiting for him? He couldn't imagine why they would want to take him there.

His more immediate concern, though, was just getting through the night. Without the use of his arms, he wouldn't be able to shift into bear skin and use his fur to keep warm. He glanced over at Roberts and eyed the heavy pack the man carried on his back. A blanket and some rolled-up object hung from the bottom of it. Since they already knew that keeping his arms shackled would prevent him from shifting, perhaps they were prepared to keep him warm. Then again, maybe they just didn't give a damn if he suffered in the cold all night. Judging from their behavior, he knew that their concern wasn't for his comfort. But were they obliged to keep him alive and healthy for whatever use they had in mind for him?

He decided that it was pointless to ask where they were taking him again. He thought he already knew. "Why have you taken me?" he asked at last.

Roberts lit a cigarette and sucked on it for a moment before peering at Marin from the corner of his eye. "How many others of your kind live in this forest?"

Marin smiled and shook his head. "You answer my question first."

Dixon struggled up alongside them and looked past Marin to stare at the other man. "Are you gonna let him pull this shit?" he asked. He was breathing heavily from the weight of the pack on his back. "Who does this asshole think he is—Grizzly Adams?"

Roberts laughed and took another drag from the cigarette. "Hey, I have no problem telling him a few things. Maybe we can both benefit from it—if you know what I mean." He gazed over at his partner and raised an eyebrow, hoping he understood.

"I still don't like it," Dixon muttered. "I'd just as soon beat the crap out of him than talk nicey nicey."

"That's because you're a sadistic little bastard," Roberts laughed, tossing the wasted butt on the ground. "But I'll tell you what. If he gives us any shit, you can go ahead and have a little fun with him."

"I take it that whatever you need me for doesn't require that I be in good condition," Marin interrupted.

"Nope, only that you be alive," Roberts said.

"What do you need me for?"

Roberts snorted and stared Marin in the eye. "How many of you are in the forest?"

Marin stared right back. "Hundreds."

Dixon stopped in his tracks and swept his chubby hand across his sweating forehead. "Holy mother of shit," he said.

Roberts stopped and yanked Marin to a halt beside him. "You dick," he said to his partner. "You don't really believe him, do you? You think he's gonna tell us the truth?"

Dixon eased the backpack off his shoulders and let it drop to the ground. Sometimes even he couldn't believe how gullible he was. He grabbed Marin by his hair and tried to force him to the ground. "You mother..."

Before Dixon even knew what hit him, Marin had kicked out his leg and swept Dixon's feet from under him. The chubby man crashed to the ground with a thud and groaned at the sharp pain stabbing through his hip. Then Marin whirled and kicked out at Roberts, but the man already had his pistol in hand and was aiming it at his chest. Marin stopped abruptly and stood still, his gaze focused on the silver gun barrel pointed at him.

Roberts looked down at Dixon and laughed. "Well, you had that coming," he snickered. "But I guess it earns you the right to teach our friend a few manners."

Dixon wobbled to his feet and panted to catch his breath. He didn't know what hurt more, his bruised hip or his ego, but either way, he wanted to make the bear man pay. He looked up at Marin, his eyes steeled with anger, and withdrew the rifle from the top of his backpack. Swinging it back past his aching hip, he rammed it forward and smashed the wooden butt into Marin's stomach.

Marin gasped as the force of the blow took his breath away. The strength left his legs and he crashed to the ground on his knees. He doubled over, trying to control the hot stabs of pain shooting into his chest and hips, but it didn't help. He wanted desperately to bring his arms forward, to wrap them around his stomach and clutch at the pain, but his arms couldn't move. The metal links of the handcuffs clinked as he struggled to free himself, but the steel was too strong. He looked up just as Dixon drew the gun back over his right shoulder and swung it down toward his head.

For a moment, Marin saw the world spinning wildly in a green tornado. Then the pain turned to ice and everything went black.

Chapter Twenty-Three

Thoren moved swiftly through the darkness, leading the search party of the seven male bears and the human woman back to the waterfall. He stopped at the side of the pool where Marin's scent was joined by the stench of humans. Even in the blackness of the forest at night, he knew their trail wouldn't be hard to follow. The human smells of sweat and tobacco fouled the pristine pine-scented air and left a track as vivid as paw prints in freshly fallen snow.

Gareth had shifted into bear skin as soon as they'd left Lindy's house and now trotted along beside her to guide her through the darkness. He stayed close, enjoying the feel of her hand on his furred shoulder as he led her along the narrow trail. Bear eyesight wasn't the best, but it bettered human sight at night. Even with her flashlight, she stumbled over rocks and logs hidden among the vegetation and cursed each time she almost fell. Gunther followed obediently on his leash, trying to stay out of her way while the bears snorted amusedly at her lack of grace, grateful for any diversion from their worry over Marin's disappearance.

While they gathered with Thoren at the pool's edge, she dumped her pack on the grass nearby and slumped down on top of it. She watched the bears stand in a circle, their heads pointing inward toward the center. Snuffles and growls rose from the group in a frantic discussion that she wished she could understand.

She reached over and grabbed the fur on Gareth's rump

to get his attention. He backed out of the circle and swung his head around to face her. "What are they saying?" she whispered, remembering that he could understand human speak even when he was in bear skin.

Gareth arched his back and rose up beside her, assuming human form faster than she could have believed possible. He gazed behind him to look at Lindy's hand on his buttock and a broad grin filled his face.

She yanked her hand away in embarrassment. "You shit!" she laughed.

"Hey, I know you can't understand my language so I thought I'd do you the favor of translating. And this is the thanks I get," he teased. He sat down beside her and huddled in the blanket she offered him from her pack. "Sorry, but this has got to be quick. It's too cold to stay like this." He motioned down at himself, indicating his bare skin.

"I understand," she said. "Just clue me in on what's happening, will you?"

Gareth moved closer to her and inclined his head until his mouth nudged her ear, not wanting to disrupt the clan's discussion. A sweet, flowery smell teased his nose, and he sniffed softly, surprised to discover that the scent came from her hair. He brushed his cheek against the soft blonde strands, pretending to move them out of the way so he could whisper in her ear. "Thoren has picked up the scent of two humans. From here, their trail leads into the woods again on the other side of the pond."

When she looked over at Gareth, he had moved so close that she felt the warmth of his breath on her face. His lips were so close she could feel their heat and they were drifting even nearer. She inhaled a sharp, nervous breath and turned her head away, afraid of what might happen. "Does he know if they're the same humans who shot you?" she asked, trying to ignore what had happened.

Gareth abruptly straightened up to move away, and Lindy couldn't tell if he was upset by her question or the fact that she'd pulled away from him.

He sighed, a slow hissing breath as if his ego was deflating and there was a coldness to his voice when he answered her. "Yes, Lindy. They're the same men."

"Oh crap," she groaned. "What do you think they'll do to him?"

He stood up and dropped the blanket to the ground at his feet. "Probably the same thing they always do to us," he said gruffly. "They kill us." Then he arched his back and reached his hands to the ground. A moment later, the cinnamon bear stalked away and joined the circle of his kin, leaving her sitting alone with her dog.

Thoren broke out of the circle and walked past her to get her attention. He nodded his grizzled head toward the forest and waited while she tucked the blanket back into her pack and stood to join them. When she was ready, they set off into the darkness.

Chapter Twenty-Four

Marin opened his eyes and thought he was looking through water. An orange glow swam before him, its color dimming and brightening in odd swirling bursts. He blinked, trying to clear the water from his eyes, but it didn't help. He blinked once more and moved to raise his hand to his face. His hand wouldn't move. He tried again, and again his hand wouldn't move.

"Well, well, looks like Sleeping Beauty's awake," someone laughed.

He turned his head toward the sound and discerned a dark shadow drifting near the orange glow. Everything was a blur and he couldn't think where he could possibly be. Then a hand came out of the darkness and slapped him across the face.

"Wake up," the man said gruffly.

Marin groaned and shook his head, his face stinging from the blow. He tried to focus on the voice, realizing that it sounded like one he'd heard before, but he couldn't place it. Its familiarity teased his memory. How did he know that voice?

The man disappeared and returned a moment later. Immediately Marin felt cold water splash over the top of his head and pour down his face in an icy rush. It seeped into his eyes and began to clear his vision and all at once Marin realized that he wasn't looking through water. He was looking through his own blood. His eyes were caked with it. Shaking his head to throw off the water, he blinked over and over until his vision improved and he could focus on the blur in front of him. Then it all came flooding back.

Dixon stood before him, just staring up into his eyes. The look on his pudgy face was pure satisfaction. He held his canteen up and waved it in Marin's face. "Refreshing, huh?" he laughed.

Rage rushed through Marin with a power he hadn't felt in years. He yanked his shoulders forward to throw a blow at the human but his arms wouldn't budge. Craning his head to the side, he saw that he was standing up against a tree with his arms pinned behind him around the trunk of the tree. Blood trickled down his left bicep and when he looked down; he saw that blood covered his chest in dark stains. His head pounded with a pain he'd never felt before. He twisted his wrists furiously, fighting to get them free, but he couldn't.

Looking forward again, he realized that the orange glow was a mound of yellow-orange flames rising from a fire twenty feet away. The other human, Roberts, sat beside it drinking from a clear bottle. The man looked up and gazed over at him.

"Leave the poor bastard alone," he called to Dixon.

"Stick to your whiskey and let me have my fun," the man replied. He looked up into Marin's eyes and grinned like a kid who'd stolen a car and gotten away with it. He looked like he was having fun. "Now where were we before you so rudely passed out on me?" he snickered in Marin's face.

Be calm, Marin told himself. *Don't aggravate him.* By now he realized that not only were his hands bound together behind the tree, but his ankles were similarly pinioned. He couldn't move more than a few inches and for the first time in his life, he was completely helpless and at the mercy of humans. Deep in his chest, his heart began to pound in erratic thumps that he was sure the man could hear, but Dixon only stood looking up at him like an idiot. He struggled against the restraints, feeling the rough bark scrape against his back. Every time he moved, his body responded with aching throbs.

Dixon dropped the canteen on the ground and swept his gaze over Marin's body before his lips curled up in a sneer. "You probably think you're quite the ladies' man with all that equipment, don't you? Oh, or should I say ladies' *bear*?" He bent over and slapped his knee, amused by his own humor. When he stood up, his fat face was flushed bright red. He swung his hand back and punched Marin hard across the face once more.

Blood splattered from the newly opened cut on his lip, spraying his neck with crimson speckles. He struggled to withhold the cry of frustration rising in his throat and for a moment he was successful. Then Dixon slammed his fist into the bruised muscles of his abdomen again and Marin couldn't stop himself from roaring with fury and pain.

Roberts lowered his bottle and stared through the darkness at the two men. He couldn't tell if the roar had come from his prisoner or from some wild animal, but it scared the hell out of him. Then he saw the blood dripping from Marin's face. "Leave him alone," he said again. It was less pity that urged him to say it than fear that Marin's voice could be heard throughout the forest. He stood up, walked to his partner and put his hand on the man's shoulder. "You asshole, you want to attract attention? Leave him be and come have a drink."

Realizing the sense in that advice, Dixon relented and nodded his agreement. "Okay," he said. Then turning back to Marin, he drew his fist back and pummeled it into his captive's stomach one more time.

Marin gasped as the breath was sucked from his lungs. He strained to double over, to ease the pain in the tortured muscles of his abdomen, but he couldn't move. The only relief he could get was to pant rapidly and wish everything away. He closed his eyes against the pain, against the face of his tormenter. One thought echoed over and over in his mind.

I...will...rip...him...apart.

He only hoped he would live long enough to have the chance.

Chapter Twenty-Five

Everyone stopped dead in their tracks. Each head turned to face toward the east, toward the horrible screaming roar that drifted from the darkness. The sound rose from deep in the forest, surging from the utter silence. It lingered for a moment in the bitter night air before fading into stillness.

Lindy's heart skipped a beat and without realizing it, she reached her hand out to touch Gareth's fur for comfort. Gunther stood trembling on her other side, his ears at full attention. A soft whine came from his throat before turning into a low growl.

"It's okay, Gunth," she said without believing it herself. She knew it was Marin. Knew that he was out there somewhere in the darkness and that they were hurting him. If he couldn't protect himself from harm at the hands of his kidnappers, she knew that he must be completely helpless. Probably for the first time in his life, he was afraid and alone. Once again, humans were reinforcing why he hated them so. Suddenly she wanted to protect him. She wanted to bring him safely home for the clan. And for the first time, she wondered if she didn't want to bring him safely home for *her*.

"Lindy?"

Gareth's voice startled her from her thoughts and she jumped. "What?"

He slipped his arm around her and pulled her close. "We'll find him. At least now we know he's not far away."

She turned and wrapped him in her arms, needing the

comfort of his embrace. "They're hurting him, Gareth. They're *hurting* him."

He put his hand on her head and ran his fingers through her hair, separating the golden strands. Human hair was a vast improvement over fur, he decided. So soft. He wanted to keep his fingers there forever, keep her in his arms forever, but he knew she wouldn't let him.

She pushed herself away and gave Gunther's leash a tug. "Come on, boy," she urged him. Then looking up at Gareth, she wiped her face of the lone tear she'd allowed herself to cry. "We don't have time to waste. Let's go get him."

They traveled swiftly, the bruins crashing heavily through the thick underbrush while she and Gunther stumbled along behind. The flashlight beam bounced a jagged path through the darkness, casting eerie shadows among the trees. It did little good. Several times she crashed to her knees on the cold ground, but each time she dragged herself back to her feet and forced herself to catch up to the bears.

She pulled her fleece jacket tighter around her neck. Frost had settled on everything in a thin white icing that sparkled when the moonlight broke free from the clouds. But most of the night, the clouds laid heavily in the sky, obscuring the moon and stars from view and withholding their light. The air grew damp, helping the cold to sink deeper into her bones.

Her feet were clad in waterproof boots, but the cold still permeated the fabric and spiked into her soles like needles. Raising her hands to her face, she blew forcefully into her palms, grateful for the few moments of warmth her breath provided. She was so focused on her hands that she almost crashed into the bears, which had come to a sudden standstill on the path in front of her.

"Ohhh, sorry," she whispered to the one whose hip she smashed with her knee. He turned and looked at her with small round eyes before turning his attention back to the group.

Gareth walked up alongside her and motioned her to silence. They stood together and peered into the darkness, waiting for someone to speak. After a few minutes, Thoren appeared out of the darkness and gathered them together. A rapid succession of growls and whines surged from his throat, spurring responsive growls from the others. They huddled together for a long time before Thoren growled his message to Gareth.

Gareth listened intently and nodded his understanding. When Thoren left, he turned to Lindy, grabbed her by the arms and pulled her close. His voice was a barely audible whisper. "Thoren has seen them up ahead. He says that Marin is bound to a tree and looks to be asleep. He wants you to free him while we take care of the humans. We have surprise on our side, but watch closely and have your gun ready in case we have any problem."

Lindy nodded solemnly. So this was it. The moment when she would prove her worth to the clan. She took a deep breath and steeled her resolve. She looked down at Gunther and saw her hand on his leash; it was shaking badly. She knew her trembling wasn't from the cold. "Let's get this over with, Gunth," she said, wishing that it was already behind them.

At once, everyone was in motion. Through the darkness ahead, she could see a faint glow. The closer they got, the clearer the glow became and she realized it was a fire. Her breath caught in her throat at the realization that the kidnappers' camp was coming into view. She wondered if they knew they were being followed. She crashed along behind the bears, her heart thumping wildly at the thought of what lay ahead. *It'll be okay*, she promised herself. *The bears will kill the men while I free Marin. Then we'll all go home, safe and sound. It will be okay.*

Then everything went to hell. Gunther bounded along behind the bears, straining at his leash and dragging Lindy behind as he tried to follow the bruins toward the camp. She was moving too slow, preventing him from keeping up, and he let out a loud, mournful howl that could've awakened the dead.

"No, Gunth!" she yelled, but she knew the damage had been done.

Sixty yards ahead, the hunters snapped to attention at the sound and whirled to face whatever was approaching from the forest. They grabbed their guns and leaped into motion. Fear surged through them at the sound of heavy steps crashing through the underbrush toward them.

"Move!" Roberts yelled, grabbing their packs. He turned and bolted for the opposite side of the campsite, dragging Dixon along with him. They had disappeared into the darkness of the woods when Thoren charged into the clearing and slid to a stop by the fire.

The bear swung his head from side to side, searching for the men. Huge white clouds of warm breath puffed from his mouth into the cold night air as he panted from his exertion, and he scanned the darkness around him, hoping that they had hidden in the thick vegetation. He knew he had just missed them and that they couldn't have gone far. He roared an order to the other bears, which quickly split into two groups and charged into the darkness beyond Marin. Only Gareth remained behind, stopped at the edge of the firelight. He had shifted into man skin again to give her Thoren's orders. She could see the sweat dripping down his skin in the yellow firelight.

"Lindy, we're going after them," he panted. "When you have Marin free, take him back to forest home. He'll be able to show you how to get there. Then wait for us there." Without waiting for her response, he stood down and shifted, his cinnamon bulk quickly disappearing into the darkness.

They had only been gone a few minutes when a gunshot echoed somewhere in the darkness. "Gareth!" she cried. "My gun!" But it was too late. Everyone was long gone.

Chapter Twenty-Six

Lindy stepped closer to the fire and gasped. On the other side of it, Marin was tied to a large tree. His head was slumped down on his chest, his shaggy hair drooping down to partially cover his face. Through the black strands, she could see patches of brownish red where blood had dried on his skin. Rivulets of it had soaked down his neck and trickled across his chest. Her breath caught in her throat. *Please be alive*, she whispered to herself.

She laid her pack and gun down and ordered Gunther to stay beside them. She skirted around the fire, wanting to run to Marin and yet afraid of what she'd find. "Marin?" she called softly. She moved closer, walking faster as the extent of his injuries became clearer.

He moaned weakly and raised his head to peer at her from beneath the wet mop of hair. Both of his eyes were encircled by red, swollen bruises. She stopped in front of him and took a careful look. The sight of him made her want to cry.

"It's you," he coughed, barely moving his aching jaw.

She couldn't tell if it was relief or disappointment that filled his voice. "Yeah, Marin, your favorite person. Can you believe that I'm the one here to rescue you?"

His eyes blinked sluggishly as he shifted position against the tree. "Lucky me."

She shook her head in amazement. Even helpless and beaten, he was still rude. "Thanks for the vote of confidence, buddy." She walked around the tree to check his bonds. *Oh shit*, she cursed. His hands weren't tied behind the tree but were chained there. A steel padlock fastened the thick links together. If it had been a rope binding him, she could have had him free in minutes. But a padlocked chain? Without a key, it would take a hacksaw to cut through the metal. She peered around the trunk and scanned the area near the fire to see if the men had left their backpacks, but they had obviously taken the packs with them when they fled. If there was a key, it was long gone now.

She stepped back in front of him and ran her gaze over his body. His left bicep was split by a jagged gash and blue-purple bruises swelled across his stomach. Deep red abrasions circled each ankle where a rough rope pinioned his legs to the tree. Welts striped his lower legs and thighs as though his captors had dragged him through the underbrush. "Is anything broken?" she asked, fighting to control the waves of anger surging through her at the thought of the beating he'd taken.

"I don't think so."

She walked back to her pack and fished through it for a moment before withdrawing a silver canteen. She returned to him and raised the spout to his mouth. "Drink some water. You're probably dehydrated." He accepted gratefully, parting his dry lips to gulp in the cool liquid. "Slowly, slowly," she whispered, easing up on the flow until it trickled into his mouth.

After a few moments, he nodded to indicate his fill and when she had pulled the canteen away, he laid his head back against the rough bark and licked his lips. "Good."

Returning to the pack again, she retrieved the first aid kit and pulled out a cleansing towel from it. She brought it to Marin and wet it lightly. "I'm going to clean you up a little bit. You'll be able to see better once the blood is out of your eyes."

He grunted but didn't speak, making her wonder if he'd rather just be left alone. She raised the cloth to his brow and dabbed gently, deciding that at least she would feel better doing this for him. Anyway, there was nothing else she could do until the clan came back. He winced beneath her touch as she wiped the towel carefully down the side of his face, but he didn't speak, didn't complain.

Lindy raised her other hand tentatively to his head and held him gently in her grasp so she could use a little more pressure. For a moment she couldn't believe she was really touching him; that she had the nerve to do it. But it felt right and she let herself continue. The blood was crusted on his cheek, forcing her to rub his skin. *Has he ever been touched by a human before?* she wondered. She'd give anything to know how he felt about her touch.

"Dammit!" he growled, turning his head away.

Well, I guess that answers my question. "Marin, hold still so I can get this blood off," she ordered, turning his head back.

"Don't touch me," he warned, his fury exploding.

"I'm sorry if it's hurting you," she began. "But..."

"I'll have no traitor touch me," he snarled.

She lowered her hand and let the towel dangle beside her, taken aback by his words. "What do you mean by that?" she asked. She wondered if he was delirious.

"I know what you did."

She shook her head back and forth, clueless as to what he was talking about. "What I did? What did I do? I have no idea what you're talking about."

"You betrayer. You led them to the waterfall. They knew I was there alone and they ambushed me."

Betrayer? She couldn't believe what he was saying, what he was accusing her of. "No, you're wrong," she said. "I would never do that to you Marin. I would never do that to Gareth or the clan."

He turned his head back to look at her and his dark eyes burned within his battered face. "I should have killed you when I had the chance."

Her breath caught in her throat at his words. If he hadn't been chained to the tree, she would have been terrified of his threat. But she was safe at the moment and all she could think of was how to convince him that she was innocent. She grabbed his head between her hands and stared hard into his eyes. "Listen to me!" she ordered. "I did not betray you."

"Then how did they find me?" he seethed.

She shook her head furiously. "I don't know. But I swear to you, I swear, Marin, that I didn't betray the clan or you."

He lowered his eyes and tried to kick his leg at her, but the rope held him fast. His helplessness infuriated him and he jerked his head back against the tree so hard it hit with a thud.

"Don't do that," she cried, feeling pity overwhelm the defensiveness she'd felt a moment before. "You're hurt bad enough already, don't you think?" She raised the cloth up again and brought it close to his face.

"What are you doing?" he snarled.

"I told you I was going to clean some of this blood out of your face. Then you'll be able to see better." She exhaled loudly, her patience wearing thin

He growled furiously and yanked his head away again. "Stop, woman. It doesn't matter!" he roared.

The ferocity of his voice took her breath away and she lowered her arms to her sides again. "I'm just trying to help you," she said.

Marin moaned and rolled his eyes until his gaze met hers. "It… doesn't matter." His voice was suddenly filled with surrender and was so unlike him that it scared her.

"What do you mean?" she asked.

For a moment he looked away, his eyes drinking in the wilderness around him before settling on her face again. He took in a slow, ragged breath. "I won't survive the night so you don't need to worry about making me look pretty."

Lindy smiled at his words. They were so crazy that she was now sure he was delusional. "What do you mean by that, Marin? You've been found. You're okay now." Then as quickly as it had come, her smile faded. Maybe he hadn't been honest with her. Maybe he was hurt worse than he'd admitted. Her face grew serious and she stared into the dark depths of his swollen eyes. "What is it? Tell me."

A groan escaped his lips and he shifted his weight to rest

more heavily on his left foot. Every part of his body ached and all he wanted to do was lay down, but the chain held his arms so tightly to the tree that he couldn't slide down against the rough bark. Standing was a struggle. Breathing was a struggle. He ached from the cold. He looked up at the sky, at the clouds drifting thickly in the darkness.

"The temperature is dropping. Frost already covers the land." He stopped and closed his eyes, picturing what was to come. "I have no protection and I can't keep myself warm. By dawn I will have frozen to death."

Her eyes widened at his explanation but she couldn't help being skeptical. "You're a bear, for God's sake, Marin. How do you survive out here at night?"

An exhausted sigh preceded his words. He was so tired he could barely force the words out. "When I'm in bear skin, I can survive the coldest winter night. But being bound like this keeps me confined to this form, and as a man I'll die from... I... don't know the word for it." When he opened his eyes again, they were empty of hope.

But she knew the word. Hypothermia. Suddenly she understood. "Oh no," she moaned. "I didn't realize...you can't shift." She thought for a moment and laid her hand gently on his shoulder. "The clan went after your captors. When they've killed them, they'll be back for us."

He shook his head and gazed at her through half-closed eyes. "No, I heard Gareth say they'd meet us at forest home. They won't come back here. And even if they did, they can't free me from this chain. I'm dead, Lindy, and there's nothing either of us can do about it."

She stood there looking helplessly at him and for the first time, despair settled over her. She looked around at the forest, at the immense dark beauty, and realized that it held immense danger, too. "Marin..." she began, but his head was low on his chest and he was silent.

She stood beside him for a long time, watching as a heavy fog appeared from the darkness and shrouded them in a thick gray blanket. Her gaze shifted from the fog to Marin's chest as she watched the slow agonized breaths shudder out of him. Finally unable to bear watching him any longer, she turned and walked over to the fire. Gunther still lay curled beside her pack, his eyes following her as she added wood to the flames until they licked skyward in the darkness. She sat down beside him and patted his head absently while her gaze settled on Marin again. He still slept, his body sagging painfully against his pinioned arms. Even from this distance, she could see him shivering. She folded her arms across her chest and exhaled deeply, watching her warm breath vaporize in the increasingly cold night air. Marin was right. The temperature was plummeting and would surely reach freezing by morning.

"Dammit," she cursed, feeling more helpless than she had ever felt in her life. Even if Marin did act like a jerk toward her, he was still the best hope the Bear People had to help them survive. Her mind raced to find a solution before it was too late. She could try to move the fire closer to him, but risked burning him alive if the wind shifted. She'd brought no extra clothes that she could share with him, and even if she had, she wouldn't be able to get them on him.

A chittering sound broke the night's silence and she looked around in the darkness to find its source. She traced the sound to the other side of the fire and realized it was his teeth chattering. Lindy jumped up and ran to him, her own panic surging. Marin's lips were pale blue. "Oh God, I can't let him die," she groaned.

She ran back to her pack and untied the rope that bound it to her sleeping bag. Inside was the red plaid blanket Gareth had insisted she bring with. Her mind raced to decide how to use it. Draping the blanket over her arm, she grabbed the sleeping bag and ran back to Marin. He shivered violently now, his breaths shallow and rapid as though his lungs couldn't overcome the shivering enough to take in deep breaths.

"Marin," she said, pushing his hair aside so she could see his face. His eyelids flickered as a groan slipped from his throat. One violent tremor after another washed over him. "Marin," she said again louder. He raised his head to look at her but seemed to have trouble focusing his eyes. She grabbed his head in her hands and pulled his face level with hers. "Listen to me," she commanded. "Lean forward, Marin. Lean toward me."

Understanding registered in his eyes and he let his body drop forward as far as the chain allowed. It wasn't much, but it was enough. She tucked one corner of the blanket behind his back and yanked it up until it slid above his head. The two side corners were bunched beneath his arms. She pulled them up until they too were free. Then leaving the blanket to dangle around him, she unrolled the sleeping bag and tucked it around his legs and feet. When it was secure around his lower body, she stood up and faced him.

Marin watched without speaking, too cold to think clearly. His eyes followed her movements, dropping from her face to her hands as she unzipped the front of her fleece jacket. She pushed the coat open and unbuttoned the front of her flannel shirt. His eyes widened slightly at the sight of her white flesh beneath a lacy black bra, but still no sound came from him other than the chattering of his teeth.

Lindy shoved her chest against him, gasping when her skin met his. He felt like ice to her touch and shivers rushed over her in an aching flood. Ignoring the discomfort, she pulled her shirt, then the jacket around her sides and over his to cover as much of their flesh as she could. Her hands shook badly with the chills. She fumbled with the blanket, struggling to pull the corners around behind her to enwrap Marin and herself together within it. When she had maneuvered the material into the best position she could manage and tied the blanket closed, she lowered her head into the valley between his neck and shoulder and shuddered. "It's the best I can do, Marin," she said, praying that her best would be good enough.

Chapter Twenty-Seven

Dawn broke over the forest in a soft yellow wave that slowly washed away the darkness and the fog. It was a welcome sight for the two men as they rushed through the pines trying to escape their pursuers. At least now they could see where the trail was and where they were going. Their breaths came fast and furious, their chests aching from the exertion, but there was no way they could stop. From the volume of the growls and crashes coming from the woods behind them, they knew the bears were hot on their trail. Dixon swung around and fired off two more shots into the darkness. He knew it was unlikely that he would hit one of the bears, but he figured it was enough to slow them down momentarily.

"I told you not to beat that asshole," Roberts cried over his shoulder to his partner, who ran a few steps behind him. "That scream of his could have raised the dead."

"Up yours," Dixon panted, flipping his partner the bird. "I didn't know that they were close enough to hear him."

"It was a fucking stupid thing to do," Roberts panted with a shake of his head. "The boss is gonna be real pissed off that we left him there. Shit, he's not gonna like it when we show up empty-handed."

"Yeah, well, we'll deliver the goods one way or the other," Dixon called back, trying to laugh despite the fear that coursed through him. He didn't want to admit it, but he was dreading the confrontation that was imminent with the man who'd hired them.

They crashed relentlessly through the vegetation, knowing that they were nearing the farmhouse and the welcoming committee that they hoped awaited them. Their legs ached from the exertion, their chests grew tight from their panting, but they couldn't stop. To do so meant certain death, and to die from mauling was not how they intended to end life. Rescue waited at the clearing on the edge of the forest and it was coming nearer minute by minute.

Finally Roberts yelled out, his voice filled with relief. "There it is! I see it!" He burst from the forest and stumbled into a meadow that was nothing more than a long-overgrown wheat field. Even years later, the rows were still evident where seeds had once been methodically and evenly planted. Now all that grew in the abandoned soil was wild grasses and thistles.

Dixon burst into the meadow just behind him and panted a sigh of relief. Just beyond the edge of the old wheat field, a battered white farmhouse rose above the vegetation. Its roof had partially collapsed and the ancient clapboard siding was barren of most of its paint, but to Dixon it looked like the prettiest thing he'd ever seen. "I see it!" he cried, pulling alongside his partner with a burst of speed that surprised them both. They ran side by side up a gravel path that led to the front door and burst inside the house.

The bears crashed out of the forest and dove into the old crop field at full speed. Foamy spittle sprayed from their gaping mouths as they panted in huge gasps, and steam rose in white wisps from their drenched coats in the freezing morning air. The men were mere yards ahead of them, but they saw the building and knew that escape was now a possibility for their prey. The farmhouse was clearly their intended destination and within moments they would be there. The bears strained to overcome them, lunging forward to take advantage of the last few feet of open space to maneuver, but suddenly they knew they had failed. They dug their paws into the weedy ground of the front yard and slid to a stop just in time to see the humans disappear inside the dilapidated building.

Thoren threw his grizzled head back and roared with anger. How could they have come so far and lost their prey at the last possible moment? He knew he couldn't rest until the kidnappers had been caught and given their due punishment. The clan needed the security of knowing that these men would never come looking for them again. He wanted more than anything to exact revenge for what the men had done to Gareth and Marin, but he also had enough sense to know that he and his kin couldn't just rush inside the house and retrieve them. They were at an impasse and he had no idea what to do.

The problem was solved for him when the front door opened and six men stepped out into the dawn sunshine. Each one carried a gun that was aimed directly at the bears.

"Welcome, bear kin," their leader said, stepping forward to point his gun at Thoren's head. "We've been expecting you."

Chapter Twenty-Eight

Lindy felt her head jerk and she snapped awake. Her left cheek burned with warmth and for a moment she couldn't fathom why. Then she saw the smooth olive skin beneath her face and everything came flooding back. She pushed herself backward and gazed up. Marin was awake and alert, his dark velvet eyes peering down into hers.

"You're alive," she whispered, not quite believing it.

The corner of his mouth upturned in a faint smile. "Cold but alive," he said.

Except for faint starlight flickering overhead, the night was still black and foggy and she wondered how long she'd been sleeping. The blanket was still drawn tightly around them and it took her a minute to realize that her hands gripped it so tightly her fingers had fallen asleep. Her back ached from standing in the same position for hours. *Lord, if I feel this bad, how does Marin feel?* she wondered. She stood motionless, suddenly embarrassed by the situation. His chest was warm and firm against hers, his breaths coming evenly and deep. She could feel the flow of air in and out of his body as if it were going in and out of her own. She noticed that his teeth had stopped chattering and from all appearances, he seemed to be feeling better.

She looked up at him and cleared her throat. "Maybe I'll uh… I'll get us some water."

"NO," he blurted out. His eyes darted away from hers as though he was caught off guard by his response. He exhaled softly. "Please, I... don't want to be cold again." There was a desperate tone, a pleading in his voice she couldn't refuse.

"Oh, okay," she said, still flustered at the position she'd put herself in. "Are you comfortable then?" As soon as she said it she knew it was a stupid question. He was chained to a tree—how could he possibly be comfortable? *Great, now he's got proof that I'm the idiot he thinks I am.* She wanted to shoot herself.

Marin blinked and licked his lips, debating how to answer. It would be so easy to humiliate her right now. But his gaze darted away and he lowered his head. "I have a...an itch on my back, to be honest," he said at last, seeming similarly embarrassed.

She exhaled slowly, relieved by his response. "Which side?"

"My left."

She took the edge of the blanket into her left hand and forced her right hand up along his shoulder blade. There was so little room to move that her knuckles felt the rough, furrowed bark beneath the blanket. Her palm flattened against his back and she could tell that every muscle in it was in peak condition. "Here?" she asked. Heat was starting to radiate in her face again and she knew she was blushing.

"Higher and toward the middle."

She opened her fingers and ran her nails lightly across his skin. A shiver swept over his flesh and she wondered if her hand was cold against him or if he was just enjoying her touch. The answer came immediately when a deep, contented rumble purred from his throat. She relaxed and let her own breath ease from her chest, pleased to be able to ease his misery if even for a few moments, and let her nails wander aimlessly across his back. He was so broad and the muscles of his back so developed that if she had been a small woman, her arms would barely have reached around him. The purr in his throat grew in intensity with each sweep of her hand across him and she felt his body relax against her.

Well, most of it. Even as his upper body relaxed, she felt the muscles of his stomach tighten and begin to twitch. He shifted slightly against her and her thigh slipped between his legs. He was growing hard, his genitals pressing against the fabric of her jeans with increasing firmness. She stood unmoving, astounded by his unexpected reaction, but he sucked in a breath and tried to move away in panic. There was no place for him to go. He tried to force himself back against the tree and squirmed against her, his embarrassment growing along with his manhood, and it was only making things worse.

"Marin, hold still," she said, trying to sound nonchalant. "It's all right."

"It is *not* all right," he retorted angrily.

She looked up at him, surprised by the harshness of his voice, but he only looked away. "There's no need to be ashamed. It's a natural reaction," she reassured him. Though she couldn't help thinking that it served him right for all the times he'd acted superior to her, she pitied his embarrassment.

Marin swung his head around and glared into her eyes. "I am repulsed by humans. Don't even dare to think that you caused this to happen!"

Lindy's lips parted and her jaw fell in shock. She looked away and tried to catch her breath, feeling as though she'd just been punched in the stomach. *The son of a bitch.* She'd stood there with her arms around him all night to keep him from freezing to death and this was how he thanked her? She was tempted to yank the blanket from around him and take it away. Fuck it. Let him freeze. But as much as she wanted to, she knew she couldn't do it. She owed it to Gareth and the rest of the clan. Marin was their Guardian and she wouldn't turn on him now. She swallowed hard and fought back the hot tears burning in her eyes. She'd be damned if she'd let him know how much his words hurt.

Marin laid his head back and closed his eyes, focusing on the feel of her body trembling against him. *Good. Humans needed to learn their place. They needed to be taught that they were no better than any other creature, despite their own misguided perceptions. They needed to be taught respect.* He breathed deeply, knowing in his mind that he was right. It felt good to finally put her in her place.

Then he felt the warm drop of liquid fall on his skin. It landed on the front of his shoulder and trickled slowly down his chest, leaving a hot trail. She brought her hand around to his skin and quickly wiped the moisture away, but it was too late. He knew it was a tear and that he had caused it, and the impact of his horrible words on her hit home.

He sighed softly. "Lindy?"

She didn't answer, didn't move.

"Answer me," he demanded.

She stood silent, her face turned away from him.

"I know you're crying. Don't cry."

She jerked her head up to look at him and he was stunned to see such pain in her eyes. "I know, Marin. Crying is such a disgusting human habit. Well you know what? Fuck you." She unwrapped the blanket from around them and stepped back, then closed it over the front of him again. Staring into his eyes, her anger seethed. "I don't want to sicken you with the feel of my human flesh anymore." She spat the words out as she redressed and walked over to the fire. A few orange embers remained and she added more wood until the flames licked toward the sky. Then she sat down beside it and drew Gunther's head into her lap. "I'll just stay over here with my dog. No doubt you can't stand him, either."

They remained quiet for a long time, neither of them willing to be the first to break the tension. Soon the darkness lifted and the first pale rays of dawn lit a path between the trees. She watched the light burning its way into the darkness and wished it could burn the agony out of her heart. *Why did his words hurt me so much when I don't even like the man?* she wondered, knowing that she was lying to herself.

"I need water."

She looked over to see him staring at her. "Get it yourself." Her voice was flat, the emotion drained.

Marin licked his swollen lips. "Please."

Silence.

"Please, Lindy."

She rolled her gaze toward him again while she debated. For someone who could be so forceful and mean, he looked pretty damn pathetic. She thought that the bruises on his face made him look like a raccoon. Exhaling with disgust at herself for being such a pushover, she rose and brought the canteen to him. Despite the painful swelling around his mouth, his lips parted eagerly and he drank well. Lindy put the cap back on it and turned to walk away.

"Wait."

She glanced from the corner of her eye and found his eyes boring into her. "I don't think so," she said, turning her back to him.

"Lindy, please." His voice was soft, almost imploring.

She'd never heard him sound like that before. "What do you want?" she asked, staring into the fire. Despite its warmth radiating into the air, she felt cold inside.

"I owe you an explanation."

She snorted softly. "You don't owe me anything, Marin. I'm just a human."

He pushed his head back against the tree in frustration and the chain rattled behind him as he strained to move his badly aching wrists. "Lindy," he groaned. "This is not easy for me." Exasperation filled his voice.

She turned slowly and lifted her head until they looked eye to eye. "It hasn't exactly been easy for me, either, you know. You've tried to make every minute I've had with the clan miserable."

He took a deep breath and shuddered. "I know."

She held her breath, waiting for an apology that never came. She turned to walk away.

"Don't think I don't know that you saved my life last night." He stopped to lick his lips again and take another slow breath, waiting until she had turned around to look at him again. Her eyes were wide. "But what happened... what happened when you were... near me..." He looked away, embarrassed by the heat of a blush creeping over his bruised cheeks. "That hasn't happened to me in a long time." His voice became barely audible. "Not since my mate died seven years ago."

Lindy felt her anger beginning to slip away and her heart soften with compassion. It was the first thing he'd ever revealed to her about himself and she could tell how painful the confession was for him. "I'm sorry about your mate, Marin. I know what it's like to lose someone special." She stopped and took a breath, groping for words to console him. "But look at it this way. What happened can be a good sign. At least you know your sex drive is still intact."

He swallowed loudly and gazed over her head into the distance. "It puts me in a bit of a predicament."

"How so?"

His gaze lowered, traveling over her face before settling on her eyes. His dark irises were swimming with moisture as though he was ready to cry. "I swore to protect my clan from those who hurt us. I've devoted my life to it, as my sire and his sire did. I just can't let down my defenses and allow myself to feel kindness or pity…or affection, for those who killed my mate."

She closed her eyes and grimaced, knowing what was coming. "Humans killed her, didn't they." It wasn't a question because she already knew the answer.

Marin was silent for a long time and when he finally spoke, he had to force the words out. They came out slowly, as if each word ripped a piece of him away. The moisture in his eyes welled until he could hardly contain it. "I heard her roars and I came after her, but I was too late." He stopped again and drew in a ragged breath. "I was too late. They were standing over her. Laughing. Joking while her blood turned the grass red. They had already started skinning her before she was even dead."

Lindy clutched her stomach and ran for the bushes, fighting down the bile rising in her throat. Gareth's words came rushing back from the night she'd rescued him. The night he'd said that someday she would understand why Marin felt the way he did about humans. "Jesus," she cried, finally vomiting. "Oh Jesus."

Chapter Twenty-Nine

"Lindy," he called again. "Answer me. Are you okay?"

She lifted her head from the ground and rested with her hands on her thighs to catch her breath. Her stomach burned as though it had been seared by a flaming brand. Panting in three deep breaths, she licked her lips and swept the damp hair back from her face. "I'm okay," she finally managed to say. She raised her face to the sky, willing the cold air to take the burning out of her lungs.

"Are you sure?" he asked again. Despite his own pain, all he could think about was Lindy doubled over in the bushes. He didn't want to care, tried to force himself not to, but he couldn't help it. He cursed his own heartlessness while his rescuer cried in pain.

His rescuer. He couldn't believe that the human had come with his clan to try and save him. After all the times he'd treated her so badly and threatened her so forcefully…after he'd almost killed her in the forest. Why would she possibly want to risk herself for him? Could she possibly have betrayed him as he suspected?

Gareth. She had come for Gareth's sake. Maybe he'd asked for her help. Maybe she did it to impress him and win his affection. Marin could only speculate why a human female would accompany the Bear People in pursuit of two members of her own species. But now it wasn't important. The fact that she had done it was all that mattered.

He leaned his head back against the tree and exhaled

slowly. He didn't know what to say, so he waited in awkward silence.

She stood up and wobbled slowly over to her backpack, feeling like she'd been hit by a train. Never in her life had she been more ashamed to be human than at this moment. Suddenly everything was clear; it made perfect sense. No wonder he hated her. She finally understood why he was revolted by her presence and the feel of her against him. She opened the canteen and poured the remaining water down her scorched throat. Now she knew that he had every right to treat her the way he did.

Marin watched carefully while she took her drink. He strained to focus his eyes on her trembling hands and the sweaty paleness of her face, wondering if her physical response was due to illness or what he'd told her. Could a human have compassion with such depth that it could make the body ill?

Lindy set the empty canteen down and patted Gunther's head before turning to walk back over to Marin. She stood before him, her face white and sullen, and looked up into his black eyes. "I'm sorry," she said, exhaling a slow heavy breath. "I'm sorry for what we did to your mate. I'm sorry for the way we've harassed and abused your clan all these years." She stopped to force down the sob rising in her throat. "And I'm sorry I let you down. I tried my best, but I've failed the clan and I've failed you."

His breath caught in his throat at the sight of tears streaming down her beautiful face. Never before had the thought of holding a human woman been so tantalizing, so tempting as it was now. But now he didn't have the option. The chain still bound his hands tightly, preventing him from doing what he had never before wanted to do. All he could do was bow his head and wish for the impossible.

She wiped the wetness from her cheeks and turned sideways to look at the fire. It had burned down and needed feeding. "I'll get more wood," she said quietly.

Marin swallowed hard and debated what to do. He

wanted to call her back to his side and ask her to put her arms around him and hold him tight. She needed to know that he didn't blame her for the actions of her kind or for the death of his mate. And although he'd never admitted it, he respected her for standing up to him when he'd put her on trial. Much like himself, she had courage and determination. And more than a touch of stubbornness.

But he held back and let her go. First and foremost, he was the Guardian and his responsibility was to protect the clan. When they freed him, as he knew they eventually would, he would resume his role with authority and dignity. Life would go back to normal. And when it came time to decide how to deal with Lindy, he knew what he would do. He would give her permission to pursue a relationship with the one she loved.

He watched her kneel by the fire and throw sticks into the growing flames. The happiness that once had graced her lovely face was gone, replaced by a deep sadness. A heavy shudder tremored through him at the sight of her and he finally, grudgingly admitted to himself what he had known for a long time. Gareth wasn't meant for her. He was.

Chapter Thirty

The man standing near Thoren shoved the gun barrel deep into the bruin's thick fur. He was a tall, well-manicured man with a handsome face and a demeanor that revealed a life free of manual labor. He was obviously accustomed to getting his own way. His gaze traveled over the rough coat of the panting bear before flicking to the other bears with him. "Stand tall," he said at last, speaking to Thoren.

Thoren blinked twice and swung his head around to look at his bear kin, wondering if they'd heard the man's words as he had. They stared back with eyes wide in surprise and he knew he'd heard correctly. The human had given them an order that only Bear People followed. Thoren turned back and looked up at the man, feigning ignorance.

The corner of the man's mouth turned up in a knowing smile, allowing an exhalation of air to slip out in disgust. He shook his head. "Come on, Pops, don't play games with me. You heard right. I said stand up. Stand tall. You know, shift. Change. Comprendo?"

Still Thoren stood immobile. His panic was growing and he didn't know what to do. Marin had always been there to advise him, but now he was on his own with the safety of the others to consider. He snuffled softly and pawed the ground, stalling.

"Okay, if you want to play this game we can play it." He swung the gun barrel up and aimed it into the sky.

Thoren watched carefully, waiting for the human's next

move.

The man's smile grew broader, forming a horizontal slit across his face. For a brief moment, he looked behind him to Dixon, who leaned against the front door of the farmhouse catching his breath. Once he had his attention, he turned back to face the clan. "Who will it be, Dix?" he asked.

Dixon wiped the sweat and dirt off his face and looked from bear to bear. "Gee, Boss, I'm kinda partial to that pretty red bear. It'll look real nice over my fireplace."

"You've got good taste," the man in front answered, lowering his gun again. This time it was aimed directly at Gareth. He pulled the trigger back until it clicked.

Thoren roared and rose up on his hind legs, throwing himself between Gareth and the gun. The air echoed with the shot as the bullet sank deep into Thoren's chest. The bruin screamed a high-pitched whine and sank to the ground at the man's feet, his paws thrashing helplessly while his blood spread in a thick red carpet around him.

No one moved. The bears watched terrified while their companion bled in front of them, not knowing what to do. Thoren's head rolled back in a spasm of pain, shocking his body into a shift. Within a matter of moments, an old man laid where the bear had been. Blood was pumping from a gaping hole in the white skin of his chest.

The bears looked at each other, knowing that nothing would save them now. One by one, they rose up from the ground and shifted into the men that their spirits ordained them to be. Gareth rushed forward and fell to the ground beside Thoren. He cradled the man's head tenderly in his lap, sobbing with anger and frustration.

"You didn't have to do this," he spat at the shooter. Rage welled so hard inside him he thought he could tear the man apart with his bare hands.

The handsome man just shrugged and cocked his head. "Hey, I told him. It's not my fault the old geezer didn't follow directions. So let this be a warning to the rest of you. You'll do what I say or one by one you'll join him in the dirt."

Gareth bent over to comfort his wounded friend, but it was too late. Thoren's eyes were open but sightless, his chest unmoving with any breath.

"Now, here's what you're going to do," the man continued as though nothing out of the ordinary had happened.

Gareth jumped up and lunged for the man, managing to grab one arm before the man jolted backward. He yanked him down and fell on top of him, pummeling the handsome face over and over with furious blows of his fists. It wasn't but a moment until two of the other humans grabbed his arms and yanked him to his feet. They quickly bound his hands together behind his back before lifting their boss off the ground.

Wiping blood from his broken nose, the man shook his head and glared at his attacker. "You son of a bitch," he muttered. For a moment, he wondered if he should just shoot Gareth now and be done with it, but deciding against it, he drew his own fist back and slammed it into the man's face. Gareth flew backward and crashed to the ground unconscious.

The other he-bears lunged forward en masse until they saw all the guns lift simultaneously and point at them. They stopped and stood frozen in place, looking at each other in fear.

The boss sighed and nodded, knowing he finally had their full attention. "As I was *saying*, here's what you're going to do." He stepped forward and thrust his finger at the he-bear nearest him. "You will return to the campsite and retrieve the Guardian. Then you will bring him back here. I have some business to finish with him."

Arlin drew back in shock. *Not me*, he breathed to himself. But it was his chest that the man's finger was digging into and he knew he had no choice but to obey. The only problem was, by now Marin and Lindy were probably back at forest home. He opened his mouth to protest but the boss cut him off.

The man snapped his fingers in the air. "Key," he said. Roberts walked up from behind him and slipped a small silver key into his outstretched hand. He thrust it toward Arlin.

"You'll need this to free him."

It took a moment before Arlin understood that the situation was not at all what the clan had expected. The one thing they'd felt reassured about was that Marin would be safely at home recovering from the humans' abuse. Now they knew that he was still at their campsite, apparently locked to that tree. He would have been unable to shift and may not have survived the night. And Lindy no doubt was helpless to free him. Arlin's head sank dejectedly onto his chest just thinking about what he'd find when he got there.

"Well, are you waiting for me to shoot you too?" the man laughed. "Get your ass going."

Arlin turned and walked slowly back toward the forest. He passed by the remaining four he-bears and glanced sidelong at each of them in turn, wondering if they would be alive when he came back. He tried to look brave but he knew they saw fear in his eyes. He saw it in their eyes, too. When he was past them, he stood down. Then digging his claws angrily into the ground, he charged away as fast as he could run.

Chapter Thirty-One

Lindy took the peanut butter sandwiches out of her backpack and placed them on top of the fabric. Unwrapping one for Gunther, she ripped it in half and fed it to him in pieces. The dog was ravenous and gulped it without chewing. The other sandwich she carried over to Marin.

"You must be starving. Do you think you can eat this sandwich?" she asked.

He eyed the food warily, never having seen something called a *sandwich* before. But by now his hunger was stronger than his caution and he licked his lips. "I'll manage," he said.

She broke off a small portion and raised it slowly to his mouth, suddenly feeling uncomfortable about feeding him this way. In her mind, she kept picturing him in his bear skin, the way his gleaming white canine teeth protruded from his snarling mouth when he'd tried to kill her the first time he saw her with Gareth. Her hand trembled and the bread tumbled from her fingers to the ground. She looked down at it in disbelief before gazing back up at Marin.

Humiliation swept through him in a vicious wave. Of all that had happened to him since he was kidnapped, none of it was worse than this single moment of helplessness. He had never depended on a female to feed him, let alone a human female. He averted his eyes to keep her from looking at them, afraid that she would see his shame. "Never mind," he whispered.

Lindy took the sandwich in one hand and raised her other

hand to his face. His dark hair had tumbled down into his eyes again and she swept it back gently, freeing her view of him. He kept looking down and she knew that he was painfully embarrassed. "Marin," she said, massaging her fingers softly through the tangled mass of hair. She didn't know why, but it felt so good, so *right* to touch him, though she knew she shouldn't do it. She lowered her head and tried to look into his eyes. "You would do this for me, so let me do it for you."

He shook his head in protest. "No I wouldn't," he replied.

Lindy smiled and let her fingers drift forward across his cheek. The bruises were ugly and swollen, but he was still handsome under it all. She took his chin in her hand and raised his face up to look at her. He didn't fight her but still kept his eyes fixed on the ground. She tore off another small chunk of sandwich, held it to his lips and waited. "I think you would," she said.

Marin stared down at the food, trying hard not to inhale the tantalizing aroma. It was a smell he recognized, a nut of some kind. Whatever this strange food was, it was made of nuts, which he loved. He closed his eyes and fought his hunger, wanting only for her to go away and take the damn food with her. But she stood there patiently waiting, as stubborn as he was.

"It's a long way back to forest home," she reminded him. "When the clan arrives to free you, you'll need every bit of strength you can muster. This little sandwich won't give you a lot of energy, but it'll help. Please eat it."

He shifted painfully against the tree and sighed, knowing that she had a valid point. Still, it didn't make this any easier. Finally giving up, he opened his mouth and parted his lips just enough for her to slip the morsel inside. The rough crust slid onto his tongue, but all he felt was the warmth of her fingertips brushing against his lips, and he moaned.

Her heart began to beat furiously when he finally looked up at her. She could see from the expression on his face that it was the feel of her fingers on his lips that had caused his response, and she kept her hand on his face a moment longer, needing to feel him and wanting him to feel her touch. His dark eyes gazed forcefully down into her own, suddenly bereft of any embarrassment. There was no doubt in her mind what it was that he was feeling, what he couldn't keep his eyes from expressing. It was *desire.*

As if he recognized that she knew, his eyes darted away to look at the forest. He chewed the food quickly and swallowed it down with a gulp, waiting silently to see what she would do.

Lindy was puzzled by his conflicting actions. One minute he seemed to enjoy and even yearn for her touch, while the next minute he tried to push her away with his coolness. If only his intention was as obvious as Gareth's, she'd know how to handle him. But Marin was an enigma and she began to wonder if *he* even knew how he felt about her. *Only time will tell me that,* she supposed.

Pushing the thought aside, she tore another piece off the sandwich and put it carefully in his mouth. It pained her to watch him chew, to see his swollen jaw move so awkwardly and slow. She wished she had an ice pack to put on his face to ease the swelling, or some pain medication to give him, but of course she didn't. "Does it taste good to you?" she asked.

He nodded yes and swallowed. "I don't think anything has ever tasted so good."

She fed him the rest of the sandwich and wiped the crumbs off his chin. "I wish I had some water left to give you but I drank it all," she apologized.

"I know," he said. "It's all right."

She stood beside him for a moment, wondering what to do next. There was nothing she could think of to do for him, nothing left to give him, but she didn't want to leave his side. Her mind raced, trying to think of some excuse to stay near him. "Are you warm enough?" she said at last.

The corner of his bruised mouth rose in a slight smile. "I'm a little cold," he lied.

"Well then, let me get you warm again," she said, opening the blanket over his chest. Then she stopped and looked up at him with a strange look on her face. “Maybe this isn’t a good idea. I mean, it made you upset before.” She stood there frozen in place, her hands still holding the blanket open.

Marin knew exactly what she was thinking about. She was remembering the way he’d yelled at her and forced her away from him after she’d kept him warm with her body all night. He knew that his cruel words were replaying over and over in her mind and he could almost feel the warm heat of her tear as it had trickled down his chest. He gulped down his regret, looked her firmly in the eye and took a slow, thoughtful breath.

“There’s something I want to tell you, Lindy.” He paused until he was sure he had her full attention. “I haven’t spoken about Terra since the day she died,” he began. A shiver swept over him and he stopped again, beginning to feel the cold that he’d just lied to her about. “I never really dealt with what happened because I just wanted to forget everything. But I never forgot the anger and as the years passed, I could feel it growing inside me. The only way I was able to go on day after day was by focusing my hatred on the ones who hurt me. Then when I saw you with Gareth that day, I went crazy. I not only wanted to kill you, but I wanted to punish him, too. I thought to myself, *how dare he flaunt a human in my face.* All I could think of was making you both hurt as much as I had been hurt.”

Lindy closed the blanket slowly over his chest and held the corners of it tightly in her hand. She looked down at the ground, unable to look him in the eyes again.

“I never believed that there was such a creature as a *good* human. The only experience I had was with those who hurt and tormented and killed my people. What reason did I have to think that you were any different? But then you gave me a reason.” He stopped and took a deep breath.

She continued to look at the ground, her mind reeling from what he was saying.

“Lindy, look at me,” he said. When she finally raised her eyes to meet his, he continued. “You gave me reason to believe that Gareth was right. I wasn’t convinced after you’d saved his life, and I still wasn't convinced when I saw you show up here last night. But I became a believer when you put your body on mine to save my life, knowing how much I frightened and intimidated you. I owe you an apology, Lindy. Thank you for what you did for me."

She smiled and gulped down the lump that had formed in her throat. Gareth's words floated back into her mind from the time he'd told her that Marin never apologized to anyone. Still, his apology didn't mean that he had *liked* the feel of her against him. "Thanks Marin," she said. "I'm glad that I was able to change your mind. And I'm glad that I could save your life last night. I understand why you said what you did, though. I guess I wouldn't like the feel of your body against me if our situations were reversed."

The chain clanked behind the tree as he tensed his arms to ball his hands into fists. He realized that he still hadn't explained himself adequately and his apology wouldn't be complete unless she understood exactly how he felt. "Lindy," he began again, laying his head back against the tree. "Don't you know that what I said to you, I said in defense? How could I admit that you did arouse me when I wasn't ready to admit it to myself? But now I've said it and we both know that it's the truth. I enjoyed the feel of you against me, Lindy. I want to enjoy it again."

She looked up at him with tears welling in her eyes, hardly believing that he felt the same way she did. "So it's okay if I share your blanket?" she asked tentatively.

He gazed down into her glistening eyes and nodded. "There's nothing I'd like more. And I promise that I'll behave better this time."

Exhaling louder than she meant to, she unzipped her jacket and slipped inside the blanket until they stood chest to chest. She felt his body relax and she snuggled harder against him, holding her palms against the muscles of his back to hold him tight. She heard him exhale slowly and then felt his chin lower gently onto the top of her head. Lindy closed her eyes and hoped that rescue would never come.

Chapter Thirty-Two

Arlin ran with his nose to the ground, following the trail back the way he had come. His large bulk swayed awkwardly above his short legs and he cursed himself for not staying in better shape. *It's no wonder the she-bears have little interest in mating with me*, he berated himself. But this was not the time to be worrying about that, he realized. The only thing that mattered at this moment was getting to Marin as quickly as possible. Then he would bring him back to the farmhouse and free the others...if the Guardian was still alive.

Morning sunlight streamed through the forest canopy in bright yellow streaks that illuminated the ground vividly before him, aiding his journey. It wasn't hard following the trail in reverse and he was confident that he could be back at the human's camp quickly. He ran harder than he had ever run in his life, urged on by the horrible thought of what the humans had done to his dear old friend Thoren. Arlin shuddered at the memory of the old man dying in Gareth's arms. What they had in store for the rest of the he-bears, he was afraid to imagine.

He panted heavily, desperate for a drink of cool water, but he refused to stop. This discomfort was nothing compared to that of his companions. Gareth had suffered from a gunshot, Marin had been badly beaten, and Thoren had been killed by the human's bullet at the farmhouse. It could just as easily have been him that the bullet killed instead of the old bear and he knew he was lucky. He figured this was his time to tough it out and show what he was made of. Maybe this was his suffering to endure, and he vowed to himself to carry the burden well. He licked his parched lips and kept running.

The sun had risen high in the morning sky when he smelled smoke from the fire and knew he was approaching the camp. He tore between the last huge pine trunks and burst into the clearing, preparing himself for what he might find. Then his eyes flew toward Marin and he roared with rage.

Marin was still bound to the tree and Lindy was with him. But the woman wasn't just standing *next* to him; she seemed to be leaning *against* him. She had her hands pressed up against his chest and was speaking directly to him while she stared at him. Arlin knew for a fact that one of the first things Gareth had taught her about the clan was never to touch a he-bear, especially Marin. And yet there she was taking advantage of his helplessness. How dare she touch the Guardian! His anger seethed at her disrespectful nerve.

He growled out a tremendous roar and arched up off the ground to shift into man skin. In a moment it was complete and he ran over to the tree and yanked Lindy viciously away. She whirled to the ground and fell on her side with a cry.

"What are you doing?" Marin yelled as he watched her land painfully on the hard ground.

"You're alive, Guardian!" he replied, quickly searching Marin's face as if to reinforce to himself that Marin was indeed talking and breathing.

Marin nodded and forced a smile to reassure the nervous he-bear. But his eyes never left the woman.

"Has she harmed you?" Arlin asked franticly, following Marin's gaze to the ground. "I saw her disrespecting you, and if she's caused you any pain, I'll rip her apart myself," he swore.

"No, you won't touch her," Marin said quickly, afraid that in his excitement, Arlin would do as he'd promised. "Help her up."

Arlin just stood and looked at him, wondering if he'd heard correctly. "But...she had her hands on you..." he murmured. "She was disrespectful to you. Are you going to allow that?"

Lindy struggled back onto her feet and stood silently behind Arlin, afraid to speak or move. All she wanted was to hear Marin's answer.

His gaze darted over to her and he motioned with his head for her to come closer to him. She didn't move, fearing that she had misunderstood his intent and afraid of what Arlin might do to her again.

"Lindy," Marin said softly to ease her worry. "Come back beside me."

She swallowed hard and stepped around Arlin to stand by Marin again.

"Are you hurt?" he asked.

She shook her head and brushed the dirt off her jacket. "No, I'm okay."

Arlin blinked his dark eyes and stared from him to her and back again. "I don't understand. Did I miss something?"

Marin laughed weakly and nodded. "You have no idea. Lindy saved my life last night."

Not knowing what to say to that, Arlin put his head down and stood silently for a moment. Then he remembered the key in his hand. "Marin, something terrible has happened."

The Guardian's eyes became alert and he shifted uncomfortably against the tree. "What is it?" He wasn't sure he wanted to know, but he had to.

A soft whine slipped from Arlin's throat along with his words. "We failed, Marin. The humans escaped into the abandoned farmhouse at the boundary of the forest. Six more of them came out with guns and are keeping our kin prisoner. They hit Gareth and bound him. And Thoren…" His voice trailed away to silence.

Marin's face wrinkled with dread. He knew by Arlin's expression that it was bad. "Thoren? What happened to Thoren?"

Arlin refused to raise his head and look Marin in the eye. "They killed him with a bullet."

Marin leaned his head back against the tree and howled

an agonized moan that seared into Lindy's heart. She wanted desperately to throw her arms around him and comfort him, but she knew she couldn't with Arlin standing there scrutinizing her behavior. She lowered her head and cursed the humans who had murdered the wise old bruin.

"Marin?" It took a moment for the Guardian to compose himself, and when he was quiet, Arlin continued. "Their leader sent me back here to free you. I have a key he told me to use."

"Oh thank God," Lindy cried. She held out her hand to take the key, but Arlin yanked his hand away.

"Give it to her," Marin ordered.

Reluctantly, Arlin handed her the silver key and watched while she slipped behind the tree and opened the heavy gray padlock. The chains clinked while she maneuvered the lock off the links and a moment later, Marin was free.

As soon as the chain slipped off his wrists, he sank to the ground. His legs felt like stone and all he could think about was lying down on the soft sleeping bag beneath him and going to sleep. Every part of his body ached from the cold and the beating. Lindy kneeled down beside him and drew the blanket over his shoulders.

"Let me see your wrists," she said, drawing his arms gently toward her. The flesh on his lower arms was raw and bloody from the chafing, but he didn't flinch when she touched him. "God, your arms are a mess. Let me clean you up." She rose and turned to get her backpack.

Arlin wheeled around to block her path. "Marin, I'm sorry but there's not time. We need to go."

Marin just looked up at him with a blank look on his face.

"Go where?" Lindy asked.

Arlin didn't want to respond to her, but remembering how Marin had rebuked him for the way he'd treated her a moment ago, he was afraid not to. "They told me to bring Marin back to them at the farmhouse."

Marin and Lindy groaned at the same time.

"Why?" she asked.

"The leader said he had some business to finish with him."

Marin struggled to sit upright and rubbed his hands across his aching thighs. The muscles felt like they hadn't been used in years and he wondered if he would even be able to walk. He shook his head slowly back and forth. "Business to finish? I don't understand. I've never had anything to do with any humans except to kill the ones…" His gaze shot up to Lindy and he decided it was best not to finish.

She laid her hand on his shoulder and squeezed it gently. "Don't worry, I understand," she said reassuringly. There was no doubt in her mind that the people he'd killed had done something to deserve their fate. "But you're in no condition to travel," she reminded him. "Even if you made it there, you don't have the strength to fight anyone. They'd just take you prisoner, too."

Marin sighed and forced himself to his feet. He wobbled so unsteadily that Lindy grabbed his arm to keep him upright. His arms and shoulders throbbed, but it was the pain shooting up his legs and through his back in searing bursts that took his breath away. He nodded gratefully when she put both arms around him and held him for support, knowing that he would tumble back to the ground without her help. "I don't have a choice. If they've asked for me, the only chance my kin may have of surviving is if I show up. Maybe they'll take me in trade for the others."

"I have a feeling these humans don't make deals," Arlin said. "They showed Thoren and Gareth no mercy when they didn't follow orders. And they don't seem like they'd take a change of plans very well."

Marin nodded thoughtfully, his mind racing to come up with a plan to save his kin. But he was so tired he couldn't think straight. His body ached; he was hungry and thirsty, and too weak to put up a decent fight. For one of the few times in his life, he didn't know what to do.

Arlin looked around at the trees aimlessly, having no idea how to help. He was completely lost when it came to things like defense and fighting, and seeing Marin like this scared him. "What should we do?" he asked helplessly.

Marin closed his eyes and hunched over, feeling utterly hopeless. Only once in his forty years had humans defeated him and killed something he loved, and he swore that it would never happen again. And yet here he was again in a similar situation. But this time if he failed he could lose almost half his clan. "I don't know what to do," he moaned, barely able to force the words out.

Lindy tightened her arms reassuringly around his shoulders. His hair had fallen down into his face again and she brushed it gently out of his eyes. Then she cupped his chin in her palm and raised his handsome face up until he looked at her. "Marin, we may a chance. You've got a weapon they don't know you have."

His brow furrowed with confusion. "I do? What is it?"

She smiled and stroked his bruised cheek tenderly. "Me."

Chapter Thirty-Three

Gareth groaned and shook his head. He felt groggy and lethargic and his face throbbed in strong, steady pulses that made him shiver. As his vision cleared and he looked around, he could see that he was inside a run-down building that appeared to be vacant. There was little furniture or signs of habitation like he had seen in Lindy's house. But there was an old sink and some cupboards in front of him and he realized that he was alone in a room that once served as a kitchen. It was the old farmhouse. They'd taken him inside.

His first impulse was to break the glass out of the dusty window above the sink and run to freedom. But when he tried to move, he couldn't. Fear began to tighten his chest when he looked down and realized that he was in man skin and was tied to a chair. His hands were bound behind him around the back of the chair and his legs were pinioned to its front legs. Panic tore through him and he struggled franticly against the ropes, discovering for the first time what it felt like to be totally helpless. A whimper leaked from his throat.

The noise of his struggling caught the attention of one of the humans, and the man walked through the open doorway of the adjacent room and stopped before Gareth. He was a stocky man with a ruddy complexion and long black hair. He carried a rifle across his shoulder and set it down on the old porcelain drain board so he could squat down by his prisoner.

"You'll only hurt yourself by struggling," he said, gazing into the he-bear's frightened eyes. He had never seen such a creature and was amazed by how human it looked. If he had seen Gareth clothed and walking down the street, he would never have suspected that the man was also a bear.

"Where are the others?" Gareth asked. He couldn't stand the thought that he might be alone with the humans. He felt his heart pounding in his chest and wondered if the man could hear it, too.

The man nodded to someplace beyond the room they were in. "Don't worry, they're still alive."

Gareth twisted his hands, desperately hoping to loosen his bonds, but the rope didn't budge.

The man smiled and shook his head, sweeping his dark hair around his shoulders. "You've got a lot of fight in you."

"What do you want with us?" Gareth demanded.

The man stood up and grabbed his gun, then hefted it over his shoulder again. "Gotta go," he said and walked toward the doorway.

"Tell me!" Gareth screamed. "Tell me!"

The man just ignored him and walked back into the other room.

Gareth ceased his struggling and sat quietly for a moment, thinking. Voices drifted in from the adjoining room but he could only hear bits and pieces of the conversation. He could tell that they were the voices of the humans; none were the voices of his kin. The human had said they were somewhere out there and still alive, so why couldn't he hear them?

"Shara?" he called out.

No answer.

"Arlin?"

Still no response. He kicked at the chair legs, fighting to free his limbs from their confinement. He knew that unless he was able to free himself, he'd be unable to shift. And if he couldn't shift, he didn't have much chance of taking down a man with a gun. Panting in several deep breaths, Gareth steeled himself for the coming pain and kept his mind focused on one thought: no matter how much it hurt or how long it took, he would fight the ropes until he worked his way free and then he would kill a human. It didn't matter that he was sure to die in the attack. As long as he took one human with him into death, it would be worth the sacrifice.

The humans sat together in the dining room and joked quietly among themselves. They smoked cigarettes one after another and played poker to pass the time while they waited. Two other men stood outside the front door of the old house with the boss, their guns resting loosely across the crooks of their arms while they smoked.

The boss sat on the weathered cement porch step and stared at his prisoners. The remaining four he-bears were tied to trees in the front yard of the farmhouse where they could be easily monitored. He watched for a moment, enjoying the way they struggled against the ropes holding them, their eyes wide with fear. He knew the hard part of his plan was over. All he had to do now was wait for the fat bear to bring the Guardian back. A ripple of excitement flooded through him at the thought of what was about to happen.

His daydream was interrupted when the dark-haired man stepped through the doorway and stood beside him.

"How's Red doing?" the boss asked.

"He's awake now. Seems to be okay," he answered.

"Keep an eye on him, then. You make sure those ropes were tight?"

The man nodded and cast his eyes on the other four he-bears in the yard. "Yeah, they're tight."

"Good. Then take a breather until the action starts. It shouldn't be too long until they get back."

The man nodded and disappeared back inside the house. The boss crossed his arms over his knees and rested his chin on his forearms to stare at the prisoners. "I can't believe this day has finally come," he said to no one in particular. He liked the way the Bear People looked back at him helplessly, their terror plain on their faces. He almost couldn't believe that they were bears at all, except that he had seen it for himself. But of course he knew that it was true. They were no less real than he himself was.

He snorted softly at the comparison. Shapeshifters sounded so exotically different, so mysterious and magical, but they were flesh and blood just like him. The only difference was that they had chosen another path in life than his people had taken. But that was about to change. History was about to be made. He could hardly wait.

Across the yard, Shara's back scraped painfully over the tree bark as he tugged his wrists harder against the rope. All he could think about was how he had felt seeing Marin bound to a tree and now he was in the same position. Even though he was the youngest adult male and one of the most powerful bears in the clan, he knew that if Marin hadn't been able to free himself from the humans' restraints, he most certainly wouldn't be able to. He closed his eyes and tried to think about something else.

He thought about Thoren, whose body had been left on the ground where he'd fallen. He wanted to avenge the senseless murder, to rip the throats out of every human who played a role in their capture and Thoren's death. Shara opened his eyes and watched the sun tracking across the morning sky, wondering how long it would be before Marin and Arlin made it back. Did they have a plan?

He glanced around him to catch the attention of his bear kin, but they also had their eyes closed. At that moment, the realization of their situation stormed into his mind and he fought back a sob of fear. They were completely helpless and dependent on Marin to rescue them again. But he had seen how beaten their Guardian was and he wondered if he would be able to help them at all.

Shara leaned his head back against the tree and tried to control the panic sweeping through him. *Someone help us*, he wanted to cry out, but he knew there was no one else.

Chapter Thirty-Four

Marin had one arm on Arlin's shoulder and the other one draped over Lindy. He'd tried hard to spare them of the burden, but he just didn't have the strength. His legs felt like dead wood dragging through the vegetation and his head throbbed from the beating. Once he'd begun walking, he had shifted immediately and tried to make the journey in bear skin, but he just couldn't get very far without crashing to the ground. So he'd shifted back into man skin and allowed them to help him. They'd been walking for hours now and he wasn't sure how much longer he could go on.

Arlin stopped abruptly and pulled his companions to a halt beside him. "We're almost there," he said, gazing at a break in the trees in the distance ahead of them. "The house is just beyond those pines."

Lindy slipped off her backpack and motioned for Gunther to sit beside it and be quiet, then helped Marin settle on the ground. "We need to get closer and take a look," she whispered. She took a few steps before realizing that Arlin wasn't with her. "Are you coming?"

"Who'll stay with Marin?" he answered, feeling like a coward the moment the words left his mouth.

Lindy shrugged her shoulders and nodded, knowing that she was probably better off leaving him behind anyway. "I'll be right back."

She moved slowly forward, slipping from tree to tree while trying to stay hidden behind the thick trunks. There was no way of knowing if the humans had posted a sentry near the farmhouse or anywhere else outside, so she moved quietly and carefully, taking her time. Seeing no one around, she bent to the ground and crawled forward on her hands and knees to enter the overgrown weeds and grasses in the old wheat field.

Dust flew up into her face and she swatted gnats away from her sweating skin, but she kept going. Somehow, she had to determine where all the humans and he-bears were if they were going to figure out a plan of attack. Marin may not have the physical strength to help with the rescue, but she was depending on the strength of his mind to develop their strategy. A voice drifted from the distance somewhere ahead and she sank to her belly on the ground. The man laughed and muttered a few words about how hungry he was getting. Lindy crawled backward a little way until she felt safer, and then raised her head slowly off the ground.

The man was about forty yards away. His red plaid flannel shirt stood out vividly against the dingy white of the farmhouse's clapboards. A cigarette dangled from his lips for a moment before he dropped it to the ground and stubbed it out with the toe of his boot. Then he strolled leisurely across the front yard and stopped in front of a tree.

Her breath caught in her throat. The man stood before Shara, who was tied to the tree. Three other gnarled old trees grew in the yard and each one had a he-bear tied to it. She strained to see if any of them were hurt, but it was difficult to tell. The wind had picked up and the plants rustled softly in her face, obscuring her view. But there was nothing she could do about it; there was no way she could risk getting any closer.

Three human men were outside the house: the one that was standing by Shara and two on the porch, one sitting with his head resting on his hands and the other standing with a gun in his arms. She was too far away to clearly see their faces, but they all appeared to be strong and fit. Her heart began to thump faster in her chest at the thought of what she was up against. Lowering herself back toward the ground, she crawled backward and made her way out of the field.

She was never so glad to see trees in her life. When the weedy ground beneath her gave way to the needle-carpeted forest floor, she threw her back against the nearest tree and shuddered. Breaths began to pant out of her uncontrollably. *I can't do this, I can't*, she whispered to herself again and again. But when she looked deeper into the woods, to the spot where Marin bravely awaited her return, she knew that she had to. If she didn't, the Bear People would die.

Lindy peeked around the tree to ensure that she hadn't been followed, then hurried back the way she'd come. Marin and Arlin were sitting quietly together, staring warily at Gunther. The dog stared back with his ears pricked up at attention. His eyes darted to her as she collapsed on the ground to make her report.

"I saw the clan. They're tied to trees in the front yard of the farmhouse. There are three men outside the house, one of them has a gun," she panted. "I didn't see the other men."

Marin looked toward the field, trying to visualize the scene. "Are they hurt?"

She shook her head and shoved the blowing strands of blonde hair from her eyes. "I was too far away to tell for sure, but I don't think so. I didn't see any blood on them. They just looked...scared." She knew that just by saying the word, Marin would know how helpless his kin were.

He looked over at Arlin and squinted in concentration. "How many humans did you say there were?"

Arlin thought for a moment, replaying the scene of their first contact in his mind. "There were the two hunters we chased from the woods, and then six more men came out of the building."

"And how many guns?"

"Every man had a gun."

Marin's head sank down on his chest at the news. How could they possibly overcome eight men, each armed with a gun?

Lindy reached over and rubbed her hand slowly on his

knee, trying to comfort him. She was keenly aware of Arlin's disapproving gaze watching her movements, but she didn't care. Marin needed encouragement and she was determined to give it to him. "We need to distract the humans," she said.

Marin raised his head and gazed into the distance, thinking. "Perhaps. But even a distraction is useless unless the odds are changed more to our favor. We need to take some of the humans out of the fight."

Lindy nodded thoughtfully, seeing his point. "If we could lure a couple of them here into the forest, I could shoot them."

"No, that would alert the others and they might panic and kill our kin."

Arlin stared at the ground for a long time before he worked up the nerve to speak. "I could help," he said hesitantly. When Marin looked over at him, he inhaled slowly and forced himself to make the offer. "I could go back and tell them that I've brought you, but you collapsed in the forest and I need help getting you the rest of the way. Then I'll lead them here where the three of us can attack them."

Marin closed his eyes to work it out in his mind and realized that Lindy had been right. They didn't know she was with them, so they wouldn't know she was waiting here in the forest. Maybe together they could overpower the humans and take their guns. *It just might work.*

Lindy looked from Arlin to Marin and nodded. "It's worth a try," she encouraged, feeling relieved to have a plan of sorts.

"Let's do it then," Marin said at last. His gaze swept over to Lindy and lingered on her beautiful face. He loved the way the sunlight made her golden hair shimmer and dance around her blue eyes. He forced a smile, comforted by the thought that if they died, at least it would be together.

Chapter Thirty-Five

Arlin burst out of the field and pawed to a stop by the porch. All three men swiveled at his approach, surprised to see his dark hulk bearing down on them. The man with the gun swung the weapon up and aimed it at Arlin's head, his finger twitching in the trigger.

The boss stood up and stared at the bear, watching with fascination as the creature lifted its paws off the ground and arched itself upright into human form. Within moments, the fat man stood before him, panting heavily from his exertion. The boss swept his gaze over the yard around them, searching.

"Where's the Guardian?" he asked gruffly. "If you've failed…"

"No, no," Arlin protested, raising his arms before him.

"Where is he?" the boss asked again, this time louder.

Arlin swallowed hard and swept the sweat off his forehead. "I brought him but he's in bad shape. He collapsed in the forest a ways back and I can't get him here by myself."

"I want him *here*," the man growled, nodding his head toward the farmhouse behind him. "It was your job to get him here."

"I *did*," Arlin whined. "But it's not my fault your bullies beat him so badly that he can hardly walk. I'll take your men to him and together we can carry him back."

The man pursed his lips disgustedly while he thought about it, but he really didn't have much choice. He turned to look at the two men flanking him and nodded toward Arlin. "Go with him and bring the Guardian back."

The unarmed man ran into the house for his gun and then joined his accomplice at Arlin's side. They trained their guns on him and followed a step behind the bear man as he led them through the waving grass of the old field and into the woods.

"Move your fat ass," one man barked at Arlin, laughing at the sight of his bare bottom. It amazed him that these weird animal-men went around naked and didn't think anything of it. He dug the barrel of his rifle into Arlin's buttock and laughed again.

Arlin bit his tongue to keep from turning around and jumping on the man. He knew that if he did, he'd be dead in a second. Then Marin and Lindy would be on their own. No, it was better to stick to their plan. Then, when the time was right, he would have his opportunity for revenge.

"Where is he?" the other man grumbled, curious to see who this Guardian was.

Arlin motioned forward with his head. "He's right over there."

They continued walking until they spied a body lying near some bushes just ahead. They could see his bare back curled on the ground, as though the person had assumed a fetal position. Even from a distance, they could see that he was badly bruised. Both men raised their guns and aimed them at the Guardian's back.

"Get him up," one of the men ordered Arlin.

Arlin stepped over to Marin and reached down to take his arm. He pulled the limb up but Marin didn't rise. He was dead weight. Arlin stood back up and looked over at the humans with a helpless look on his face. "He's unconscious."

"Son of a bitch," the man replied. Wanting to see for himself, he stalked over beside Arlin and gazed down at the body on the ground.

"NOW!" Arlin said as loud as he dared.

Marin rolled over and yanked the man's feet from under him. The man crashed to the ground, the gun still in his hands. At the same instant, Lindy burst out of the bushes and slammed a heavy tree limb over the other man's head. Lindy's victim sank to the ground, groaning in semi-consciousness, but Marin's victim was still alert. Arlin jumped on him and slammed his fist into the man's face until his eyes rolled up in his head and he blacked out.

"Now what do we do with them? Lindy asked breathlessly. There was no rope to tie them up with and nothing to use as gags.

Marin looked up at Arlin with his dark eyes burning. "Will you do it?" he asked without further explanation.

Arlin nodded. Without another word, each he-bear grabbed the head of the man nearest him and gave it a vicious yank, breaking the neck with a sharp *snap*. Lindy whirled away and clutched her stomach, sickened by their actions.

"It had to be done," Marin said emotionlessly, struggling to his feet. They'd had no options, and even if they had, he knew he wouldn't have used them.

Lindy nodded and swallowed, forcing the bile back down. "I know. I just didn't think it would be so...gross."

Marin couldn't help but smile. She was so naïve in so many ways, but that was a good thing. It meant she had been spared some of the agonizing things that had made him the way he was. The way he hated being.

"Now what?" Arlin asked, wiping his hands on the sides of his legs as though ridding himself of the feel of human.

Lindy picked up the two guns and handed one to each he-bear. "You guys ever handle one of these?"

When they both shook their heads no, she explained to them how to aim using the sight and how to pull the trigger to fire the bullet. When she was confident that they understood, she took all three guns and laid them on the ground beside her. She reached up and put her arms around Marin, feeling how cold and tense he was when she pulled him close against her. He hugged her back and quickly pulled away, needing to get on with things before his strength failed completely. He turned and began walking determinedly through the woods toward the old field.

"Be careful," she called softly after him.

Raising one hand in reply, he walked on without bothering to look back.

Chapter Thirty-Six

“Where the hell are they?” the boss groaned, looking at the gold Rolex on his wrist. Fifteen minutes had passed and there was still no sign of his men or the two bear men they had been sent to recover.

“They’ve been gone an awful long time for just helping that wounded Guardian back here,” the other man agreed.

The boss looked down at his watch again when he heard a whistling breath come from his accomplice. He looked up to see what the problem was and choked out a cough.

A large naked man was walking through the golden weeds in the field. When the wind blew his shaggy dark hair away from his face, they could see that his skin was swollen and distorted with bruises. Cuts scarred one of his upper arms and lines of scarlet stains fell across his chest. Large circular bruises swelled on his abdomen. But even in this condition, his size and power were intimidating.

“Who the hell is that?” the man asked.

“I believe that is our Guardian,” the boss said through a grin. “Hey boys, you’d better get out here,” he called to the men in the house.

One after another, the men came out of the farmhouse and gathered around the boss to watch the arrival. Dixon and Roberts snickered at the sight of their old friend Marin approaching them, but the other men just stood staring in shock. A few of the men were alert enough to keep their weapons trained on him, but the rest just let them droop across their arms in their amazement.

After a few moments, Marin walked into the front yard and stopped before the group of men. He looked around at each of them in turn, unsure who was in charge, and waited. When no one spoke, he breathed deeply and forced himself to speak with strength in his voice.

"I am the Guardian."

A soft, slow laugh erupted from one of the men in the group. Marin looked at him and cocked his head to one side.

"And you, I presume, are the one who has taken my kin?"

The boss stepped forward and looked Marin up and down. He was already impressed by the Guardian, but he couldn't let him know that. "I am."

Marin glanced past the men to the trees in the yard where the he-bears were bound. His kin were alert and attentive, their eyes wide with fear. "Let them go," he demanded.

The boss snorted out a laugh and shook his head at Marin's boldness. "You think I've gone to all this trouble to arrange our little meeting so you can march in here and tell me what to do? I don't think so."

Marin looked at the man again and glared. "What do you want with us?"

"Not so fast," the boss said. "What happened to my men and the other shapeshifter that was with you?"

Marin answered without flinching. "They're dead."

The boss stared back, unsure whether to believe the explanation, but either way it caused him no concern. All that mattered was that the Guardian was here.

"Now tell me," Marin growled again, eyeing the human. The man was tall and handsome with smooth hands and nice clothes that bespoke his life of privilege. "Why have you taken the Bear People?"

Chapter Thirty-Seven

Lindy and Arlin crawled through the tall grass, making their way around the perimeter of the yard. They didn't take their sight off Marin and the group of men gathered around him. They couldn't hear what he was saying, but he had the mens' full attention and that was what they were counting on as their only opportunity to free the he-bears from their ropes. When they had circled around to the rear of the yard, they sneaked up behind the trees. Lindy went to Shara first.

"Shhh," Lindy quickly warned to avoid scaring him. "Don't look behind you or you'll alert them to my presence," she said. Working feverishly, she unknotted the rope and freed his hands. "Keep your hands behind you until we give the signal," she explained. "That way they won't know you're free."

She moved on to free the he-bear at the next tree while Arlin freed the other two. Then she and Arlin slipped back into the field and disappeared into the tall grass. When they were halfway around the house, Lindy motioned for Arlin to stop. "Right here, this is good. We'll be able to see and hear what they're saying to Marin," she whispered. They both crouched low on the ground and listened.

The boss crossed his arms over his chest and glared at Marin. "What's your name?"

He glared back, refusing to show the slightest hint of fear. "I am Marin."

Nodding slowly, his sandy blond hair drifting attractively across his forehead in the wind, the boss moved a step closer.

"Marin. So you're the grandson of Marowin. Or is it *great*-grandson?"

Marin was stunned. Had he heard correctly? Had the human spoken the name of his great-grandsire? He couldn't respond, but stood quietly.

"Ah," the human continued. "I see that I'm correct."

"But how… how did you…know?" Marin fumbled for words, still reeling in shock.

The man tipped his head back and laughed, and when the sound came out it was slow and lush like thick rich syrup. Like Marin's laugh. "I'm surprised. You don't recognize your own kin?"

Every head swiveled simultaneously to look at the boss. Until this moment, no one had known the man's secret and now that they knew, they couldn't believe it.

Marin shook his head as though ridding his ears of water. "You're lying. You're human; I can smell it in you."

A sneer rose on the man's face as he took another step closer. "And I can smell it in *you*."

Marin recoiled, disgusted by the man's words. The human must be mad, his words made no sense. But how did he know great-grandsire's name? "But Marowin?" he said.

The boss's sneer lifted to a smile and his arms uncrossed as he planted his hands on his hips. "Ah, Marowin," he murmured, his words breathy and soft. "My dear great-grandsire."

Marin's eyes narrowed suspiciously. Now he *knew* the human was crazy and he became fearful that he'd react irrationally if provoked. He calmed himself before speaking. "Marowin is *my* ancestor."

The human's face lit with delight and he moved closer until he was mere inches from Marin's face. "And *mine*."

Chapter Thirty-Eight

Lindy gasped without realizing what she had done. Before Arlin could slam his hand over her mouth, the men in the group swung around and aimed their rifles in the direction of the sound. Three of them rushed over to the edge of the yard and fanned out into the tall grass. It was only a moment before one of them called out.

"Hey boss, you'll never guess what I found," he said. He reached down and yanked Lindy to her feet by one arm.

"Two for the price of one," the man next to him laughed, pulling Arlin up to stand beside Lindy. He grabbed their rifles and threw them into the yard. Then training their own weapons on the prisoners, the men led them back to the yard where the others stood guarding Marin.

The boss shook his head at the sight of the chubby he-bear. He looked back at Marin and frowned. "And you told me he was dead. My cousin the liar."

Marin closed his eyes, his heart sinking at their capture. Now what would they do? Whatever hope had been in him vanished. When he opened his eyes again, he glared at the annoying human taunting him. "You are not my kin."

"We can debate genetics later," the man hissed, "but right now let me greet my new guests." He turned around to face the prisoners.

Lindy gasped again and couldn't stop her jaw from falling open. "Dr. Dean?"

The man laughed and swept his gaze up and down her

body. He didn't remember her looking so lovely. "Mrs. Anderson. I presume the medicine I gave you saved your bear's life? Which one is he?" He swept his arm out to the side, indicating the four he-bears tied to the trees. Then he sucked in his lower lip with mock concern. "Oh, I hope it wasn't the old boar that I shot."

Lindy lunged at Dean but he deftly stepped back and let his men pin her arms roughly behind her back. "You bastard," she muttered. "You're an embarrassment to humankind."

"Ooow, I'm smarting from that one," he roared, spurring the men into laughter along with him. Then his expression grew serious again. "But back to business." He turned back to Marin and started speaking as though there had been no interruption. "I know you have so many questions that I won't keep you waiting any longer."

The men forced the three prisoners to sit on the ground in front of Dean, who stood before them like a Shakespearean actor geared up to say his lines. He had clearly prepared for this moment and was relishing every bit of it.

"Despite what you want to believe, Guardian, I know all about Marowin. He was Guardian of the clan, just as your father and his father before him were. That was at a time when immigrants first settled near this lake with the intention of logging the forest. During their explorations of this area, they stumbled across the Bear People and became terrified of them, so one night they planned an attack. They decided to kill the clan. But a woman, her name was Emma, disagreed with their plan."

The wind had picked up with dark clouds drifting into the sky from the north, and he swept his hair from his forehead with a dramatic flair before continuing. "So one night, Emma left the settlement and wandered into the forest in search of the Bear People, wanting to warn them. It was Marowin who found her and heard her warning, and together they saved the clan from destruction at the hands of the immigrants."

"But when Emma returned to her home, she couldn't get

Marowin out of her mind, and over time she went back to him again and again. He began to have feelings for her, too, and eventually they mated. But when the clan discovered that the human was carrying Marowin's child, they couldn't accept it. They attacked the settlement and tried to kill her."

Marin jumped angrily to his feet. "Lies!" he screamed, more furious than anyone had ever seen him. The men pushed him roughly down and drew their fists back with a promise to hit him if he continued his interruption.

Dean merely smiled and continued. "But gallant Marowin came to her rescue. He arrived in time to warn her, so the clan failed to kill her and pregnant Emma survived. Her husband took her away and raised the child, never knowing that it wasn't his own. Of course, Emma never let the child know of its heritage and so it never realized that it had the ability to shift. No one in the family knew, until I found Emma's diary. My *great-grandmother's* diary."

Marin snickered at the man's stupidity. "That hardly makes us kin, human," he growled.

"I'm afraid it does. You see, through her diary, I learned that Emma gave birth to twins that day. She brought one to Marowin to raise as his own, a little parting gift, shall we say? That half-breed child was your grandfather. That makes *you* part human and us cousins."

Lindy's mouth was still wide open when she looked to her left at Marin. From the look on his face, she knew he was equally stunned. He didn't move, but appeared frozen in place. She could see that he was trying to work it out in his mind, trying to put all the pieces together, and he was realizing that everything made sense.

"Okay," she said after a moment. "So even if you and Marin are related, what do you want the Bear People for? Why did you ask for Marin?"

Dean turned to stare down at her with a look that was pure annoyance. "Isn't it obvious? This clan is responsible for denying me my heritage. All these years I've had the power to shapeshift, to become something else entirely, and I never knew.

I *never knew*!" His voice grew loud and angry as he swung around to face Marin again. "It's all because of you and your damn family of Guardians. They forced Emma away and denied me the right to know my own kin. They ruined my life."

Marin licked his parched lips and gazed down at the ground around him before raising his head to Dean again. "I can understand why you want me, why you want revenge for my bloodline, but why the others? They've done nothing to you."

Dean laughed again and stooped down so he could look Marin in the eye. "You're right. I'll have my revenge when I'm looking at your dead body. The others..." he rolled his eyes to cast his glance their way. "They're going to make me famous."

"Famous?" Marin asked, not understanding his meaning.

"Yeah. Just imagine, a small town veterinarian announcing to the world that he's discovered a new creature, an animal that's part human and part bear. It'll be the biggest story this planet has ever seen. Do you have any idea what scientists would pay for such a creature? What implications an animal like that would have on the future of medical research? I'll be rich. The money from the tabloids alone will make me a millionaire. I'll never have to look at another dog's ass again."

"They don't deserve it," Marin said. "You can't hold them responsible for something their ancestors did."

"Watch me," Dean retorted with a laugh. "The way I look at it, theirs is the same blood that ran through their grandparents' veins, and that makes them equally guilty."

"But what about her?" Marin said, indicating Lindy. "What does she have to do with this?" In the back of his mind, the question of her culpability lingered. Was she responsible for leading the hunters to him at the waterfall? He didn't want to believe that she was, but he had to know.

Dean stood up and walked a tight circle around the woman. Then he bent low and traced his index finger slowly beneath her jaw and down her neck, pushing open the top of her shirt with his whole hand. He gazed down inside the fabric and stared at her breasts. "Such a pretty little pain in the ass," he murmured. "Since you've decided to involve yourself, you're guilty, too. That means I can punish you however I see fit." He took her shirt in his hands and ripped the front apart until her bra was fully exposed. His eyes rose back up to her face with delight. "I'll handle you after I take care of the boys. And I do mean *handle* you," he smirked.

Marin couldn't restrain his anger any longer. He lunged for the man with all the strength he had, only to be knocked back to the ground by the butt of Dixon's rifle. He grunted in pain and held his throbbing ribs. "Let her go. I'll do anything you want, but leave her alone," he groaned.

Dean gazed down at Marin and snorted contemptuously. "Let her go so she can run to the Sheriff? It's her own damn fault for sticking her nose where it doesn't belong. If she hadn't taken that cinnamon bear into her house that night, my men would have had him and this would have been over a long time ago. But she interfered, she's part of this mess and she pays. Simple as that."

Marin groaned and looked over at Lindy. The expression on her face was pure terror but she didn't complain or shed a single tear. His heart swelled at her strength and how bravely she faced what was imminent. "I'm sorry," he whispered to her, wanting more than ever before to pull her into his arms. "I'm so sorry."

When she looked at him, she felt her courage soar. If there was one thing she was sure of, it was that she hadn't come this far to watch it all end this way. She took a slow steady breath and smiled. Then she opened her mouth and screamed.

"NOW!"

Chapter Thirty-Nine

As one, Marin, Arlin and Lindy leaped up and grabbed for the guns in the hands of the men nearest them. Marin quickly had a weapon in his hands but Lindy and Arlin were struggling with the humans in a desperate tug of war. Suddenly, from across the front yard, roars echoed as the four he-bears dashed away from the trees and charged toward their kidnappers.

The men stared in shock, momentarily paralyzed when they realized that the shapeshifters were no longer bound to the trees. By the time they had their guns raised, the he-bears were upon them and forcing them to the ground. In the confusion, no one noticed Dean slip away and disappear inside the house.

Marin had the head of one man in his hands and with a quick jerk, snapped his neck. Arlin wasn't so lucky. The human he fought had wiggled out of his grasp and now lunged on top of him, trying to work his rifle into position to get off a shot. Arlin screamed and bucked until the man flew off. The heavy he-bear was surprised by his own agility as he flipped over and threw himself down on the man. He stared down at the panicked human face and quickly put him out of his misery.

Shara growled and jumped on the back of a man about his own age. He had never been in a fight in man skin before and was amazed by the power of his hands as weapons. The human flipped Shara over his back and slammed the young he-bear onto the ground, knocking the wind out of him, but Shara retaliated by knocking the man's feet out from beneath him with one blow of his arm. When the man crashed to the ground, Shara followed Marin's lead and snapped the man's neck.

Marin climbed off the human's corpse and looked around, unable to find Lindy. He knew she had to be right there, but he couldn't see her. Then a muffled scream came from the ground at the edge of the field and he knew it was her. He suddenly realized why he couldn't see her. A human was straddling her body and his hands were tightening on her throat in a strangling hold.

With a roar of anger, Marin grabbed the man by the shoulder and tried to pull him away, but his strength was gone and he knew he couldn't hold on. The man screamed as Marin's fingers dug into his soft flesh, but he wriggled out of his grasp, determined to finish what he'd started. Marin could feel his legs giving way beneath him and he knew that it would only be a moment before he crashed to the ground. He forced himself forward toward the man, reaching for his arms to stop him from strangling Lindy, but he couldn't. Unable to stand one minute more, Marin slumped down with a grunt of exhaustion.

"Lindy," he called weakly. He wanted her to know that he was there, that he was by her side at the end. He hoped that she would forgive his weakness before she died. Then suddenly he saw her attacker fly backward and roll painfully on the ground. When the human stopped moving, Shara took him by the neck and finished him. Marin fell on his back upon the ground and breathed a sigh of relief.

Arlin wandered over to Lindy and helped her to her feet. They simultaneously groaned with pain and looked each other in the eye, laughing out loud at their bedraggled condition. Arlin looked around the yard and yelled with joy at the sight of his bear kin alive and victorious over the humans. Even Shara celebrated by rushing to him and throwing his arms around the chubby he-bear for a victory hug.

Lindy turned away and knelt down on the ground beside Marin. He was soaked in sweat and breathing painfully, every bit of energy drained from his body. "It's going to be okay now," she whispered, running her palms across his burning cheeks.

He wouldn't look at her and didn't reply.

"Marin, are you all right?" she asked again. He had turned his face away and she knew instantly that he was blaming himself for not rescuing her. She bent down lower and huddled on his chest, feeling the steady pound of his anguished heart. "I know what you're thinking and there was nothing else you could have done. You're exhausted, Marin, you need medical care."

He rolled his head angrily across the ground in protest. "It should have been me, Lindy. Not Shara. It should have been me that saved you."

She sat up and tried to pull him upright beside her. "This is not the time to argue. We need to get out of here and get you some help…"

Before she could finish, a gunshot echoed through the air. Lindy swung around to see who had fired the shot. She closed her eyes and swore under her breath.

Gareth stood on the front porch. His hands were tied behind him and his eyes were wide with terror. Without moving, he shifted his gaze to look at the pistol pointed at his neck. Dean fingered the trigger and grabbed Gareth's arm tighter.

"Hey kids," he called down to the clan. "It ain't over till it's over. And this party ain't over."

Chapter Forty

Gareth had no choice but to let Dean drag him down the stairs and force him to a halt on the ground at the bottom of the porch. The gun barrel sank deeply into his neck and there was no doubt in his mind that if he struggled, he'd be dead. He tried to speak but blood had crusted over the wounds on his face and they cracked open painfully when he moved his lips. All he could do was stand silently in terror.

Dean looked at the devastation around him through narrowed eyes. It was hard to believe that not one of his men had survived the fight. *Worthless bunch of dipshits*, he told himself. *They weren't worth half the money I paid them.* Then he looked again and his expression wrinkled with confusion. There were only four bodies. He quickly scanned the faces of the corpses and then it hit him who was missing.

"You looking for me?"

Dean started to turn and look behind him when he felt the gun barrel poke into his back. "Johnny," he said.

The young Indian pushed the gun harder into Dean's back. "Put your gun down and let the shapeshifter go."

A soft chuckle slid from Dean's throat as he whirled himself around to face Johnny, taking Gareth with him as he turned. The gun never moved from Gareth's neck. "You put your gun down, Johnny," Dean answered.

The two men stood facing each other only feet apart. Sweat broke out on Gareth's forehead; he knew that no matter who fired, he was dead. He tried to control his trembling but he couldn't.

The clan stood stone faced and helpless, not daring to move or even speak for fear that one of the humans would pull the trigger. All they could do was wait and watch and hope for a miracle.

"Now Johnny, don't tell me I didn't pay you enough," Dean smirked as he struggled to hold the he-bear closer to him. Gareth's legs had begun to tremble and he wasn't about to let him slip out of his grasp. He only needed one live specimen to show the world as proof of his discovery and he was determined that it would be the cinnamon bear in his grasp.

Johnny just shook his head and glared at the man. "It's not about the money."

"Then what do you want? Fame? Women? You want to be a celebrity?"

"You don't get it, do you?" Johnny sighed. He glanced over at the clan and nodded their way. "You think you can just come in here and take what you want, but you can't. These people have a right to live their lives in peace."

Dean snorted and tossed his head back, pissed off by what he was hearing. "People? You call these things *people*? They're not human. They're animals and I intend to use them to my advantage. So back off. All I want is to take this one with me. You and the others can go home."

Johnny shifted his weight and waved his gun toward Dean's head. "You know something? They're more human than you'll ever be."

The smirk returned to Dean's face and he tensed his finger on the trigger of the gun. Gareth squirmed against him, fighting the rope around his wrists, but it didn't budge. He cast his glance toward the clan, needing to see them one more time. They looked as scared as he was. He looked at Lindy and saw her kneeling beside Marin with her hand on his shoulder. There was so much he wanted to tell her and he knew he'd never get the chance.

Lindy stared back at Gareth and smiled, willing him not to give up. Like Dean said, it wasn't over till it was over. Then suddenly she pursed her lips and let out a loud, shrill whistle.

Everyone turned and looked at her as though she'd lost her mind. They just continued to stare while she whistled with every ounce of breath she had.

"Stop that annoying sound!" Dean demanded at last. He swung the gun away from Gareth's neck and waved it in Lindy's direction. "Shut up before I shut you up."

Lindy did as he ordered, but another sound had suddenly appeared. Something was crashing through the tall weeds of the old field and it was heading in their direction.

"What the hell is that?" Dean said.

The noise grew closer and louder, rustling the winter-dried stems as it passed. Every head turned to stare at the field, at whatever was coming closer to them.

Gunther burst out of the weeds and bounded into the yard, his large ears perked up at alert and his eyes wide as he searched for his mistress. He found her and his gaze followed her outstretched arm as she pointed to the man by the porch.

"Attack!" she ordered.

The German Shepherd's long legs flew across the ground, covering the distance to the house in a matter of seconds. With a growl of determination, he jumped and lunged the last few yards toward Dean and Gareth.

Johnny grabbed Gareth and yanked him away just as Dean swung his gun down at the dog. He managed to squeeze off one shot before the animal was on him but the dog was too quick and knocked him to the ground. Dean screamed at the agony of Gunther's sharp canines sinking into his arms as he flailed them helplessly to shield his face. The Shepherd snapped at the man's face again and again, sending bloody flecks flying into the air around them.

Shara rushed over and grabbed the gun from the ground where Dean had dropped it. He watched fascinated as the dog continued its relentless attack.

"Make him stop!" Dean cried, his face a bloody mess from the bites that had shredded his flesh.

"Off Gunther!" Lindy ordered. "Off!" Immediately the

dog ceased his attack and trotted back to sit beside his mistress. The brown fur of his muzzle was soaked crimson with blood.

"What are you going to do with him?" Johnny asked, pointing his weapon at the sobbing man.

Shara thrust his head up proudly. "Let me take care of him." Then he quickly arched over and shifted into bear skin with only one thing in mind. He opened his mouth, showing the huge curved teeth that filled his muzzle. The others turned away to let him finish it.

Lindy ran to Gareth and pulled him into her arms. "Oh my God, I thought I'd never see you again," she sobbed. "Are you okay? What did they do to you?"

He forced himself to control his trembling and waited impatiently while Arlin untied the rope that bound him. As soon as he was free, he threw his arms around her and buried his face in her neck. There were no words to speak. The only thing that mattered now was holding her.

"Uh, I hate to interrupt the reunion," Johnny said softly, "but we need to do something about this mess. And soon." He nodded his head toward the corpses littering the ground around them.

Everyone turned to look at Marin for his advice. Of them all, he was the one with the most experience in these matters. Marin leaned weakly against Arlin and looked over at the farmhouse, trying to decide what would be best. "If we get the bodies inside, can you burn the house down?" he asked Johnny.

The man nodded his head without speaking. Motioning for the he-bears to help him, they lifted the first body off the ground and carried it into the building.

Lindy pushed herself away from Gareth and stood by Marin again. "I have matches in my backpack. I'll get them." She took off at a run and disappeared into the forest, returning a minute later with the matches. She handed them to Johnny and gave him a hug. "I don't know who you are," she panted. "But thanks for your help."

Johnny took the matches from her hand and smiled back,

feeling a bit sheepish. "Lady, I appreciate your gratitude but you did just fine without me." Then he turned and walked into the house. A few minutes later, he came back out and smoke began to billow from the front door. It wasn't long until yellow flames licked up the outside of the building, consuming the dry weathered clapboards in a crackling frenzy.

When the flames shot skyward through the battered roof, Lindy looked at the he-bears around her and sighed. The tears wanted to come but she forced them back, needing to feel the safety of her own home around her when her emotions collapsed. She bent down and helped Marin struggle to his feet.

"Let's go home, guys," she said, her exhaustion finally taking its toll. "I just want to go home."

Chapter Forty-One

Lilea paced nervously at the edge of the clearing, too worked up to even think about eating or sleeping. It seemed like forever since the he-bears had left to find Marin and all she could think about was whether the Guardian was alive or dead. She didn't know what the clan would do without him, what she would do without him, if they'd lost him.

She brushed a fly from her nose and sat down for a moment to calm her thoughts. She was still upset that the clan had voted to ask the human woman for help. Even though she knew Lindy was their best chance to retrieve Marin successfully, she couldn't help but be jealous by the woman's involvement in his rescue. The thought of her out there alone with all the he-bears, of her playing a role that Lilea herself had not been asked to play… it made her so angry she wanted to roar.

But after a moment, she realized that there was another reason for her anger. She hadn't been oblivious to the he-bears' conversations when they'd discussed Lindy's exotic sensual appeal. She knew how much Gareth desired the human and wanted to have a relationship with her, and deep down, she suspected that Marin did, too. More than once, she'd seen the glow in both Marin and Lindy's eyes when they gazed at each other and it was this that broke her heart.

Not that she had a chance with the Guardian, anyway. So many springs, she'd strutted past him, flaunting her scent to entice him into mating with her, and each time, Marin had only closed his eyes and walked away. She knew that something in his soul had died the day Terra was killed and he'd never been able to bring that part of him back to life. Deep sadness filled her at the knowledge that she had been unable to help him recover it, either.

In fact, she admitted, none of the she-bears had been able to heal Marin's wounds. It wasn't for lack of trying. Everyone wanted him, whether for his superior intelligence, his handsome physique, or his astonishing strength and power. But he had accepted no one, preferring to spend his last seven years sexually isolated.

Lilea growled a sigh and lay down with her head on the soft grass, wondering if Marin had suffered at the hands of the humans again. He didn't deserve any more pain. He'd given so much, sacrificed so much for the sake of the clan, for her sake, that she knew she'd do anything to help him if he came back alive. She promised herself that she would do whatever it took to heal him and make him whole again, even if it meant denying her own desire for him and giving him to the woman whose life she had reluctantly saved.

Chapter Forty-Two

"Here they come!" Notch cried. "Here they come!

The she-bears whirled away from the berries they were eating and loped across the meadow in the direction that the cub had indicated. After a moment, they saw the bears approaching out of the darkness of the forest.

Lilea gazed desperately into the shadows, straining to see who was present, and moaned with relief when she saw the faces of the bears lumbering into the clearing. Then she shook her head and growled slowly as they approached. "Thoren?"

Arlin shook his furry head and pressed his side comfortingly against her own, sharing her sadness at the loss of their old friend. Then he nudged her to turn and walked with her back to the boulder in the center of forest home.

Lilea swung her head back to look behind her while she walked. She could see Marin riding on Shara's back. He was in man skin and seemed so weak that he could barely hold on to Shara's fur. The woman walked alongside Marin, her arm wrapped around his shoulder to keep him from falling. As Lilea swept her gaze over him, she shuddered at the sight of the hideous purple bruises swelling all over his body.

When they reached the rock, the entire clan gathered together and the she-bears clamored to hear the story of what had happened. Arlin surprised himself by assuming the authority to tell the tale. He praised the he-bears for their courage and determination, especially Shara for his outstanding act of bravery in rescuing Lindy. His growls and roars grew more animated as he told how the humans had held Marin and Gareth captive and how he and the others had rescued them and killed the kidnappers. For the first time in his life, Arlin gloated with pride while the she-bears oohed and aahed at his story and his own acts of courage.

Gareth turned to Lindy and motioned with his head for her to come and stand beside him. She let her arm slip off Marin's shoulder and made her way around the gathered bears until she stood next to Gareth. He shifted into man skin so she could hear what he was about to say to the clan. Placing his arm around her waist, he turned to face his kin. "None of us would be here if not for this human. I told you that she had a good heart and she proved it more than once during this rescue." He pulled her closer and cast a grateful smile her way. "If any of you had doubts about the depth of our friendship, you'll have to reconsider. Lindy isn't just my friend; she's the *clan's* friend."

Lena snorted softly after considering Gareth's words. Nudging her cub ahead of her, she waddled up to Lindy and opened her mouth. Lindy stepped back, fearing that the bear was about to bite her, but Lena only extended her long pink tongue and licked the back of Lindy's hand. Then Notch scrambled out from between his mother's paws and stretched up as tall as he could make himself to lick her hand as his mother had done. When he backed away, every clan member came forward one by one to pay their respects to the human.

Shara watched from the outside of the circle until he could wait no longer. He growled loudly, interrupting the proceedings to get Gareth's attention. Gareth looked over and cried out, distressed by what he saw. Marin was unconscious and had fallen forward on Shara's back, ready to fall off the bear completely.

Lindy ran back to him just as Marin started slipping off Shara. She caught him in her arms and tried to push him back onto Shara's broad back, barely able to manage his weight by herself. Gareth ran to help her and together they returned Marin to his perch. "We need to get him help," she cried to

Gareth, unable to control the urgency in her voice.

Gareth put his head down and debated silently. He knew in his heart what had to be done, but it was the one thing he would give anything not to do. When he raised his head again, he looked at Marin and forced himself to admit that the only one who could help their Guardian now was the woman they both wanted.

"Take Marin home," Gareth said to her after a long moment of silence. "Take him to your home and make him well." Then he pulled his lower lip inside his mouth and bit down to keep from changing his mind.

Chapter Forty-Three

Marin opened his eyes and looked around. He had no idea where he was. There was nothing near him that looked familiar or even vaguely identifiable. All he knew was that he was inside a building of some kind and it appeared that he was alone.

He sat up slowly, raising his hand to his aching head, and looked down around him. He was laying on a soft platform with a sheet of fabric and a blanket drawn up over him. Although he'd never seen one, he assumed he was in a bed and he hoped that he knew whose bed it was. "Lindy?" he called tentatively.

After a moment, her head appeared in the doorway as she peeked into the room. "You're awake!" she said. "I thought I heard you call me." She walked across the carpeted floor and sat down beside him, her eyes making a quick sweep over the parts of him that weren't covered by the blanket. "How do you feel?"

Marin rubbed his forehead, trying to ease the pounding that was sweeping through his head. He pushed himself backward on the mattress until his back rested against the wooden headboard and was surprised by how smooth and cool the wood felt against his skin. "Not bad," he lied, trying to ignore the aches that throbbed all over his body.

The corner of her mouth rose slightly in a skeptical smile. "Right. So you're ready to go out and run a marathon, huh?"

He looked at her blankly. "What?"

"Sorry," she said. "Bad joke. Did you know you've been asleep for almost two days?"

The expression on his face was disbelief when he cocked his head to look at her. "Two days?"

She nodded with a smile. "You were exhausted. Sometimes sleep is the best medicine." She reached over and smoothed the part of the blanket that lay over his legs. "You look like you could use some water."

He nodded and licked his parched lips. When she handed him the filled glass from the bedside table, he drained it in a long gulp and handed it back to her, pretending not to notice how her fingertips trembled when they brushed across his. He swung his head away and looked around him, amazed by how confining human habitations felt. "How did I get here?"

She set the glass back down on the table and let her hands rest in her lap. Marin's jet hair stuck out wildly around his head and she struggled to keep herself from reaching out and running her fingers through it. But she sensed that he was uncomfortable enough being in a strange place without her making it worse by forcing her touch on him. "Shara brought you here on his back."

"I don't remember it," he grunted, sounding disgusted with himself.

She shook her head. He was always too hard on people, including himself. "You were unconscious at the time. You wouldn't remember."

"Is the clan safe?"

"Yes. They're all back at forest home enjoying Gareth's storytelling."

He exhaled softly and played with the silk that edged the top of the blanket. "Does Gareth know I'm here?"

She laughed and raised her eyebrows at him. He really didn't remember. "Gareth is the one who sent you here."

Marin's face screwed up with surprise. "He did?"

"Yeah, he asked me to take care of you."

"I can't believe it. He's so possessive about..." He let the thought die away unspoken, sure that she already knew what he'd intended to say anyway.

She exhaled slowly, wondering how to respond to his comment without making her feelings embarrassingly obvious. "I know he can be a little overbearing when it comes to me. He just cares about me, that's all. But he also cares about you, Marin. I saw it in his face and in his actions when he went to rescue you. You mean a great deal to him. And he knows that I can take better care of you than they can; he knows that you need to be here."

Marin settled his dark eyes on hers. They were barely visible beneath the swelling and bruises, but they still demanded her attention. "He shouldn't have imposed on you like this. I'll be well in a day or two and the clan can take care of me until then."

She bit her cheek for a moment, trying not to show her disappointment. "Is that what you want, Marin, for the clan to take care of you instead of me?"

His gaze dropped away from her eyes and rested on her hands. One thing he clearly remembered was the way her fingers swept tenderly across his face at the campsite, how they felt brushing his hair away from his eyes. "It's just that you've done so much for me already…"

"Marin," she said again. "Is that what you want?"

When he looked up, he was sure she could see the truth in his eyes. She had to; he felt that strongly about it. "No." He shook his head gently back and forth. "No, it's not what I want."

The smile returned to her face. "I'm glad to hear that because I really want you to be here. I want to take care of you."

He could scarcely believe her words. *She wants to take care of me.* It had been so long since someone had said that to him that he almost didn't want to believe it. He looked away without answering.

She cleared her throat softly and tried to catch his eyes with her own. "Is something wrong?" she asked.

Still, he couldn't force the doubt from his mind. "I haven't treated you very well," he said quietly. "I don't know how you can even be civil to me."

She scooted closer to him and laid her hand on top of his, feeling the strength of his fingers as they clenched the silk. She thought he might pull his hand away, but he didn't. He merely gazed back at her, waiting. "I know you were just doing your job. But I won't lie to you. You scared the hell out of me so many times I wondered if I'd ever really have a chance to get to know the clan. Then that night when you told me about Terra, I began to understand why you feel the way you do and why my presence among your kin is so irritating to you. I don't blame you a bit, Marin. Really I don't."

"I'm glad you understand," he said, still not moving. "I'll try not to be too much trouble for you anymore."

Lindy shook her head and smiled. "You're no trouble. Now why don't you lie down and let me clean you up like I had intended to."

He slid carefully back down on the mattress and watched while she left the room and returned a minute later with the supplies she needed. She set a bowl of warm water and some small towels on the bedside table and laid a first aid kit on the mattress behind her. When she was ready, she pulled the blanket and sheet down to his waist and let her gaze linger on his blood-stained chest.

She cleared her throat again, trying to control the desire tightening inside her body. "I'll try not to hurt you, but if I do just tell me and I'll stop."

He felt his heart begin to race and he nodded, knowing that he wouldn't care if there was pain or not, as long as she was touching him.

She dipped a towel in the water, raised it to his head and abruptly stopped. There were so many bruises and cuts she didn't know where to start first. It pained her just to look at his poor face and she couldn't imagine how badly it must have hurt when the bastards hit him. She decided to start on the worst side, the one closest to her, and laid the towel carefully against his right temple.

Marin held his breath as the cloth swept gently across his

temple and down his cheek. Her fingers were so close to his skin that he could feel their heat. When he realized that he was holding his breath, he forced himself to exhale slowly so she didn't know how nervous he was. He felt the cloth go lower, dabbing the blood off his chin, and then rise up to his mouth.

The blood had crusted around his lips and it wasn't coming off easily. Lindy knew she'd need to use firmer pressure and she leaned forward to get more leverage. Her chest hovered so close to his that she could see tiny beads of sweat glisten on his skin. "Am I hurting you?" she asked.

His heart beat harder with every inch closer she came to him. He'd never felt anything like this before, had never been unable to control the heat rising inside of him. He swallowed hard and shook his head slightly. "I'm fine."

Lindy moved closer again until her head was inches from his. She could see the dried blood clearly, the way it crinkled at the corner of his mouth and dug uncomfortably into his skin every time he talked. She pressed the edge of the warm towel firmly into the blood and slowly wiped it away. His lips parted slightly with the pressure and her breath caught in her throat. Suddenly all she could think of was what his lips would feel like against her own, how his mouth would feel pressing firmly over hers, and she uttered a soft whimper.

His eyes widened with panic and she yanked herself back, realizing that he had been thinking the same thing she had. But instead of feeling the desire that she felt, she was certain that he was only feeling fear. He had never wanted a human, never even liked humans, and now she had put him in a situation that he was totally unprepared for.

They both took a deep breath and looked away from each other. Lindy mechanically dipped the bloody cloth back in the bowl and rinsed it clean, then began wiping him again, being careful to keep her distance. After a moment, he seemed more relaxed and began to watch while she wiped the blood from the other side of his face.

"Doesn't it bother you to clean my blood?" he asked, wanting more to break their awkward silence than to know her answer.

She ran the towel down his neck and across his broad shoulders until the thick scarlet stains were gone and clean olive skin appeared. "No, not really." She was still reeling with embarrassment and didn't know what else to say, so she worked without speaking. The cut on his bicep had begun to heal and was protected by a large protruding scab. She skirted the area, dragging the towel down his muscular arms to his wrists. Blue linear bruises encircled both wrists where he'd strained against the chain and her heart throbbed at the memory of his body sagging so heavily against it.

"What are you thinking?"

His voice pulled her back to the moment and she gazed down into his eyes, feeling the moisture beginning to appear in her own eyes. She ran her fingers gently over his wrist, tracing the blue marks with her fingertips. "I was just thinking about how you suffered. And about how brave you are."

For a moment he lay quietly and thought about his response. No one had ever called him brave before. He just was what he was. But it flattered him that she thought so much of him. At last he gazed up at her and flashed a small smile. "I guess I wouldn't be much of a Guardian if I was afraid of everything."

Her eyes met his in a smoldering stare. "Is there anything you're afraid of, Marin?" she asked. "Everyone is afraid of something."

His eyes locked on hers. *I'm afraid of spending my life alone*, he wanted to cry out to her, but he couldn't. This intimacy with a human was all too new, too strange for him to open himself up any more than he already had. He'd never meant to tell her about Terra, but he hadn't been able to stop himself. And he'd certainly never wanted to feel himself becoming attracted to Lindy, but he hadn't been able to stop that, either. But this was just too much too fast and he couldn't bring himself to utter the words. All he could do was turn his head away and stare at the wall without answering.

She was unsure what to make of his silence but she knew

better than to press him. It was better just to let the subject drop. She knew that if and when he wanted to tell her, he would, just as he had revealed to her why his hatred of humans ran so deep.

She rinsed the cloth again and laid it across his chest, watching how the damp fabric clung to the curve of his pectoral muscle and draped down across his side. She rubbed it lightly and finally removed the last stains of blood from his skin. She moved to pull the cloth away when his hand came down on top of hers and held it firmly in place against him.

"Do you like touching me?" he asked. His tone was so naively boyish that he sounded like a young man experiencing love for the first time.

A lump had formed in her throat and she realized that she wasn't breathing. Taking in a sharp breath, she stared at his hand on hers, almost unable to believe that he had done it. He had touched her. His skin burned against hers and she felt the power in his fingers as they closed tightly over hers. When she looked at him, his eyes were boring into hers, patiently waiting.

She licked her lips and knew she had to answer.

"Yes, Marin," she said so softly her words were barely audible. "Yes I do."

He nodded without releasing her hand and became quiet for a moment. Then his eyes flicked away and gazed out the window before settling on her face again. "But you enjoy touching Gareth too."

The look on his face was a mixture of confusion and pain. Wrinkles gathered at the corners of his eyes and his battered lips drew tightly together. The brown-black irises of his eyes seemed clouded as though they wanted to find the truth but couldn't. All he could do was ask her and hope that she would give him the truth.

Lindy struggled to hold back the tears that were burning in her eyes. It hurt so badly to think how his confusion was tearing him apart. He'd seen her with Gareth so many times, seen the way they acted when they were together. She had never acted romantically toward him or allowed him to act that way with her, but everyone believed that they were attracted to each other. Everyone in the clan knew that Gareth loved her and they assumed that she was in love with him. There was nothing else Marin *could* think but that she loved Gareth. But she knew better.

"Can I tell you something?" she asked. "When I found Gareth outside and brought him in to take care of him, I found out that he was something special. He was warm, and kind, and very open with me about who and *what* he was. I had every reason to fear him but I never did because of the way he treated me. So sweet and gentle. Over time, we've developed a very special bond unlike anything I've ever experienced before."

Marin rolled his head to the side and closed his eyes, unwilling to look at her face while she broke his heart. It felt like a weight was crushing his chest, making it hard to breathe. He started to pull his hand off hers but she grabbed it with her other hand and held it firmly between her palms.

"But there's a difference between caring for someone and being in love with someone. I care for Gareth, I enjoy his friendship, but I'm not in love with him. Do you understand, Marin? I don't love him."

Very slowly, Marin opened his eyes and turned back toward her. She was looking down at him, her soft blue eyes searching his own. *She doesn't love him.* He repeated the words over and over in his mind. *She doesn't love Gareth.* He felt her hands squeeze tightly around his hand and he tilted his head back into the pillow and sighed. The boulder rolled from his chest and he could breathe again.

She squeezed his hand once more and smiled. The expression on his face had changed dramatically and she knew that he understood what she was trying to tell him. Unsure what to say, she raised his hand to her mouth and kissed it softly. Then she laid it back by his side and took the first aid kit from behind her. When it was in her lap, she took the antibiotic ointment and spread it on his cuts, praying a silent prayer that he wouldn't get an infection the way Gareth had. She never wanted to see another veterinarian in her life. When she finished, she pulled the sheet and blanket back over him and tucked it carefully around his shoulders. "Are you warm enough?" she asked.

It took him several moments to answer. Finally he tilted his head sideways and looked up at her. "What if I said no?"

His response stumped her. From the way he'd taken his time to answer, he was obviously considering something and she wasn't quite sure how he wanted her to reply. "I could get you another blanket," she said. Then lowering her head a bit, she saw the gleam in his eyes and knew exactly what he wanted. "Or, I could use something else to keep you warm."

Marin stared at her without replying. Then his hand swept out from beneath the covers and he pulled them over to his left side. He scooted himself over in the bed, making room.

Lindy knew she had a dumbfounded look on her face, but she didn't care. All that mattered was being next to him again. She lowered herself onto the mattress and pressed herself gently up next to him. When she was settled, he pulled the covers back over both of them and took her left hand gently in his right. "Now I'm warm," he said contentedly. Within moments he was deeply asleep.

Lindy turned on her side and laid her arm carefully across his chest. She could feel the pulse of his heart and the rhythmic rise and fall of his chest against her. She closed her eyes, feeling happier than she had in years. "And I'll have good dreams," she murmured, and joined him in sleep.

Chapter Forty-Four

Johnny sat down across from his uncle and withdrew the medallion from inside his shirt. He let it dangle before his face and swing in endless circles like the earth rotating on its axis. The wood was polished from the touch of many generations of hands and it glowed softly in the single beam of sunlight drifting through the dusty window.

"Is it done?" the old man asked, keeping his lone eye on the spinning orb.

He nodded slowly and leaned back in the chair, relieved to finally have it over. He let out a low whistle. "I wish you could have been there, Uncle. I can't even begin to explain what they're like. They look so human, you would never know they weren't."

"Did you see them change?"

Johnny nodded, picturing how the bear men shifted between bodies so easily. "Like night to day, only faster. They made it look so effortless, yet it seemed so impossible when I watched them. And you were exactly right, as men, they can't change unless they reach for the ground."

There was a gleam in Jack's eye when he smiled, and he was pleased that he had correctly remembered his father's instruction about the Bear People after all these years. "Did you identify yourself?"

"There wasn't time," Johnny said, flipping his long hair away from his neck. It was warm in the trading post, but he knew the warmth flooding through him was from the excitement of what had happened that day, not the still air.

Jack nodded thoughtfully, his few remaining white hairs sifting softly down across his eyebrows. “They need to know that they have a Protector again. You should have told them.”

“Like I said, there wasn’t time. And anyway, I’m not sure I want to be the one.”

Jack forced his thin lips together and stared at his nephew forcefully. He had to make him understand his obligation. “But you *are* the one, Johnny. You must be. You’re the only one that can be.”

The young man shook his head as a thought ran through his mind. Maybe there was another possibility, but it would take some effort to convince his uncle. He decided to try another tactic. “Would you like to meet them?”

Jack’s eye opened wide in surprise. “Can it be done?”

“There was a human woman who helped them during the rescue. I know where she lives, over on Otter Lake just outside the national forest. The Wilke’s old log cabin. She took their Guardian to her home to heal him because he was so injured. If I take you there, maybe she’ll let you meet him.”

Jack smiled so broadly his face seemed to shatter like an old mirror. “I’ve dreamed of it all my life. I’d gladly meet any of the Bearwalkers, you know, but the *Guardian*! Yes, I want to meet him.”

And I want you to meet her, Johnny thought. He smiled and put the medallion back inside his shirt. “Let me see what I can do.”

Chapter Forty-Five

She was soaked in sweat. Unbearable heat radiated around her and even half asleep she knew something wasn't right. She slowly opened her eyes, and then jerked herself back so hard she almost fell off the side of the bed. Untangling the sheet from around her, she slipped off the mattress and stood on the floor, just staring down at the bed.

Her abrupt movement woke Marin from his dreams. He opened his eyes and uttered a sound that was half groan and half growl. He could see Lindy hovering above him beside the bed and couldn't for the life of him figure out why she had that shocked look on her face. Then suddenly he knew why and he felt like an idiot. He had shifted during his sleep and she had awoken to find herself sleeping with a bear.

Rolling his eyes in embarrassment, he slipped to the floor on the other side of the bed and arched his back, forcing himself to shift. He stood up, prepared to apologize for what had happened, but he saw that he didn't need to. Her face was wrinkled with merriment and she was giggling. Her reaction was such a surprise that he just cocked his head to look at her.

"Oh my God, I just slept with a bear!" she laughed, her head shaking so hard that her blonde hair bounced around her face.

Marin's eyes were wide at the sight of her laughter. "I…I didn't mean to do it," he said, unsure whether to feel defensive or relieved.

She walked around the bed and placed her hands on his upper arms, pulling him close enough to lay her head down on his chest. "Oh, Marin, sometimes I forget who you really are. I never know what to expect from you."

"I'm sorry," he said, somewhat bewildered.

"Don't be sorry," she laughed. "Life would be awfully boring without a few surprises from time to time." She felt his body relax against her and she held him tightly for a moment. Then she pushed him back and swept her gaze up and down over his body. He seemed stronger already and some of the bruises were beginning to fade. "Do you think you can eat something? I'll make us breakfast."

Feeling rested and more at ease now, he nodded yes and followed her into the kitchen. When she offered him a chair, he sat down tentatively, unsure if the fragile looking thing would hold his weight. He looked around, mystified by all the strange things around him, the very things that Gareth had told the clan about. He was most curious about the water source and he watched in fascination while she filled glasses of water for them from the faucet.

She stood beside his chair and looked down at him. The morning sun gleamed on his golden shoulders, making her want to run her hands across his smooth skin. She shoved them into her pockets instead. "What would you like? Bacon and eggs? Pancakes and sausage?" From the look on his face, she knew he had no idea what she was talking about. It was easy to forget that these human things needed clarification. "I mean, what kind of meat do you want? You know, pork? Pig?"

He shook his head, looking vaguely squeamish. "We're mainly vegetarian, you know. Fruit, berries. Maybe some ants or fish. I've never eaten pig and honestly, Lindy, it doesn't sound very appetizing."

She sat down in the chair adjacent to his and folded her arms before her with her elbows on the table. "I wasn't thinking," she admitted. "Jeez, I've lived here all my life, I know what bears eat. But you see what I mean? I look at you and think you're just a normal guy."

He forced a smile, but deep down he knew that she had just put her finger on their problem without even realizing it. He wasn't a normal human man. He was one of the Bear People. He would never be fully human, no matter how much she might want him to be.

"Well, how about some blueberries and cereal? I have bread and honey, too."

That brought a real smile to his face. It had been two days since he'd eaten the sandwich at the humans' camp and he was ravenous. "That would be good."

They sat quietly and ate, merely enjoying each other's company. Gunther trotted in from the family room and plopped down on the floor beside Marin's chair. He stared up at the bear man with a strange look in his eyes but didn't growl or bare his fangs. His ears flicked now and then as though he was expecting to hear something from the man.

"I think Gunth likes you," Lindy said.

Marin eyed the dog warily, not too sure if he could return the feeling. "Tell me something," he said, returning his attention to the woman. "When we were at the farmhouse, he came when you whistled. How did you manage that?"

She smiled at his naivete, it was so charming. "Humans often train dogs to perform certain jobs. Some canines help people who are blind or deaf, some sniff out drugs, some search for lost people. Gunther was trained for protection. Believe me, where I lived before, I needed it. Dogs are really smart, amazing animals and good companions. You should give them a chance."

He grunted and shook his head, still mystified why humans would take wolves into their homes. It was a bizarre practice that he figured he'd never understand. Then it occurred to him that he'd never seen a human take a bear into his home as a companion and a chuckle slid from his throat at the thought of it.

"What?" she asked.

"I was just wondering why humans don't take bears for companions like they do dogs."

Her eyebrows raised and she winked at him with a devilish smile on her face. "There's always a first time."

He wasn't sure if she was making him an offer or just making a frivolous statement, so he sat silent and watched while she cleared the dishes and excused herself to take a shower. When she was gone, he got up and wandered cautiously through the house, hoping to explore and identify each room from the way Gareth had described it. Just beyond the kitchen was the room where she could build a fire. He saw the hole in the wall, smelled the burned ashes settled on the floor inside it and knew that it must be the fireplace that Gareth had spoken about. Marin looked down at his feet, feeling soft fabric beneath them, and shuddered at the thought that this was where she'd laid Gareth the night he was shot. He couldn't see any blood on it; but he could smell it. She would have had her arm around him as she led him here and eased him down to rest and warm up.

He turned away and looked around the room. Gareth was right about her love of bears. They were everywhere. He laughed at the silly way they were represented in the decorations; most of them didn't seem very lifelike at all. He saw a narrow hallway leading to another room and followed it, tracing his hand against the rough curves of the log walls. Why humans chose to build homes out of trees he couldn't fathom, when a warm earthen den served equally well and was much less work. At the end of the hall, he opened the door and wandered into the room. There was another bed inside of it. Beside the bed was a table with a picture of Lindy and her sisters, just as Gareth had said, and he realized that he was in her bedroom.

The thought suddenly occurred to him that when they'd brought him into the house, he'd been put into the other bedroom. Was it because she didn't want him in her own bed? Where had Gareth been during his healing time—in which bed? He sat down on the mattress and sniffed her pillow, immediately recognizing her feminine scent. It was hers alone with no trace of bear scent. The thought began to nag him.

Why didn't she want him in her bed?

The bathroom door opened and Lindy stepped out. A damp blue towel was wrapped around her body and her hair was wet but neatly combed into long, straight strands. She froze when she saw Marin sitting on her bed.

He turned around and stared at her. Her shoulders were bare and glistening with dampness, and below the bottom edge of the towel, a few droplets of water trickled down her thighs. He watched the drops fall toward the back of her knee and disappear behind her shapely calf. His eyes grew round and he opened his mouth but couldn't make a sound.

They both remained where they were, momentarily frozen. Then she grabbed the top edge of the towel and pulled it up higher over her breasts. She saw his eyes follow every move she made, and for a moment she felt a pang of fear.

"Why are you in here?" she asked.

He blinked a couple times and forced his eyes away. For the first time since he'd met her, he was embarrassed for staring at *her* body. "I...I was just looking around. I didn't realize where the *shower* was. I'm sorry. I'll go." He stood up and took a step toward the door.

"Wait."

He stopped without turning around. "What?"

"Do you want to see me?"

Marin felt sudden heat rising up through him, a raging warmth he hadn't felt in so very long. *Of course I want to see you. I've dreamed of seeing your body*, he wanted to confess. He wanted to turn around and watch her slip that towel off her body. But he knew if he did, he would lose control and do something he'd regret. He was a bear. And bears and humans didn't mix.

"Marin? Did you hear me?"

He turned around and hung his head low to his chest to avoid staring at the tops of her breasts above the towel. "I can't, Lindy," he said softly. "I want to, but I can't. I'm concerned about how I might react. About what might happen."

The momentary fear she had felt was gone, replaced by

desire. She took a step toward him and reached out her hand. "It's all right, you know. It's okay if you see me. I'm not worried about what could happen."

He shook his head, feeling the desire growing inside him like wind before a storm. "You don't understand. It's not right for us to want each other. You need your kind and I need mine. That's the way it was meant to be."

"It hasn't always been that way," she protested. "Look at Marowin and Emma."

"And look what happened to them," he replied curtly, holding his head higher so she could see how seriously he felt about it. "It's not right, Lindy. It's not normal."

She gazed at the carpet beneath her feet and swallowed down the lump in her throat. "Are you saying that we can't have a relationship of *any* kind?

"No, that's not what I'm saying at all. But just as I warned you about becoming too friendly with Gareth, you and I need to keep our distance, too. We all need to stick with our own species."

"Is that why you've gone without sex for seven years, Marin? Is it because you can't find someone suitable of your own species?"

Anger raged through him at the nerve of her comment. How dare she criticize his life when she had so little knowledge of him? "What does it matter to you, anyway?" he roared. "If you want me so much, why didn't you put me in your own bed when you brought me in!"

She held the towel with one hand and threw her other hand angrily on her hip. "I thought you didn't want to be in my bed, Bear Man. I'm not your species, remember? I guess I'm damned no matter what I do."

They both stood there and stared at each other, shocked by the harshness of what they were hearing. Marin let his gaze drop slowly from her face and linger on the floor. Lindy exhaled loudly, unable to contain her frustration, and slowly walked over to him. She put her arms around his neck.

"I'm sorry for what I said, Marin. It was mean and

thoughtless." She leaned back and looked up into his eyes, but he showed no emotion. "What you do in your personal life is none of my business."

He stood motionless, unable to put his arms around her. It wasn't her words that ran through his mind and bothered him so much as his own words. He was the one who'd just pushed her away with his self righteous comments about sticking to their own species and now he was contradicting himself by whining about not being in her bed. He knew he sounded like a love-struck fool.

He pulled away from her and walked out the door to return to his own bedroom, leaving her feeling like a bullet had struck her own chest.

Chapter Forty-Six

Gunther raced through the house to bark at the front door. Someone was knocking loudly.

Lindy put down her magazine and rose from the couch to look out the window. At first she didn't recognize the men who stood together outside the door. Both were Indians, one young and one very old. But the more she looked at the younger man, the more he looked familiar. Suddenly it came to her who he was.

She opened the door and stared at him. "It's you," she said.

"Yes Ma'am," he said. "My name is Johnny Thundermaker. This is my Uncle Jack."

"Please come in," she said, waving her arm toward the sofa. "Have a seat."

They came in side by side, the younger man helping the older one shuffle unsteadily across the floor. When they reached the sofa, Johnny took his uncle's hand and lowered him to the cushion. Then he sat down beside him and watched as Lindy took a seat on the chair nearby.

"Johnny?" she repeated. "I'm Lindy Anderson." She reached over and shook the hands of both men. Despite his age, the old man had a firm grip and a gleam in the one eye remaining to him.

Johnny nodded politely. His long dark hair was pulled back in a ponytail and he played with it for a moment before speaking. "I hope we're not bothering you."

"No, no," she assured them. "Would you like something to drink?"

They both refused before Johnny spoke again. "I've brought my uncle here to see the Bear Man, but I guess that first I need to explain something about what happened that day."

Putting her hand up in the air to stop him, Lindy quickly stood up. "Can you wait just a minute?" When he nodded yes, she left the room and entered Marin's bedroom.

He looked up from the bed and gazed at her. "Who's here?"

"Our friend from the farmhouse. He's here to explain some things and I thought you might want to hear this, too."

"I would."

"Maybe you should put something over you," she suggested.

Marin slipped out of bed and stood still while Lindy pulled the blanket off and wrapped it around him. When they were ready, he followed her into the family room and waited while she pulled another chair up beside hers. He sat down and stared at the men, recognizing the young man instantly.

A grin grew on the old man's face as he scanned his eye across Marin. He peered hard at the man's face, trying to find a single clue that would give away the fact that he was a bear, but he couldn't find one. "He looks so human," he whispered to Johnny at last, as though Marin couldn't hear him.

"Why are you here?" Marin asked brusquely. He was in no mood to be gawked at.

Johnny settled his gaze on Lindy's face and nervously inhaled a big breath of air. The Guardian had frightened him at the farmhouse and he frightened him now, too. All he wanted was to get this over with and let his life get back to normal. "I was hired by Dean to capture a shapeshifter."

"Whaaat?" Lindy asked. She couldn't believe what she'd heard.

"I was…acquaintances with Paul Roberts, one of the hunters that shot the bear man you rescued. We used to have drinks down at the bar on weekends. He was drunk one night and told me about how Dean hired him and some of the other locals to catch a Bearwalker for him. I convinced him to have Dean hire me, too."

Lindy leaned forward in the chair with her forearms crossed over each other. "But I don't understand. Why did you ask him to hire you and then turn against him and help us?"

The old man chuckled and leaned slightly forward, too, trying to get a closer look at Marin's face again. He thought it was a handsome face. "Because I told him to."

Marin snorted. The men were obviously crazy. He was beginning to wonder if it was a common trait among human males.

"Please go on," Lindy urged, shooting a warning look at Marin.

Johnny pulled his uncle back and ran his fingers through his ponytail again. "I had to protect the Bear People. The best way to do that was to be there when they made the capture."

"Protect us?" Marin laughed sarcastically. "You call roping my kin to a tree *protecting them*? You call killing Thoren *protecting him*?"

"I'm sorry about the old bear," Johnny said. "There was nothing I could do about that. But the others were unharmed, weren't they? And we got Dean before he took your young bear man away."

Marin grew silent; he couldn't deny that the man was right about that.

"I'm confused about the protecting part, too," Lindy said. "Why did you think you needed to protect them? How do you even know about the Bear People?"

"I'll let my uncle explain that," Johnny said.

For a long time, Lindy and Marin sat silent while Jack told the story of the beginning of the Bear People and how his ancestors had vowed to help them. He motioned for Johnny to show them the medallion and told them how the Protector wore it as proof of his commitment to help the clan. His voice grew strong and animated the longer he spoke, and it was clear to them that he firmly believed what he was saying.

"I've never heard of such a thing," Marin growled when Jack was done speaking. "No Protector has ever shown himself to me."

"My father was the last one to meet the Bear People," Jack admitted, "because they decided they didn't want humans around anymore. I don't know why, they'd had a good relationship for so long. They even had a name for the Protectors: they called them 'People of the Bear'. They were treated like members of the clan, but they were human."

"I know why," Lindy said, looking to Marin. "It's because of what happened with Emma. The clan was so angry that they separated themselves from all human contact after that, even taking the Protector's help away from the Guardians. They ended a long history of cooperation…and friendship, by doing that."

Marin nodded thoughtfully, considering the possibility. "So you're saying that at one time, the Guardian of the Bear People and a human Protector worked together to safeguard the clan?"

"Yes," Jack said, his face beaming. "My line and your line. Together."

"I never knew. No one ever told me," he said. There was a touch of sadness to his voice, along with a hint of anger that his grand-sire had hidden this information from him.

"So you're the Protector now?" Lindy asked Johnny.

His lips pressed together in a semi-frown. "I am. But I think I'm the wrong one."

Everyone turned to look at him.

"Why?" Jack asked

He looked at his uncle and shook his head, swinging his black hair from side to side. "They already have a Protector." He took the medallion string from around his neck and held it out to Lindy. "You've done a better job than I have. This should belong to you."

She stared at it dumfounded. She was no Protector. She

knew nothing about protecting anyone.

"The boy is right. You've broken the long silence between our two peoples and proved yourself to the clan. You should take this." Jack motioned with his gnarled hand for her to take it.

"Marin?" she said, looking to him for direction. But he was as lost as she was and could only look helplessly from one face to another.

Johnny sighed, obviously relieved to have it done with. He patted his uncle's hand. "We should go," he said.

An anguished look filled the old man's face. "But you said…"

Johnny tapped his hand lightly against his forehead, remembering his promise to his uncle. He looked at Marin and then at Lindy. "Before we go, could I ask a favor of you? All my life, my uncle has heard the story of the Bear People and he's waited for our bond to be reconnected. He's never seen how a shapeshifter changes and he was wondering if…"

Marin growled to cut off his words. He was tired and sore and ready to go back to bed. But when he looked at the old man's face, at the one clouded eye that remained, he saw something in it that softened his heart. It was something he'd rarely seen in a human before. It was *wonder.* He shook his head, knowing he'd just talked himself into doing it.

He pushed himself out of the chair and stood up, letting the blanket drop to the floor. The men swept their gazes over him and were clearly astonished by the power of his physique. When they'd had their look, he arched his back and reached his hands toward the floor. The mens' breaths hissed simultaneously at the sight of fur sprouting from beneath Marin's skin. They stared in astonishment as the man became a bear.

Jack reached out his hand to touch Marin but Lindy grabbed him and pulled him back. "That's not a good idea," she advised. "He's a little grumpy." He nodded understandingly and continued to watch while Marin reversed the process and immediately returned to man skin.

"Amazing, isn't it, Uncle?" Johnny said when Marin sank back into the chair.

Jack nodded excitedly, shaking the white wisp of hair on his head wildly. "Amazing."

"Thank you," Johnny said, nodding to both Marin and Lindy. "I should get Uncle back before dark." He stood up and helped the old man to his feet. They started for the door when Johnny turned around. He walked back to the sofa and laid the medallion on the end table beside it. "I don't need this anymore," he said, looking at Lindy.

She walked with them to the door, still thinking about the medallion lying on the table.

Grabbing Johnny's arm, she pulled him gently around so she could see his face. "Thank you for what you did," she said. "Things would have turned out differently without your help."

He returned the smile and gazed over at his medallion. "Like I said, you really didn't need my help. You did just fine by yourself." The he turned and helped his uncle out the door.

Lindy watched them go. When she turned around, the medallion was still on the table but Marin was gone. She looked over in time to see his bedroom door closing softly shut behind him.

Chapter Forty-Seven

Lindy looked out the door at the beautiful spring morning. Taking Marin by the hand, she led him across the yard to the shore of the lake. Waves lapped softly against the grassy bank, propelled by a warm southerly breeze, and sparkled with each rise and fall of the water beneath. She stepped onto the weathered wooden pier, headed for a bench at its end where she could sit and gaze out at the scenery. Marin pulled to a stop behind her and eyed the pier suspiciously. He had never walked on water before.

"It's okay," she said. "It's sturdy enough to hold us."

He grunted skeptically but finally accepted her assurance and let her lead him to the bench. When they sat down, he noticed that she'd positioned herself close enough to him for their arms to touch. He just didn't know if she did it to comfort him or because she wanted to touch him.

"Isn't it beautiful?" she asked. The water was dark and sparkling beneath the bright sun.

Marin ignored the water and gazed across its surface to the forest on the opposite shore. Somewhere over there, his kin were napping in the warm morning sun or searching the bushes for sweet berries to eat. He couldn't help but wonder how the clan was faring without him, or if they even missed him. Sometimes the five days he'd been gone seemed like forever; other times it seemed like mere moments. He sighed without realizing he'd done it.

Lindy looked at him and saw the wistful look in his eyes.

Though he was right beside her, he seemed a hundred miles away. “Are you okay? You look like you have something on your mind.”

He shook his head without looking at her. “I’m fine.”

She slipped her hand over his as it rested on his thigh. His olive skin glowed dark gold in the light like a bronze statue. “Are you missing home?”

He thought for a moment before answering. “This is the first time I’ve ever been away— other than when I was taken by the humans. It’s strange how I get so tired of watching over my clan every minute of every day, but now that they’re gone from me I miss them.”

Lindy laughed softly and squeezed his fingers, feeling the strength in them beneath her own delicate fingers. “It’s sort of like being married. You can get on each other’s nerves, but then you miss him when he’s gone.”

Marin tipped his head to look at her. “Gareth said that you once had a mate. What happened?”

“Gareth told you about that?”

“Gareth told us many things about you. So why aren’t you together anymore?”

“Well,” she sighed, “It’s a long boring story that you probably don’t want to hear. So to put it simply, I loved him more than he loved me. He ended up with another woman and I ended up with Gunther.”

He gazed into her eyes and saw for the first time how dark flecks sparkled within the lighter shade of blue when the light hit just right. The breeze blew her hair softly in shimmering golden drifts that framed her face and lit up her eyes. She was so beautiful he could hardly speak. “Then your mate was a fool,” he said at last.

From the tone of his voice, she could tell that he really meant it and she blushed. “Thanks Marin.” Then she looked away and gazed at the water again.

They sat quietly for a moment. A loon called somewhere down the lake, its haunting cry sending a ripple down Lindy’s back as it echoed eerily over the surface of the water.

Marin felt her fingers squeeze tighter over his and he smiled. There were times when she was so brave, and other times like this when she seemed to rely on him for strength. She never failed to surprise him. Like the way she'd come up with a plan to rescue the clan and then followed through without apparent concern for her own safety. His thoughts drifted back to the Indian man who had helped them in the rescue and his visit to her house the previous day. "Do you think that they spoke the truth?" he asked her.

"Who?"

"The young man and his kin."

She brushed the hair from her eyes and nodded. "Yes I do. That medallion looked pretty old, like it's been passed down through a lot of generations. Besides, why would they make up a story like that? And even if they did, how would they know about your people?"

Marin sighed softly, sounding like he was conceding defeat. "Then it means that my kind and your kind have known each other for a very long time."

"Not just known each other," she corrected. "Worked together. Helped each other. Cared about each other. It could happen again, you know."

He swung his head to look at her and saw the hope on her face. "The young human doesn't want to wear the medallion."

She nodded. "I know."

"Someone else would have to take it"

"Yes. It would have to be someone that you were willing to work with. Someone who respected your authority as Guardian."

"But also someone with the intelligence to make decisions on his own. With the courage to go up against his own people if necessary. Someone willing to devote his life to us."

Lindy fell silent, feeling the excited thump of her heart grinding to a halt inside her chest. *His, his, his.* Marin was making it painfully clear to her that he wanted a *man* to assume the Protector role. She obviously wasn't good enough.

Pulling her hand off his, she raised it to her forehead to shield her eyes from the glare of the sun on the water.

Marin looked at her, waiting for her to speak again, but she said nothing. "Well," he said after a long awkward pause. He didn't know why she had pulled her hand away so abruptly, but he wasn't sure he was ready to ask her. "My head hurts. I'm going inside to rest."

"Oh, okay," she said, her voice cool. He stood and walked carefully down the pier, the hesitancy still showing on his face.

When he had gone inside the house, Lindy lowered her head to her chest and cried.

Chapter Forty-Eight

Gareth sat in the meadow with his back pressed up against the boulder. The sun beat down on the stone and radiated heat into his shoulder in a steady flow. The wound had healed well but there were times when an ache suddenly pulsed to life deep inside it. He supposed it would always be there, an unwanted reminder of the terrible thing that had happened to him. And the wonderful thing.

Closing his eyes, he tried to picture Lindy at home and imagine what she was doing. He could see her kneeling on the kitchen floor with her arms around Gunther. She was rubbing the coarse fur at his neck while she spoke softly to him. It was funny how much she loved that wolf. Then suddenly the wolf was gone and it was Marin in her arms. She was gazing into his eyes and her fingers were caressing his back in delicate little circles.

He laid his head back against the hard stone and forced the picture from his mind. There was nothing he could do to change the situation and dwelling on it would only make him more miserable than he already was. He had no one to blame but himself. He was the one who'd sent Marin to her in the first place, even though he suspected that feelings were growing between them. He'd seen it in their eyes and in the way she touched him so tenderly and so often during the rescue.

For a moment, his anger swelled at Marin's hypocrisy. The Guardian had virtually threatened him when he'd shown an interest and possessiveness toward her. 'Humans and bears don't mix' he had preached again and again. But Marin himself had accepted her help and compassion without hesitation, and now it was he who was alone with her in her home.

"Why are you growling?" a voice asked him from nearby.

Gareth opened his eyes and gazed up to see Lilea standing beside him. She was panting heavily in the warmth of the sun, and waves of heat were rising from the fur on her back, but she was too curious about his behavior to move into the shade.

"I didn't know I *was* growling," he mumbled.

"Can I join you?" she asked.

"I guess."

Lilea shifted into man skin and sat down on the grass beside him. She could tell from the look on his face that he was upset about something. "You're thinking about her again, aren't you?"

"Who?" he replied sharply.

She laughed and slapped his arm softly. "You know who. Don't be so grouchy."

"Is it that obvious?" Gareth looked at her and had to smile. Lilea was petite and lovely, the prettiest of the she-bears, in his opinion. Her dark hair shimmered seductively in the afternoon light, framing her dark eyes as they bored into him. She was sweet and fun-loving, and quite the tease. An unexpected shiver of excitement rippled through him.

"I know you don't want to hear this and it's none of my business, but you need to let her go."

"You're right," he agreed. "It is none of your business."

She wasn't put off by his rudeness. In fact, it only encouraged her more. "You fell for her because she's different and exciting, and she took care of you, that's all. She's a good woman, for a human, but you know it wouldn't work out."

"Why is that?" he asked dryly.

"Because she needs a mate that will be with her *only*. You told us about how her mate was with another woman and she couldn't accept that. That's how humans are. What do they call it…monotonous?"

"Monogamous," he said, trying to hide his smile.

"But you're not that way, Gareth. I've seen you with my sister bears; I know what kind of guy you are. You need variety. *Our* kind of variety."

There was a gleam in her eye when he looked at her. "You know that for a fact, do you?"

She nodded confidently. "Females know these things."

He folded his arms across his chest and looked away with a sullen expression on his face. "I suppose you're right. Besides, I think I've already lost her to Marin."

Lilea sighed and rubbed her arm up against him, liking the feel of him very much. Until the kidnapping, she'd never realized how brave and strong he was. "I think so, too."

Gareth looked at her, trying to decipher the emotion in her voice. It held a sadness that echoed his own. "You want Marin, don't you?"

She snorted softly and pursed her pouty lips. "Are you kidding? Who doesn't?" Then her voice grew soft and filled with regret for what might have been. "I couldn't give him what he needs. Neither could any of the others. He's never been the same since Terra died, you know. Marin needs…well, he needs something special."

"Something like Lindy?" he said.

"Yeah. Like Lindy." She laid her hand gently on his forearm. "You need to let her go, Gareth."

It was a long moment before he answered, and when he did, there was a finality in his voice that sounded painful. "I know."

"Will you then? For Marin's sake?"

He inhaled deeply and sighed out a long, slow breath full of regret. "Yes," he said, gazing into Lilea's sympathetic eyes. "For Marin's sake, and for hers, I'll let her go."

Chapter Forty-Nine

Marin finished his dinner and stared across the kitchen table at Lindy, pondering how human females differed so dramatically from the she-bears. Ever since he'd arrived at her home, Lindy had taken care of him. From the minute she helped him out of bed in the morning to the time she helped him back in at the end of the day, he was never in need of anything. She was constantly feeding him or bandaging his wounds, or merely giving her sympathy to ease the sense of loss he felt over Thoren's death.

He'd never been treated so well and he wasn't sure if he should try to reciprocate her kindness or just accept it as a gift she was giving him. She-bears never expected anything in return when they did something nice for a he-bear. If they offered a bunch of wild strawberries, the recipient had merely to eat them. He wasn't expected to return the favor. But whether humans operated the same way, he wasn't sure.

He pushed the chair back and turned to stand up when a searing pain shot through the muscles in his back. He yelped in agony and sank back down in the chair, clutching behind him at a spot he couldn't reach. Ever since he was chained to the tree, his back protested with burning spasms when he changed positions too quickly, and he just wasn't accustomed to being cautious when he moved. He realized that would have to change.

Lindy ran over and bent down beside him with a concerned look on her face. "Is it your back again?"

He nodded and growled through the pain. "How can I stop these damn things?" he hissed, bending his chest toward his knees to try and ease the spasm.

"I wish I could help you," she said. Then she had an idea. "It might help if you soak in the tub. Heat can do wonders for sore muscles."

"Soak in a what?" he growled. He had no idea what a *tub* was.

"It's like a pool of water, but it's inside the house. I can make the water hot and if you just sit in it and relax, it might make the spasm go away."

He was willing to put up with anything to end the discomfort. "Fine. I'll try it."

She left to run the bath water and reappeared a minute later to help him into the bathroom. She felt so sorry for him, walking hunched over like an old man. He held on to her arm as she led him slowly toward the tub and waited impatiently while she checked the temperature of the water. When she thought it was comfortable, she helped him climb in.

He sank down into the steaming liquid and within moments, closed his eyes.

He was amazed. He had never been in water that was hot and he couldn't believe how wonderful it felt. His body seemed to melt as the heat seeped into each sore muscle, and every part of him began to relax. Even the sound of the water was soothing the way it lapped gently against his skin with the slightest movement. Tipping his head back, he let the warmth creep up his neck and absorb into the mass of his hair. It felt better than anything he'd ever experienced.

He sat quietly in the warmth for a long time before realizing that Lindy was still beside him. He opened his eyes and saw her sitting on the side of the tub watching him. He thought the expression on her face was the sweetest look he'd ever seen, a look that said more to him than any words ever could. She looked so happy, so comfortable with him there, as though it was natural for him to be there. He sat up straighter and smiled.

"Is it helping?" she asked.

He nodded slowly, almost too relaxed to answer. "Uh-hum."

She knelt down on the floor beside the tub and put her hand in the water. Cupping it full, she splashed water carefully up across his shoulders. He moaned softly and closed his eyes again as the moisture spread heat over the tops of his broad shoulders. For a moment she held both her hands in the water until they radiated with heat and then ran them slowly down his upper arms, spreading the warmth through him even more. She moved to his chest, feeling the smooth curve of his muscles beneath her fingers, and then swept her hand up his neck to his face.

It was almost more than he could handle. As she moved her fingers softly against his cheek, he felt the ardor rising in him uncontrollably. Despite his relaxation, he could feel his groin tighten and grow hard and he knew that if she turned, she would see his body responding to her touch. He knew he should ask her to leave, even push her away if he must, but he couldn't. He wanted her to stay, wanted her to keep touching him.

Lindy ran her fingers over his cheek and swept them back through his hair. The dark strands curled softly in the steamy air and tangled around her fingers as if refusing to let them go. His neck stretched back and he laid his head against the porcelain, raising his chest and hips higher up in the water. She followed the trail of the water as it rolled off his pectorals and drifted down across his rippling abdomen. Then she saw what she was doing to him and gasped.

Marin raised his head up and opened his eyes. He saw her gaze shift from his groin back to his face and he couldn't figure out why she had gasped. She shouldn't have been surprised by his body's response, knowing that she had caused it once before. And he doubted that she was embarrassed by it since she'd never seen him when he *wasn't* naked. He decided to wait for her to speak before he said anything.

Her face grew flushed as she looked at him. She expected

him to gruffly order her away with his usual explanation about bears and humans not mixing, but he lay there without speaking. She waited momentarily, allowing him more time, but still he didn't speak. He just looked at her with those dark eyes of his pouring into hers like syrup. Finally she couldn't stand the silence any longer. "I...I thought you would tell me to leave," she mumbled.

Marin watched her face while she spoke, seeing how tiny wrinkles of worry gathered at the corners of her eyes and her lips pressed tightly together in anticipation of his response. He thought back to the first time she had touched him, the night she'd saved him from freezing by holding her body against him, and remembered how he'd screamed at her in anger over his own frustrating lack of control. He'd realized it then and it was still true now. He wanted her, needed her, the way he had wanted and needed Terra. And now he knew he had the strength to admit it.

"Kiss me."

She cocked her head to look at him. "What?"

"I want you to kiss me. That is the name of that thing humans do with their lips, isn't it?"

She nodded without speaking but her eyes had flared wide open.

Marin's mouth curled up in a smile and he reached his hand out of the tub and placed it behind her neck. He drew her close until her shoulders were over the water and her face was inches from his. Then he waited. He had never kissed a woman and a woman had never kissed him. It was not a thing Bear People did, and so he waited for her to take the lead. He saw her eyes close and he did the same.

Suddenly there was a warm pressure against his mouth and he jolted slightly back in surprise. He felt her pulling away and he tightened his grip on the back of her neck, refusing to let her go. This time he pulled her close enough that his lips met hers and immediately felt her warm mouth moving firmly on his.

He couldn't believe how wonderful it was. He'd heard

talk about the strange things humans did to show affection, but they hadn't sounded very appealing to him. Now here he was in the midst of his first kiss and all he could think about was wanting more. The feel of her mouth against his was more stimulating than he could ever have imagined and he pulled her hard against him until he realized he wasn't breathing. He released his hold on her neck and drew his head back to gasp in a breath.

Lindy opened her eyes and gazed at him in disbelief. His eyes were still closed and his face had an almost blissful expression as he breathed in deeply and slowly. Finally his eyes opened and when he looked at her, she saw something she had never seen in him before. He looked *contented.* There was no sign of the struggle that she knew had been raging through him since he'd met her. No sign of anger at his physical response to her. And no longer a need to push her away.

Finally catching his breath, Marin cleared his throat softly and gazed down at the side of the tub. "I guess I shouldn't have criticized human customs without trying them," he chuckled, making fun of himself.

"Did you…*like* that?" she asked, hardly daring to hope that he had.

His smile grew larger and he raised his hand out of the water to run his fingers through her hair. She was so beautiful that it almost scared him to think that she could want him for her own. "Yes, Lindy," he said. "I did."

She realized then that *she* wasn't breathing and she took in a slow breath. He was touching her hair, running his fingers through the golden strands over and over and he wasn't displaying the least bit of apprehension. She closed her eyes and prayed that the wall between them had finally come down, but she knew that only time would tell for sure. What had happened between them just now was only a baby step on a journey that she hoped would bring them much closer. Still, she knew he'd need time and she vowed to herself to give it to him.

"Lindy?"

She opened her eyes again. “Hmmm?”

“Thank you.”

She crossed her arms on the edge of the tub and rested her chin on her hands. “For what?”

He pursed his lips while he thought. “Where do I start? Thank you for saving me from freezing. For saving me from Dean and his men. And mainly for saving me from myself.”

Her eyes squinted when she looked at him. “I don’t understand that last one.”

He laid his head back against the tub and slid down deeper into the water, looking at her from under half-closed eyelids. “When Terra died, I promised myself that I would never care for someone that way again. I vowed to spare myself from the pain of losing someone I loved. But what I was really doing was insulating myself from life. I stopped feeling, stopped caring. I stopped living. Then you gave me my life back. And I was so angry and self-righteous that I almost stopped you. Lucky for me you’re so stubborn.”

She laughed softly. “Not stubborn. Just…persistent.”

He grew quiet and gazed down at the opposite end of the tub. “I need to go back to them, you know.”

Lindy drew her bottom lip into her mouth and chewed on it for a moment. “I know.” She didn’t want to think about it and could hardly force the words out.

“I need to go soon.”

She nodded and closed her eyes to keep the tears in. “When?”

“Tomorrow.”

She rose up and stared at him. Her chest was beginning to ache. “That soon? Are you sure you’re ready? You still have some swelling and…”

“Lindy.” He had to cut her off before she talked him out of it. “My place is with the clan. They need me. You’ve done a good job taking care of me and I’m ready to go.”

“But your back?”

He nodded thoughtfully, acknowledging her concern. “There’s not much I can do about that. At least I know where to come when I need help with it." His eyebrows rose hopefully.

"You know you'll always be welcome here." She leaned forward and placed her hand tenderly on his chest, needing to feel the pulse of his heart. "You will come back here sometimes, won't you, Marin?"

He placed his hand on top of hers and swallowed down the lump that had risen in his throat. "How could I stay away?" Then he leaned forward and kissed her one last time.

Chapter Fifty

"Oh my, oh my," Lena said through a mouthful of leaves. She raised her shaggy head and turned around to get the clan's attention. "Look who's coming."

The bears ran up beside her and watched excitedly as Marin and Lindy walked together on the path toward forest home. He ambled beside her with a stiff gait that revealed some remaining muscle pain and his face was still swollen above his dark muzzle. Lindy had her hand on his massive shoulder, her fingers buried deeply in his fur as though they were attached to each other. When they came closer, the clan could see that both of them were smiling.

Gareth arched up into man skin and ran out to greet them. "Welcome back, both of you." He pulled Lindy into his arms for a quick embrace before backing away to address Marin. "How are you feeling, Guardian?"

Marin arched up and when he stood as a man, he smiled and looked at his kin standing around him. He was never as glad to see them as he was at this moment. "I'm well," he beamed, turning to look at Lindy. "Very well."

The bears nudged forward to rub their sides or muzzles against Marin in a show of affection. It was clear on their faces and in their actions how much they loved and had missed him, and for the first time, Marin felt truly appreciated by the clan. They clamored around him, begging him to tell his story of capture and escape.

His muscles ached from the long walk home but watching his kin's excitement gave him the energy to do as they asked. He climbed on top of the granite boulder and sat carefully down while motioning for Lindy to sit on the ground at his feet. He looked at the bears around him and had a sudden thought.

"Stand tall," he ordered, addressing the group. "I will talk in man-speak for the benefit of our guest."

One by one, the bears arched up off the ground and assumed their human forms. Then they sat or lay stretched out on the warm grass to hear Marin's story.

He cleared his throat and looked over their heads into the forest. The woods were cool and green, the air so fresh he couldn't breathe it in fast enough. "This story really begins long ago," he said, drawing looks of confusion from the clan. "Many generations before us, the Bear People came into this forest and changed their energy to allow themselves to shift between bear and man form. They did this because the humans hunted them and treated them with disrespect. They thought they could go away where humans wouldn't bother them. But they were wrong."

A hush had fallen over the clan and they listened intently.

"The humans pursued them even here into forest home and the Bear People had nowhere else to go. Then something wonderful happened. Some of the humans decided that it was right to help the clan, and they did this by choosing someone brave and honorable to defend them against the other humans. They called him 'Protector' and considered him a person of the bear clan. The Protector and the Guardian worked side by side to keep the clan safe. This," he said, pointing to a wooden circle hanging around his neck, "this is the mark of the human Protector."

Gasps rose from the circle of Bear People on the ground. This story seemed too unbelievable to possibly be true. Humans working with bears to protect them? But if Marin was saying it, they knew it must be the truth.

He held the medallion up in front of his face so they could see it better, and then lowered it down to rest on his chest again. “Humans and bears had a good relationship, a strong friendship for many years. Then the actions of two individuals changed everything. A human woman called Emma and the Guardian Marowin came together and…” he paused, gathering the courage to say the word, “mated.”

Roars lifted up around him. Even though they had heard this from Arlin when he’d returned from the farmhouse, they hadn’t really believed it. They didn’t want to believe that such a thing had happened or accept the implications of it.

Marin lowered his head for a moment to take a couple deep breaths. “As you know, Marowin was my great-grandsire. And as I’m sure Arlin has already told you, the human woman bore two young. She took one with her when she went away and the other she left with its father, Marowin. The blood of that child runs through me and I confess before you now that I…” He stopped, unable to finish the sentence.

Lindy looked up him, tears brimming in her eyes for the pain and humiliation he was feeling. “Marin, you must,” she urged him, knowing that the sooner it was said, the sooner he could move on.

He looked down at her and nodded, then lifted his face to speak to his kin again. “I am part human.”

The clan was too stunned to speak. So it was really true. Everything Arlin had told them about the revelations at the farmhouse was true. Lilea looked away from Marin, unable to watch the pain on his face. The others coughed quietly or shifted uncomfortably on the ground, but no one spoke a word.

Marin looked back down at the ground and swallowed hard before he continued. “After that, the Guardian decided that there should be no more connection with the humans and all contact was lost. Until the rescue at the farmhouse, when we met the one called Johnny who is kin of the last Protector.”

“When I was recovering at Lindy’s house, this man and his uncle came to see me. They told me about the Protectors and how they thought the time was right for a reconnection to be made between humans and Bear People. I never would have agreed with such an idea, but after what happened to Gareth and then to me, and finally Thoren… well, I think the time *is* right to find a human who will help us again. We should find someone to wear this medallion."

He slipped it off his neck and let it dangle from his hand without raising his gaze from the ground. He had never felt so ashamed in his life. Forcing himself to look up, he gazed into the eyes of his clan and nodded. "There is only one human who has shown the courage and honor to fulfill what is required of a Protector. Someone who has taken great risks for us, and for me."

He bent down and tapped Lindy on the shoulder. When she turned to look up at him, she saw that his eyes were wet with moisture. "Come and stand beside me," he said.

Her heart began to race as she took his hand and let him help her onto the rock. When she stood beside him, he turned back to face the clan. "I owe Gareth an apology." He gazed down at the man who stood nearby with a shocked expression on his face. "You were right, Gareth. Lindy is no ordinary human. She has integrity, courage, compassion. She has proved to us that she won't betray us and she honors the Bear People by her treatment of us. Forgive me for doubting your judgment."

Gareth just nodded, too shaken by Marin's apology to respond.

Marin swung his head to address Lindy. "And I owe my apology to you, as well. I was wrong about you in every way. I ask you to accept this medallion and become our Protector and the first of a new line of People of the Bear. Will you accept?"

The words wouldn't come. All she could do was gaze up into his eyes and nod her head furiously. Finally, after a few awkward moments, she licked her lips and smiled. "I'd be honored."

Marin turned back to face the clan. "We will need to vote on this. I will hear either aye or nay from each of you and then announce the decision." Then starting on his left, he called on each person to hear his or her vote. One after another, exuberant ayes rose into the air until the vote was complete. The decision was unanimous.

He took the string and placed it gently over Lindy's head. His fingers slid down its length and held the wood briefly before he placed it on her chest. His fingers lingered for a moment, feeling the pulse of her heart thumping wildly beneath his hand. Then he pulled away and looked out at the clan.

"There is something else I wish to say," he said. The clan looked up expectantly, wondering what other news he had to offer them. He cleared his throat again and looked up at the sky. It was as bright and blue as Lindy's eyes. "In light of the discovery about my heritage, I am stepping down as Guardian of this clan."

Chapter Fifty-One

Everyone gasped as one. What had he said? Had they heard correctly? Marin would no longer be Guardian?

Lindy turned and grabbed him by the arm. "Noooo!" she cried, her voice full of panic. She stared at him, trying to get him to look at her, but he wouldn't. "Marin, why?"

His head sank down on his chest. "Everything has changed. I know now that my great-grandsire was responsible for the hatred that ran so deeply between humans and the clan. He did the unspeakable by mating with the human, and now her blood runs in me. Lindy, I'm Guardian in title only, my bloodline isn't pure. Others in this clan have more right to claim that title now than I do."

Lindy kept shaking her head, refusing to believe he meant what he said. But the look on his face told it all. He wanted to step down and let someone else assume the role that he had spent his life playing. But she wanted to work with him, be with *him*, and she wasn't about to give up now.

She whirled around and spoke loudly to the clan, forcing herself to speak with authority. "There is only one Guardian of the Bear People. There is only one who has spent his life protecting you and watching over you. Even when he felt his own life end with the death of his mate, he put you first and refused to give in to his despair. He has risked his life and safety again and again to protect you. He has earned the right to be Guardian. Marin *is* your Guardian. What say you?"

All eyes were glued spellbound to her as Lindy declared

her belief in Marin. When she finished speaking, they looked around at each other in silence. No one spoke. Then Gareth took a step forward and pointed up to Marin.

"We have only one Guardian. MARIN!"

The others joined in and roared their agreement. "MARIN! MARIN! MARIN!" they chanted over and over. Tears slipped from his eyes and he turned around to hide them from the clan, but he couldn't hide them from Lindy.

She pulled him into her arms and rubbed her hand gently across the back of his head. Bringing her mouth up against his ear, she kissed him softly and whispered. "I'll do everything in my power to keep the clan safe. But the one thing I can promise you, Marin, is that you'll always be safe in my arms."

"And you, Protector, will always be safe in mine," he whispered back.

ABOUT THE AUTHOR

Being followed by a black bear in Wisconsin's Northwoods was the inspiration behind Lori Johnson's fascination with the lore and natural history of these beautiful creatures, and the impetus behind her first book, *People of the Bear.*

After earning a Biology degree from Valparaiso University, she combined her love of nature and writing to publish numerous nonfiction articles in local and national magazines. She lives in Illinois with her husband, daughter and a menagerie of pets.

Explore Lori's world of black bears at:
www.lori-johnson.com

Printed in the United States
116263LV00001B/16/P

9 781594 264665